SARASOTA SUNRISE

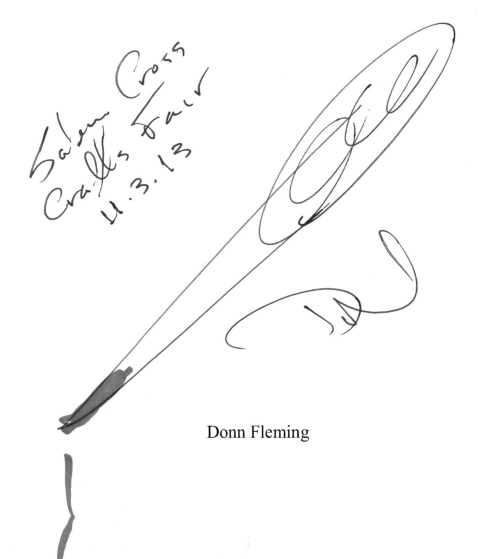

Donn Fleming

SARASOTA SUNRISE
Copyright © 2010 by Donn Fleming

FIRST EDITION

Published by
PALMWIND PRESS
P.O. 222 West Brookfield, MA 01585

Printed in the United States of America

Cover Design: dosEnes
Cover Artist: Charlene Gilbert
Author photo: Aversa
Text Layout: Eli Blyden
ISBN: 978-0-578-04390-6

Author correspondence: FLEMWRIGHT@AOL.com

For Pop

The biggest man in my life

IV

ONE

The rental car pulled into the convenience store parking lot on the corner of M.L.K. Blvd and U.S. 301. Not the most glamorous area of Sarasota. Across the street in the corner park that the city had long ago surrendered to the neighborhood, a group of men, young and old, were perched on a picnic table centered in the gazebo. Above them a naked light bulb hung from a five-bladed ceiling fan that swirled in an off-balance circle, round and round, squeaking unnoticed in the thick air of the night. A bench in front of the store was occupied by three men drinking, two of them passing a bottle in a paper bag between them, the other one holding onto a pint of his own, no bag, some generic brand of cheap whiskey.

Every city has an underbelly. Shadowy networks of the night where nocturnal roadmaps point the way to sin, debauchery and evil indulgence. Treacherous pathways that drop you into unlit catacombs of black twilight where you can get anything you want – for a price. Drugs, prostitution, even murder. The oldest businesses in the world and none of them in the phone book.

The man pulled on the front door. There were bars on it. It opened heavily. A large girl with salty sweat stains on the armpits of her brown tee shirt sat behind the counter on a stool much too small for her frame. She was talking on the phone and filing the edges of her long, airbrushed fingernails. When she laughed the gold work on her front teeth showed. He waited. "Hold on, Baby," she said into the phone. She focused on the stranger. "May I help you?"

"I wondered if you could call me a cab."

"Across the street," she pointed to a gas station. There were no lights on.

"It looks like it's closed."

With an effort she got off her stool and looked out the window in the space between the lottery poster and a Christmas ad of the Budweiser Clydesdales pulling a sled of thirty-packs through the snow. It seemed out of place in Florida. "He's right there," she stabbed the window with one of her stiletto-shaped nails, "on the side near the dumpster."

"Thank you."

He waited for the traffic to break and jogged across the four-lane boulevard. When he got about ten feet from the cab, an interior light went on. He opened the rear door. "Are you for hire?"

"Sure am," the cabbie said.

The man got in. The front passenger door opened and a girl slid out. He hadn't noticed her sitting there before. She shut the door and walked away. The cabbie adjusted himself in the front seat. "Where to mister?" He grabbed a clipboard and pulled a pen down from the visor.

The man handed a crisp hundred-dollar bill through the Plexiglas window. "Don't log it, just drive around the corner."

"Hey, mister. I don't do that kind of ..."

Another C note came over his shoulder. He grabbed it and started the cab.

"I'm looking for someone to do some work for me," the man said.

"What kinda work?"

"Light work. Nothing heavy. Couple of hours at most. I need something disposed of."

The cabbie drove out of the lot and merged into the traffic on 301 North. He watched his rearview mirror as the man spoke. It was dark in the backseat. The man wore a baseball cap, low, hiding his face.

"It's not what you're thinking," the man said. "No one gets hurt, no bodies, just laundry I'd like to get rid of."

They were a block up. The light was red. They sat.

"Take a right."

A vacant field behind a faded realtor's sign sat neglected in the night.

"Pull in here." The cab rolled off the road and drove into the field and stopped. "Do you know of anyone?"

The cabbie tore a sheet of paper off a pad and wrote on it. He passed it through the window into the back seat. "Call this number after midnight. It's a phone booth. Let it ring. Someone will answer. Tell him what you need. He'll set it up."

"A phone booth?"

"Yeah, remember those? There's a few of them left."

Another hundred-dollar bill passed through the window. "I'll get out here. Drive around for a half hour. Forget this conversation."

The cabbie took the money, "Never happened, mister."

The man got out and walked across the field.

TWO

She hadn't slept well during the night. She had been too anxious in the loneliness of her bed. She had tossed and turned, her mind whirling both scenarios over and over, her emotions buckling her into an inescapable roller coaster ride through the single hours of the night.

The instructions suggested taking the pregnancy test first thing in the morning. That would be when the urine would contain the most growth hormone; the hCG or human Gonadotropin the body produces even on the first day of a missed period. This wasn't the first day. In fact she was two weeks late. The latest she had ever been before was two days. She'd put off taking the test, trying to rationalize it away with too much stress in her life. That had worked until the third day. Then she'd allowed herself to get a little worried. Still, she believed it would come. Until the seventh day. Then it had hit her that the possibility might be real. It took her another week to muster the courage to go to CVS and purchase the kit.

At six a.m. she couldn't wait any longer. She got up and started a pot of coffee. Then she went into the bathroom and sat on the toilet. Her hand was shaking as she tore the foil pack and removed the test stick. Ten seconds. That was how long she had to hold the absorbent end of the test stick in the flow of her urine. She didn't know if she could pee that long. Oh God, she said, her eyes squeezed shut, her whole body trembling.

She opened her eyes and spread her legs, placing the absorbent tip downward. Her bladder released her urine and she began to count; one thousand … two thousand … three thousand. At seven thousand she felt the stream weakening and she pushed with her stomach muscles to pee harder, just another three seconds. She wanted an accurate test; she didn't think she could do this twice. Her urine stopped at eleven thousand. She carefully replaced the cap back onto the test stick, covering the absorbent tip as instructed. *Wait three minutes.* She wiped herself and went into the kitchen to pour a cup of coffee.

She tried to place the test stick on the counter but couldn't release it. She held onto it as she poured the coffee into her favorite mug, the one with the hand-painted flowers that always made her smile. She remembered the Arts Fest they had gone to on the Island and the pottery booth where he had bought it for her and the way his hands looked when he first picked it up, turning it in the sunlight, marveling at the artwork. The second hand on the kitchen clock turned on its never-ending journey. Two more minutes.

She thought she had gone into the living room to sit on the couch and wait, but she never left the kitchen, never took a single sip of her morning coffee. Her eyes, her whole life, were focused on the clock. At the three-minute mark she took a deep breath, closed her eyes and pulled off the tip. She didn't know which result she wanted the most. *God help me.* She exhaled slowly and opened her eyes.

THREE

"Where *is* she?!'

"She'll be here."

"That's what you said five minutes ago."

"You asked me five seconds ago."

Andre curled his bare toes in the beach sand and looked at his watch for the millionth time in the last minute. He was a nervous man by nature, even more so when he was behind schedule. He looked downright angry beneath his wide-brimmed Panama hat.

"She isn't Marilyn fucking Monroe, y'know," he yelled at his first assistant. His teeth were clenched and his perturbed voice roared above the rolling tide. "Look at this," he spread his arms toward the production people standing by their equipment. "This is costing me two thousand dollars an hour. And she's already an hour late." Another look at his watch. "That's two grand I just spent so all these people could stand around getting a fucking suntan!"

These people were the film crew of Andre Chateauguy Productions, the best fashion photographers in the business. They were set up on Lido Key Beach in Sarasota, Florida. It was two hours past sunrise and Andre had been there two hours before that, making sure the countless cameras and the myriad pieces of equipment were all set to his satisfaction. They were, but he had no control over the models. And there were a dozen of them, running and playing in the foamy tide like the teenagers that they were.

"No sweating!" Andre yelled at them. "Put that goddamn beach ball down and get out of the sun 'til we start shooting!"

The early morning sun was already hot on Lido Key, a thin strip of Barrier Island floating off the southwest coast of Florida. The beach has some of the finest white sand in the world. Pure quartz pulverized into sugary powder by an eternity of emerald waves rolling in from the Gulf of Mexico. Even beneath the tormenting sun the textured sand is always cool and soothing on the soles of your feet. Andre kicked his bare feet in the sand.

"Dammit Dodge! Get these girls under control!"

Dodge was Dodge Maddison, world famous fashion designer. The models were his domain. They were there shooting his summer catalogue in sunny Sarasota this December. Dodge was overseeing the production with the hands-on approach he exhibited in all aspects of his business. Not that he didn't trust Andre - it was just his work ethic. He'd struggled too hard for the past twenty years to get where he was and he knew no other way to conduct himself besides being involved in everything to do with his baby, *Lady Maddison*. Customers paid worthy prices for his designs and Dodge Maddison had made a promise early on, when he was young and alone designing and sewing his early pieces in a worn-down building he was renting in a yet to be discovered part of Soho, New York City. He promised himself that if he ever made it big, he would never forget how he got there, he'd always keep in touch with the roots. Never take his soul from the pulse of his market. And if that meant making time to be on the photo shoots, then he would be there.

Andre continued his fuming, but Dodge didn't notice. He was fifty yards up the shore beneath a large white cotton canopy. He and his assistant Harlow were going through racks of clothing, picking out the outfits that he wanted his models to wear this morning.

"So, where did you go off to last night?" he asked Harlow.

"Oh, I had another engagement."

"At midnight?"

Dodge had gone out to dinner at The Columbia on St. Armands Circle with Harlow, Andre, and Fletcher Ross, Fashion Coordinator for *Lady Maddison*. The Circle had been busy with the locals strolling the evening sidewalks, exercising their claim to their favorite cafes and boutiques before the onslaught of the snowbirds hit on the New Year. Then the locals would hide for three months from the congestive traffic, opulent arrogance, and the wild, mismatched ensembles of the northerners who ravaged, like a plague of locusts, the quaint little keys with the pristine beaches that floated offshore their paradise city.

"I went for a midnight stroll along the beach, the moon was beautiful."

"Hmm," Dodge pulled out a sheer silk dress. "I think Karyn should wear this strapless one."

"Good choice. Her square shoulders will present it well."

"Do you think the color will look good on her?"

"Yes, any color looks good on her. Her olive skin carries colors extremely well."

"Did you stay long?" she asked him.

"Long enough for Andre to smoke one of his disgusting cigars."

Harlow pulled out a bright summery two-piece, "Isabella?"

"Perfect."

"Are you okay?" Dodge asked her.

"Sure. Why?"

"You seemed distant last night at dinner. It's not like you to walk off like that, without saying good-bye even."

Harlow put the dress back on the rack and made a show of searching for another one. She didn't want to get into this right now. "I got caught up in the air I guess. New York is so cold it was nice to be sitting outside for a change. And the night was so warm and the moon so bright. I guess the beach was beckoning me when I came out of the ladies room, so I strolled over to it and got lost for awhile."

Dodge had seen her coming toward the table and then turn and walk down the sidewalk, cross the street and walk onto the beach. He watched her slip off her shoes and walk toward the water, her provocative body an attractive silhouette in the moonlight. He half thought about joining her but didn't. There was still something between them that needed to be worked out.

"Why didn't you come back?" he asked her.

"Lost concept of time, I guess. Then before I knew it, I'd walked all the way back to the hotel. I figured you boys would be sipping your brandy by then anyway, so I decided to call it a night."

"Dodge," it was Fletcher Ross, "Andre's freaking out. He's yelling at the girls and he just stabbed a beach ball with his pen. Says if we don't start shooting soon it'll be too late."

"What's the holdup?"

"Dana."

"She hasn't shown up yet?"

"No."

Tall, lean and Hollywood handsome, Dodge Maddison ducked his wavy blonde hair beneath the scalloped edge of the canopy. He squinted at the sun, donned the sunglasses dangling from the cord around his neck and looked toward the newly completed Ritz-Carlton standing, in all its two-hundred-million-dollar glory on the edge of the beach beyond the tall sea grass. No one was exiting through the revolving glass doors at the lobby. His gaze rose upward. He saw his corner penthouse suite with the sliding doors open and the light sea breeze swaying the loose folds of the exquisite drapery. He could see Dana's suite next door where the doors were closed and the curtains were still drawn. He turned, and as he reentered the tent, saw Andre coming up from the shore.

"How late is she?" he asked Fletcher Ross.

"Over an hour."

Harlow shuffled clothing on the rack.

"Have you called her cell?"

"About twenty times, no answer. Goes right into voice-mail. She must have it off."

"Try her again."

Fletcher flipped his phone open and hit redial.

"I can't fuck around like this!" Andre barged into the pavilion. "If she doesn't get her skinny ass onto this beach within the next two minutes I'm outta here." He took off his straw hat and wiped the sweat from his forehead with his bare arm, running it over the top of his baldhead. "Do we have anything to drink?"

Harlow went to a cooler sitting in the sand beneath the shade of the canopy.

Andre put his hat back on. "The sun is crawling Dodge, and if it gets much higher, *and it will get higher I assure you,* I won't be able to keep the light right. Then we're fucked."

Harlow handed him a water.

"Water? I need something stronger than water!" He twisted the cap off and took a long swig.

Dodge looked at Fletcher who was closing his phone and shaking his head. Andre caught the gesture.

"I told you this would happen," he said. "Didn't I? Last night, I told you this would happen."

"She's never this late," Dodge said.

Harlow allowed herself a private smirk.

"Look," Andre said, "here's where we're at. We can wait for her and lose the shoot, or shoot without her. I say we forget the fucking primadonna and get to work. We've only got a couple hours before the sun's too high and I'm going to need *all* of that. If we start right now I can wrap this thing up by noontime and we can all go to a cool bar and have margaritas for lunch."

"I'll go get her," Dodge said.

"Oh Christ!"

"She's the cover, Andre. I need her on the cover."

"Fucking supermodels," Andre downed the rest of his bottled water.

"Go ahead and start shooting the girls," Dodge said. "By the time you get everything rolling I'll be back and we'll get her into the shots."

"All right, but hurry the fuck up! I'm gonna lose this light."

"I'll be back in ten minutes. Come on Fletch."

Andre screwed the cap back onto the empty water bottle and looked for a place to discard it.

"Here, give it to me," Harlow said.

"I don't understand why he lets her walk all over him like that. She's getting the big money, she's got all the contracts, and she's living the life of luxury. You'd think she'd be more responsible."

"Andre, she's twenty years old."

"Well I guess that explains a lot of things, doesn't it." There was an undertone in his comment.

"What are you implying, Andre?"

"You know damn well. You of all people."

Harlow turned her back to him and resumed fanning through the racks.

"Still carrying that torch, eh?" Andre left the tent.

FOUR

Dodge Maddison and Fletcher Ross strode from the sandy beach onto the brick pathway beneath the shade of majestic Royal Palms lining the entranceway of the Ritz-Carlton. They entered the building and were met with a refreshing blast of cool air. They quickly crossed the Italian marble floor and approached the front desk.

"I need a key to Penthouse II, please," Dodge said.

"I'm sorry sir, I cannot hand out a key, but I'll be happy to ring that room for you."

"I don't need you to ring the room, I just need a passkey."

"Sir, I ..."

"Listen," Dodge said in a commanding voice, "I'm renting the entire top floor of penthouse suites and I need a key for one of them. Is there a problem ..." he glanced at the clerk's nametag, "... Richard?"

"No sir, its just that I'm not allowed to ..."

"Do you know who this is?" Fletcher Ross said.

"Yes, I know that Mr. Maddison is a VIP guest of the hotel, but I still can't ..."

A cold chiseled look came over the usually calm countenance of the designer. Dodge had lost his patience with this palace guard. "Give me the fucking key Richard!"

Richard sighed and reluctantly opened a drawer in front of him and retrieved a magnetic card. Dodge snapped it from his hand and darted toward the elevator bank. Richard picked up the phone and dialed a three-digit number.

The door to Penthouse II was locked. Dodge slid the card into the slot on top of the handle and entered - Fletcher close behind. The foyer was dark. The living area wore a soft glow from twin Tiffany lamps sitting on polished Chippendale end tables.

"Dana?" Dodge said as he crossed the room. He went to the far wall and yanked the cord that opened the drapes of the sliding glass doors at the balcony. He could see Andre down on the beach already busy positioning the models and snapping pictures. Fletcher had gone into the kitchen to pour himself a glass of water.

"Dana!"

The door to the bedroom was open. The room was dark. Dodge walked in and saw her form on the bed.

"Geesus, Dana, get up!" He flipped the light switch on the wall. "We've been waiting for you for over …"

The letter opener was sticking straight into her naked chest, the overhead light reflecting off the sterling silver handle. There was very little blood, just a crimson trickle between her breasts.

"Dana …" Dodge whispered through the constriction in his throat. Slowly, as if Andre was directing him to approach her in slow motion, he made his way to the bed. Standing in shock before her, Dodge realized that she was dead. And even in her death he couldn't help but see her ethereal beauty, her trademark body. For a second he felt the warmth of her embrace. All the intimate moments they had shared together flashed before his watering eyes, and the passion of their lovemaking came alive with an inexplicable and inappropriate sharpness in his loins.

His knees weakened and he slumped onto the edge of the bed. His hands went to her shoulders to pull her to him but the letter opener was in the way. Inadvertently he reached for it to release it from her breast and his fingers encircled the handle.

"Don't touch …" Fletcher warned.

But it was too late. Dodge had already removed it and thrown it onto the bed. The long red blade lay on the white satin sheets. The trickle of blood between Dana's breasts became a pasty current running down her stomach, blending into the fabric of Dodge Maddison's linen shirt as he held her embraced in his arms, rocking her willowy form back and forth.

Fletcher Ross had to think quickly. He went to the bathroom and grabbed a hand towel. He stepped to the bed and reached for the letter opener.

13

"I wouldn't do that if I were you," a stern voice came from the bedroom doorway.

A man dressed in a dark suit came at him and pulled the towel from his hands. He had the Ritz-Carlton crest prominently embroidered on the front breast pocket of his navy blazer. "Nobody move please," he said. He placed the fingers of his right hand strategically on the side of the woman's neck. Her carotid artery was still. He lifted a walkie-talkie off his belt and spoke into it, "Charley, I want a total shutdown. All entranceways, house elevators, freight elevators, all points of egress. Nobody moves in or out of the hotel without me knowing about it. Copy?"

"Got it, Captain," a voice crackled through the walkie-talkie. "What's up?"

"We've got a dead body in P II."

"Holy ..."

"Then call S.P.D. and alert homicide, extension 203. Ask for Lieutenant MacLaren. Tell him I need him here quick. Tell him I'm detaining two gentlemen at the scene. You with me?"

"With you, Captain."

"Tell MacLaren to bring forensics and the M.E., and Charley...?"

"Yeah?"

"No sirens."

Captain Eddie Frank was chief of security for the Ritz-Carlton. He was no rent-a-cop. The Ritz hired heavy, and Frank had been a heavy hitter on the Sarasota Police Department. He'd been a decorated sergeant with a solid record of diligence, hard work, and a no-nonsense approach to his job. He got things done well and right, with no room for slack. In Sarasota, head of security at the Ritz was a prestigious job that far out-paid any salary on the S.P.D. force. The hotel had a reputation to protect. And now, it had its first homicide to contend with. Captain Eddie Frank was taking no chances on botching this up.

"Sir," he said to the man on the bed with the deceased in his arms, "please release the victim. Slowly lay her back on the bed, please."

Dodge Maddison couldn't hear him.

"Sir..." Captain Eddie Frank laid a forceful hand on Maddison's shoulder.

The designer looked up and nodded his head to the man. Carefully he released Dana from his arms and let her body return to the pillows that had been gathered around her.

"Step away from the bed please."

Maddison obliged.

Captain Frank gestured with his outstretched arm to the suite's living room. "Could I have you gentlemen join me in the other room, please?"

FIVE

Scoop and a half of caffeinated, scoop and a half of decaf. The four-cup coffee maker took only a couple of minutes, just enough time for Big Ben to let the dog out and put down fresh food and water. A scratch sounded on the back door. "Didn't spend much time out there this morning did ya Joe Dog?" He saw the yellow spot in the snow not two feet from the back steps. A cold shiver came through the doorway. "Brrr," Ben said. Joe went right to his dog dish and scooped a mouthful of fresh nuggets and sat on his rump crunching away, his doe-like Cocker Spaniel eyes watching dad's daily ritual of making mom's morning cup of coffee. Three teaspoons of Splenda and a splash of Half & Half.

Joe Cocker led the way, racing down the hallway, scurrying around the doorway and leaping onto the bed in a single bound. Carlene was on her back, still asleep. The room was warm with the eastern sun streaming through the windows and she lay with the covers down to her waist and her breasts exposed. Ben loved that she slept naked, loved the way she looked in the morning. He stood over his wife with the coffee mugs in his hands and smiled to himself. He lowered her cup to her face, allowing the aroma to waft before her. Carlene curled her lips. "Mmmm."

Ben placed the cup on her nightstand and kissed her forehead. "Morning, Sugarplum."

"Good morning," she said softly, raising the pillows against her back and reaching for her mug. She took a sip. "Mmm, you make the best coffee."

Ben had crawled back into bed and sat scratching Joe's favorite spot behind his ears. "It's cold out."

"Kids get off to school okay?"

"Yeah, the bus was pulling away when I got up."

"Why does the high school bus come so damn early?"

"I'm surprised they didn't cancel with this storm coming," Ben sipped his coffee. "I'd better get down to the station early, make sure the town's getting ready."

The dog had snuggled in between them and fallen back to sleep. Ben stopped petting the dog. His right hand was free. "You'd better cover those things up," he said.

Carlene was holding her cup in both her hands just above her breasts. "But I'm not cold, Poppa," she said demurely.

"Are you sure? It looks like you're getting cold." Carlene's nipples were thickening.

She placed her coffee cup onto the nightstand and slid down into the comforter, raising it so he could see more of her nakedness. "Maybe I *am* a bit cold down here."

"Maybe you need a little something to warm you up," he said.

"How about a big something?" she teased.

"Time to get out of the way, puppy," Ben pushed the dog down to the end of the bed, "The big dog's moving in!" And he crawled beneath the covers.

Two hours later, Big Ben walked out of the police station and stood at the top of the stairs in the cold air. He held his gloves in his teeth and zipped up his coat. His frozen breath streamed from his nostrils like a thoroughbred panting in the early morning frost. The sky looked threatening. High white clouds spread in a thick monochrome sheet across the skyline from east to west and north to south. The storm was definitely coming. A Nor'easter. The weatherman was predicting two feet of snow, fast and heavy, starting late morning. Ben had spoken to the Boston P.D. earlier. It had already started there. Boston was an hour east. The storm was coming off the Atlantic. Cape Cod was already under six inches of it and the worst was yet to come. And it was all coming his way.

Benjamin J. Benson, Chief of Police in Bryce Corner, Massachusetts, descended the stone steps of the town hall slash police department and climbed into his cruiser, a 4x4 Ford Expedition. You needed a big SUV like that in New England, especially in the small hilly town that Ben oversaw, especially in wintertime, fraught with snow and ice and the obligatory blizzards, especially if you were the size Ben was. A big man, a husband, a father, a townie, literally a pillar of the community. Six two, two hundred and seventy-five pounds, still mostly muscle from his high school days playing defensive linebacker for the Bryce Corner Wildcats. He was the biggest player on the team and they had nicknamed him Big Ben, like the famous bell tower with the clock outside London's Parliament. When it became time for a blitz, the fans would chant 'What time is it? ... Time for Big Ben!' and the coach would send him in for the blitz. The fans would roar in admiration of their favorite, fearless hero. Legendary stories still abounded some twenty-odd years later of how Big Ben had lead the Wildcats to the glory of State Championship (their one and only such title) by blitzing the rival Tigers line late in the fourth quarter, getting the ball on a fumble and chugging his big frame fifty-five yards to the end zone for the game deciding touchdown. Ironically, the summer after graduation, with a football scholarship to UMASS in the lineup for the coming September, Ben acquired an ACL tear when he sustained a nasty knee injury, not on the football field, but in the woods falling off his ATV and grotesquely twisting his leg in the process. Every football player's nightmare, an Anterior Cruciate Ligament tear pretty much takes out your knee - along with your future. Surgery and rehab restored ninety percent of movement, but left him ten percent shy of ever being in the game again.

No matter. Ben was too resilient a guy to let a life-changing injury change his life, so he turned his focus onto his second passion. As a kid the only other thing Ben liked to play besides football was Cops and Robbers. His uncle had been a cop who seemed to lead an adventurous life full of danger and cool stories, so Ben decided to go to the Police Academy and become a police officer. During this time he married his high school sweetheart, settled into an old house off the common and started a family. After graduating from the Academy, Ben secured a position on the local police force and steadfastly, methodically put in his time climbing the ladder all the way to Chief of Police.

He fit well into the position and the town. He was respected and well liked. Chief Ben Benson was your typical staunch, no nonsense New Englander, not afraid to tell you what you should be doing or what you were doing wrong. One of his goals was to impart his weighty opinions to his teen-aged son and daughter, although he was having an easier time imparting his words of wisdom to his dog Joe Cocker - who would listen to anything Ben had to say as long as he had a treat in his hand.

Life was good for Chief Ben Benson. He was a happy man, thankful for all the wonderful things that he had, Carlene and the kids, his home, career, a great dog, and good friends. And he was excited because his best friend was moving back to town. Ben and Dodge Maddison had grown up together in Bryce Corner. Raced hot rods, chased girls, gotten drunk together before the legal age, way before, and had always been there for each other when one of them got into a jam. And now, Big Ben was to be best man for Dodge's upcoming wedding, although he didn't think Dodge was marrying the right girl.

But he knew Dodge would do what he wanted to do. He always had. They were polar opposites at times. Ben was a cop, Dodge was a fashion designer. Ben lived in Bryce Corner and traveled his jurisdiction; Dodge lived in New York City and traveled the world. Where Ben was as reliable and steadfast as the bell he was nicknamed after, Dodge was impulsive and ever changing like the fashions that he designed. Where Ben was monogamous and happy with one woman, Dodge seemed to need variety. Ben thought his best friend too reckless and shallow with his choices, but he guessed that was all part of the creative energy Dodge possessed and maybe needed to be as creative and successful as he was. He had worked long and hard to get to the top of the fashion world and Ben had to give him that. But he also gave Dodge his shoot-from-the-hip opinions on his relationships, and not all of them supportive. Chasing hot fashion models was certainly glamorous, and being romantically hooked-up with a super model of Dana's caliber was prestigious and had to be a lot of fun, but in Ben's mind, Harlow was the best catch. He'd told Dodge more than once that he'd have snagged Harlow in a heartbeat if he weren't so damned in love with Carlene. And now Dodge was finally getting married, to a woman he'd only known for a very brief time, and settling down in Bryce Corner again? Ben would have to see that to believe it.

The Police Chief pulled into the yard of the highway department at the edge of town down by the railroad tracks that ran along the river. Nate Moreland, the highway superintendent, was in the loader dumping sand into one of the plow trucks. Ben went over and climbed onto the side of the loader, standing in the step well and hanging onto the mirror frame, and rode with Barlow as he maneuvered between the sand pile and the trucks.

"Ready for this one, Nate?"

"Ready as we'll ever be. Gonna be an all-niter for sure."

"Got enough men?"

"Full force. Got all my guys on and six auxiliary trucks. Actually, McRevey's got an extra ten-wheeler on his farm he says we can use. Just need a driver. You up for it?"

"Hell, Nate, you know I'm up for it, but the selectmen'd have a heart attack, you know that."

"Yeah, I know. Fuckin' town politics, worse than the federal government."

"Good luck tonight Nate," Ben jumped down and walked back to the cruiser.

"Yeah, you too, and Chief..."

"Yeah?"

"Keep everybody off the roads tonight will ya?"

"No problem," Ben laughed. "If there's vehicles in your way, just plow 'em under – you've got my okay."

SIX

MacLaren was a fourth generation cop. A Scot descended from one of the clans that had sailed to Sarasota in the late eighteen hundreds. Actually he was a detective. Lieutenant. Homicide. Medium in stature with dark hair graying at the temples, he had a ruddy face permanently tanned from his 40 yrs in the sun. And a moderate potbelly from his long relationship with all things ale. MacLaren liked homicide. Liked getting the riff-raff off his streets. Liked keeping his sunshine city clean.

He drove his gray Chrysler 300 Magnum over the Ringling Causeway, past exclusive Bird Key, circled St. Armands ritzy shopping district and roared beyond the thirty mile-per-hour speed limits along the beach road. This was his first time out to the new Ritz and he was looking forward to checking it out. MacLaren slowed and turned onto the red brick carpet leading to the colorfully gardened roundabout at the front of the hotel. The doorman and a security man met him immediately. Happy that he didn't have to wear a sportcoat and tie like they did, he felt comfortable and cool in his khaki slacks and short sleeve island print shirt from the sale rack at Tommy Bahama's.

MacLaren liked the feeling of richness that greeted him inside the lobby, the level of respect shown him as he was politely escorted to the elevator and ascended to the penthouse suites. A far cry from the seedy hotel on Tamiami Trail where he had been last night on a messy drug related murder-suicide. This should be easy, he thought.

"Lieutenant," Captain Eddie Frank greeted MacLaren.

"Sergeant," MacLaren responded.

Both men had served on the Sarasota police force at the same time. As a lieutenant, MacLaren had out-ranked Eddie Frank and when Frank had accepted the position at the Ritz and gotten the title of Captain of Security, the guys on the force had kidded him about the cushy job with the honorary title. MacLaren couldn't bring himself to call Eddie Frank a captain.

"What've we got here?" MacLaren asked.

Eddie Frank didn't answer. He led MacLaren through the living room past the two men sitting on the couch and into the bedroom. MacLaren saw the naked woman on the bed with the bloody chest. He immediately recognized her from the various magazine covers she had graced, particularly the Sports Illustrated swimsuit edition on his desktop.

"Holy shit! That's whats-her-name, the model chick."

"Yeah. Dana. Haven't gotten her last name yet, but I expect she's got one."

Without touching anything, MacLaren perused the bed, the sheets, the letter opener and the body. He leaned in close to investigate the entry wound between Dana's breasts.

"Who's the guy with the blood all over his shirt?"

"Fashion designer that's doing the photography with the models down on the beach," Frank pointed out the window. MacLaren went to it and surveyed the scene. Andre Chateauguy Productions was busy doing its thing, oblivious to the proceedings high above them in Penthouse II.

"I'll need to speak to everyone down there when I'm done here." MacLaren looked again at the two men in the living room. "Ralph Lauren, right?"

"No, Dodge Maddison."

"They all look the same. Talk to me about the bloody shirt."

"I got a call from the front desk that Maddison had bullied the clerk into giving him a key to this penthouse suite."

"What time was that?"

"About five minutes before I had my security man call you."

MacLaren looked at his watch, pulled a small leather-bound pad out of his pants pocket and jotted down a note.

"When I got up here," Eddie Frank continued, "the door was wide open. Maddison was sitting on the bed cradling the model in his arms, sort of rocking her back and forth."

"So he disturbed the body."

"Yeah."

"Where was the blade?"

"Right where it is now."

"Where was the other guy?"

"Approaching the bed with a towel in his hands."

"Towel?"

"Looked like he was about to wipe the blade clean."

MacLaren looked over to the couch and saw Fletcher consoling Dodge Maddison.

"Who is he?"

"Fletcher Ross. Says he's a fashion designer that works for Maddison."

"Are they gay?"

"Maddison's not. There have always been rumors about him with women. Think he may have been involved with our model here."

"Hmm. How far have you gotten into interviewing them?"

"Just names and occupations. I knew you'd be here quick, so I've just been babysitting them. Maddison seems pretty upset. The other guy, hard to read."

"Did he know her?"

"Don't know for sure, but I expect so. They're all in the same business, and they are all here doing the photo shoot. He's got the next penthouse down. Maddison's is next door."

"I'll need a complete list of all guests in the hotel, especially the penthouse floor. Let's go have a talk with them."

SEVEN

Harlow looked at her reflection in the mirror. A wary set of eyes stared back at her. She'd had a long day of travel. From her home on Long Island she'd battled the early traffic on the hectic Long Island Expressway to get to the office in Manhattan. After a few hours at the office, she made the ride to the airport, boarding the flight from JFK to Tampa. There, a shiny limo took her down the coast past Clearwater, over the Sunshine Skyway bridge and south into Sarasota.

She was meeting Dodge who had left New York earlier in the week to check on some piece goods in Miami before flying into Sarasota for the photo shoot. Harlow had stayed at the office in New York doing what she did best, overseeing the day-to-day functioning of *Lady Maddison*, which she had done for the past ten years. She was Dodge Maddison's right hand man, an inextricably important component of their ever-challenging yet lucrative multi-million-dollar business of fashion design. Theirs was a working relationship that kept them close to each other on a daily basis. Somehow they had managed to keep it purely professional for the past decade. But recently their passion for the tangible elements of fashion had transgressed to the more human fabric of emotions. A new design had entered their relationship.

In the ladies room of the Columbia restaurant she touched up her lipstick, checked her profiles in the mirror then exited and walked back towards the table. She stopped in the middle of the restaurant. She saw Dodge sitting at their sidewalk table with Fletcher Ross and Andre Chateauguy. Andre was animating a conversation with his waving arms. Harlow found her feet taking her out of the restaurant, across the narrow boulevard and onto the boardwalk. She leaned against the railing, took her low-heeled shoes off, and, swinging them by the straps, walked barefoot onto the sandy beach. Dodge Maddison had watched her from his alfresco table.

Not long ago, in his small New England hometown of Bryce Corner, Massachusetts, Dodge had buried his beloved grandparents, the last vestige of his family. They were the only family he had. His parents died in an airline accident when he was five. Gramma Emma and Jedediah had raised him, nurtured him and proudly sponsored his education at London's Royal Academy of Fashion Design. They had been there every step of the way, crafting his career. Their loss was devastating for Maddison and it was a time of vulnerability for him. Perhaps welcomed vulnerability. And he fell into the arms of the woman he had been the closest to. They consummated their relationship. It had been sweet and passionate, but short-lived. Harlow, frightened by the spontaneity of it all, had gone back to the City after the funeral to address these new unleashed feelings. Dodge had stayed in Massachusetts to settle the estate. But before she had left, they'd talked about it, mostly at Harlow's urging, and decided to harbor the union as a happy memorable moment and revert back to their safe, platonic relationship in order to protect the business, or at least, for Harlow, to protect her heart. She needed to bide time while she wrestled with these feelings for her boss.

The moon was high and nearly full, shining like a midnight sun directly above the white beach. Night Herons sat on the transoms of berthed fishing boats like silent black ravens as Harlow approached the docks of the Ritz-Carlton's marina.

Down deep, she knew she was in love with him, but had been surprised and frightened by the spontaneous way the consummation had presented itself - lusty, abandoned sex in a dark restaurant parking lot the night before his grandparent's funeral. Sure there'd been a bottle of wine at dinner, and yes they were alone and long away from the pressures of the business and the rat race of the City. And the late summer evening with its clear sky and flirting stars had added a romantic enticement to tearing down the wall they'd erected between them so carefully over the years. Country setting, warm summer night, the coolness of the car hood on her back as Dodge pressed into her, bringing them into a world of unrestrained ecstasy. Then again, at his lakeside cottage that night, with the wind carrying the echoes of their lovemaking across the still waters and into the rising colors of a new horizon.

But that had been the one time, a lifetime of weeks ago in a New England Indian summer that had passed quickly into autumn. And she had supported it hadn't she? Hadn't she been the one to suggest writing it off to the moment, an inevitability for them that they, as mature adults, could accept and rise above? *Let's not let a few moments of passion jeopardize a decade of work together*, she'd said. *We need to protect the strength of our business relationship first. Last night will always be my fondest memory.* Thus she had convinced him it was the best thing for them to do.

But Harlow hadn't been prepared for the power of her passion for him. Now her heart was unleashed and running wild like the patient hunting dog finally free to chase the fox. So she opted to hide in familiar territory, the lonely land of denial where she could keep her composure and secret dreams. She had convinced him with her pragmatism and fooled herself with her own emotional insecurity. But she had done it well. So well in fact that Dodge bought into it. Believed that she was right. Trusted her judgment about their emotions, as he was accustomed to trusting her judgment in their business life. She had tempted chance, and by fooling herself and running scared, Harlow had inadvertently pushed Dodge away, away and into the wiles of an unforeseen rival, another woman, Annison Barrett.

EIGHT

Annison Barrett was at the farmhouse in Bryce Corner, Massachusetts. The carpenters were upstairs refurbishing one of the bedrooms in the multi-roomed Victorian. When that was completed they would start the installation of the additional bathroom needed in order to meet the building code for a Bed & Breakfast.

Initially Dodge had intended to sell his grandparent's home. He felt he had no use for the Maddison farmhouse that he had grown up in. Besides, his business was centered in the fashion capital of the world and he lived and worked in New York City. Being the only heir, he envisioned a quick settlement of the estate. There were no other relatives, siblings, wives, nor ex-wives to contend with. Only him. Only the farmhouse with its contents, the barn with the farming equipment, and the acreage. Years ago, as a boy, Dodge had inherited his parent's cottage on the lake at the northern end of town, and he would always keep that. Always keep the memory of their short time they'd shared together. But he felt it was right to sell off the farm to someone who had a use for it. Not a developer, but perhaps a young couple interested in farming, if there were any of those left in New England.

But all of those plans had been before Annison Barrett had changed his life. Two things happened almost simultaneously. First, while spending the time settling the estate, he got caught up in the charisma of his hometown, his childhood friends, the slower pace of life, and the warmth of good memories. He realized he'd been away too long from the things that were dearest to him. He was still, after all, a small town New England boy at heart.

The second thing was the intervention of fate. Annison had been staying at a friend's cabin on the lake. She had taken a sabbatical from her business to do some introspection. Her life was changing. She was taking some time for herself to shake off a bad marriage and to plot a course for her future. Fate threw the two of them together in one of its peculiar ways. Dodge had been out rowing on the lake one dawn, a faulty flue had filled the log cabin Annison was sleeping in with smoke, a black billowy cloud of it emanated from the structure, about to catch fire. He rowed to her rescue and saved her life.

They became caught up in each other. Inseparable. In love the way it sometimes happens - old souls wandering through life unaware of each other until their time to meet. And then it's a revelation. A communion. A mission without consequences to throw caution to the wind and make up for lost time. It became a whirlwind romance by the standards of conventional wisdom. But a few weeks was all it took for Dodge Maddison and Annison Barrett to fall deeply in love, and what's wrong with just a few weeks if you believe you've known each other all your life? They planned a new life together, to marry and settle down in Bryce Corner and to convert the Maddison farmhouse into a Bed & Breakfast. They were both still young, just over forty, a perfect age to start anew. Some might mention mid-life crisis, but they didn't have their hearts, didn't feel the depth of the love and attraction the two of them felt.

"Hello? Anybody home?" The Chief of Police entered through the mudroom off the kitchen.

"Good morning, Ben. Coffee?"

"Please."

"Have a seat. Just made a fresh pot of decaf - that okay?"

"Perfect. Carlene's trying to get me to cut back on my caffeine anyway. How's the conversion coming?"

"A little slower than we expected, but they're doing a nice job."

Ben sat with his coffee at the kitchen table. It was a familiar table to him. He'd been at it many times in his life. The

Maddison's were the grandparents of his best friend who had grown up in this house. He and Dodge had spent many of their years horsing around this farm.

"Be quite a change for you won't it?" he asked her.

"A change for the better I think. Much smaller than the Inn, but less stressful, no daily staffing problems, fewer guests, but more time to focus on them. And, I'll even be able to cook again. A passion I've missed for a long time. I'm actually really looking forward to it."

Annison had spent her career running The Inn at Barrett's Bluff, an expansive historic property on the coast of Connecticut that belonged to her husband's family. With the marriage over and her two children grown and living in other areas of the country, Annison found herself ready to concentrate on herself. Meeting Dodge had been unexpected but fascinating. She was in love again, perhaps for the first time in her life. She was excited about planning the B&B together and thrilled at the prospect of marrying Dodge, who had never really been married to anyone but his business.

Dodge too was looking forward to spending more time with Annison. They had even talked about children. He was planning on handing more control of his business over to Fletcher Ross, his top designer and protégé. And with Harlow running the numbers end of things, Dodge felt he'd have the opportunity to scale down his workload and move away from New York City.

"Still planning on opening by the holidays?" Ben asked Annison.

"I don't know. My intuition says probably not. It's entailing a lot more than we thought. Dodge is still in Florida doing the catalogue for his summer line and then he's going back to Milan to pick out piece goods. I think spring is more realistic."

"Always was a busy bastard. I thought he was going to slow down the pace?"

"He still wants to. We're going to set up the attic as an office away from the office so he can operate the business from here and maybe only have to go to New York for a day or two every other week."

"That'd be great. Be good to have my ole pal back in town again."

Annison sat across from Ben and stirred her coffee. She had gotten to know him and his wife Carlene quite well in the past couple months. She liked them. Liked being in Bryce Corner. Liked being with Dodge. Liked the fact that they were going off on this new adventure together.

"How was Florida?" Ben knew that Annison had accompanied Dodge to Miami.

"Wonderful. We spent a couple days in Miami, he worked with some vendors mostly, but we did find some time to shop Coconut Grove and lay around South Beach."

"South Beach as wild as ever?"

"More so."

"He doing the catalogue there?"

"Sarasota."

"That's near Ft. Lauderdale, right?"

"No. It's on the other side, southwest coast. Very pretty."

"Did you go there?"

"No, when he went to Sarasota I drove down to Key Largo to spend the weekend visiting a girlfriend. Then I flew back yesterday."

"Never been to the Keys. My extent of Florida has been a Spring Break in Ft. Lauderdale in my younger years and then a trip to Disney with 'Lene and the kids."

Ben's cell phone went off and he spoke into it for a few minutes.

"Gotta go," he said. "Thanks for the coffee."

"Want a to-go mug?"

"Naw, I've had too much this morning anyway. Dodge home this weekend?"

"I hope so. They're supposed to wrap up the photo shoot today or tomorrow, then he was going to New York for the rest of the week before coming home. I'd really like him to see the progress on the house."

"Well, let me know. Maybe we can all go out to dinner Saturday night."

"We'd love that."

"Stay warm," Ben said. "Supposed to get snow later today. A Nor'easter's coming in."

"I'll stay in and bundle up with a good book."

Big Ben Benson stood on the back porch putting his gloves on. Sometimes New England December's were warm, sometimes not. This one was cold. He made his way down the steps wondering about his friend Dodge. He'd known him all his life. He respected him and he loved him, but he didn't always agree with the things he did. And he wasn't sure Dodge was doing the right thing with this Annison Barrett. She was a nice enough lady, but Ben thought the romance was too sudden. That Dodge was at a low point with the death of his only family and the extensive workload he'd been carrying for too many years. Ben would be happier for him if Dodge'd take his time, think things through a little longer. He knew he was involved with the model girl, Dana, and had kidded him about it for the past year, chasing middle age with a woman half his age.

And then there was Harlow. Something was amiss there. Ben had always thought they worked too close in the business and that she, Harlow, was holding a candle for him, but Dodge had denied it. Carlene, Ben's wife, and Harlow had become close friends over the years. Carlene had a warm spot in her heart for a Dodge/Harlow pairing. She too wasn't clear about the new Dodge/Annison romance.

Well, ole buddy, Ben said to himself, I hope you know what you're doin'.

Big Ben climbed into his 4x4 police SUV. He looked at the sky. It was white and heavy. There'd definitely be snow.

31

NINE

Something was wrong. She knew it. They were taking too long. She walked up the beach to get a better look at the entranceway of the hotel. She saw the SUV with the *Sarasota County Medical Examiner* logo parked in the circular driveway. Harlow reached for her cell phone. She held down a familiar speed-dial key. It rang once and then went immediately into voice mail. Dammit! He must have his phone off again. Dodge sometimes did that when he was concentrating on his work. Actually his cell was sitting on the dresser in Penthouse I. He'd left it there this morning on purpose. The photo shoot was too important to him. He wanted to focus on it and wrap it up today. He was thinking he'd fly back to Logan Airport and take a cab from Boston to Bryce Corner and surprise Annison tonight. Harlow started walking along the white sand toward the hotel. She called Fletcher's cell phone.

"Why did you come up here in such a hurried fashion?" MacLaren asked.

"She was late," Dodge spoke slowly, the weight of the situation upon him. "We were waiting for her on the beach. We couldn't get through to her cell phone."

"Did you try the room phone?"

He hadn't thought of that. "No."

"Hm." MacLaren made a note.

A series of chimes entered the room. Fletcher Ross stood and reached for his cell phone.

"Don't answer that."

"What?"

"Not while I'm conducting this investigation."

"You can't ..."

"Oh yes I can. If you answer that call, I'll confiscate your phone."

Fletcher glared at the Lieutenant. MacLaren glared back. Fletcher let it ring.

"I want a lawyer present."

"Why do you want a lawyer? Have you done something wrong?"

"No I haven't done anything wrong."

"What were you doing with the towel?"

"What towel?"

"The towel Mr. Frank saw you approaching the bed with. Were you going to wipe the blade?"

"No, I ... listen I don't think your line of questioning is proper, and I certainly don't like what you're implying Lieutenant. I don't think we have anything further to say to you." Fletcher looked at Dodge Maddison, "I think we should leave."

"Okay," MacLaren said. "Let's all calm down. I realize this is traumatic for you both. I've only got a few more questions then you can go. I'm just asking for your help, okay?" he addressed this to Dodge.

"Go ahead, Lieutenant."

Fletcher moved away from the couch and paced in the vastness of the suite.

The Medical Examiner entered carrying a briefcase. It was black, the size of a medium suitcase. He nodded to MacLaren who simply said, "Bedroom."

"Talk to me about your relationship with Dana," MacLaren addressed Dodge Maddison.

"I ..." Dodge was sitting on the edge of the couch, elbows on his knees, hands clasped. The blotches of red blood on his shirt like an ill-omened tie-dye.

"Professional?.. Private?.. Personal?.." MacLaren prompted.

"All of those," the designer rose and walked to the sliding glass door. He stood looking down at the beach. He saw Harlow crossing the courtyard.

"Intimate?"

"We were involved for about a year. It ended about two months ago."

"How did it end?"

"Amicably."

"Why did it end?"

Dodge turned to face the lieutenant. "The relationship just happened. May have been superficial, as you may imagine."

"I'm not judging you, Mr. Maddison, just gathering facts."

"It ended because I fell in love with another woman."

"How did Dana take that?"

"Okay. As best as she could, I guess. I think we both knew the relationship was one of mutual admiration. We were both very busy in our careers. The likelihood of it becoming permanent never appeared to us. We never talked about things like that. The limelight found us and we shared a time in it together."

"What did she do when she found out you had another love interest?"

"Moved on. She is young … was. She had other men in her life."

"Who?"

Dodge had seen Dana in London shortly after they had broken up. A handsome man accompanied her, her age, a videographer. What was his name? "Santiago," he whispered.

Fletcher caught the name. So did MacLaren.

"Santiago?" the lieutenant prodded.

"I was introduced to him when I bumped into Dana in Harrod's in London awhile back. It was a few weeks after we had split up. She seemed happy. Happier."

Fletcher knew that Santiago was part of Andre's production crew. He also knew he was on the beach operating his equipment. From the window he could see him in the distance, sitting in a boom chair, his thick black hair pulled back in a ponytail.

"Do you know his last name?"

"No, I'm sorry."

"Carlos," Fletcher offered. "His name is Carlos Santiago. Everyone calls him Santiago."

MacLaren added the note to his notepad.

"Security one, come in," came over Captain Eddie Frank's walkie-talkie.

"Go ahead Charlie."

"There's a lady down here who says she's that designer guy's associate and needs to speak with him. Should I send her up?"

"No," MacLaren interrupted Eddie Frank. "Tell him to detain her in the lobby. We'll be down in a few minutes."

Eddie Frank relayed the message.

"Okay. Also, there's a bunch of cops coming through the doors now. What do I tell them?"

MacLaren reached his hand out for the walkie-talkie, "May I?" he asked the security captain.

"Be my guest."

"Send them up," he spoke into it. "There should be a Sergeant Reynolds there. Could you put him on please?"

"Hang on."

Fletcher Ross went to Dodge Maddison. He laid a hand on his shoulder and spoke into his ear. MacLaren couldn't hear them, but he watched.

"Lieutenant?"

"Reynolds," MacLaren said, "there's a group of people on the beach, models and a film crew. Gather them all together in the lobby. I'll be down in a couple minutes."

"Roger."

"And Reynolds, while you've got them there, you may as well print them all."

"Will do."

The Medical Examiner came out of the bedroom. "Got a minute, Lieutenant?"

"Yeah." He passed by the security captain. "Keep an eye on these two. Don't let 'em touch anything."

"They already have."

"I know, I know, but don't let them wander around. Especially that Ross guy. I don't like his attitude."

"He's right you know. You can't confiscate his cell phone."

"I know that and you know that, but he doesn't."

"Just think you should be careful. You wouldn't want to mess up your investigation on a technicality, would you?"

"You're right about one thing, Frank. It's my investigation."

Eddie Frank knew MacLaren was a show-off. He had a reputation for unorthodox behavior. He prided himself in quick resolutions to his homicides. Frank thought he was too hasty. That he held other aspirations, like advancement and power, above solid police work. But MacLaren was right. It was his investigation and he, Eddie Frank, captain of Ritz-Carlton security, would stand down. He reminded himself why he'd left the Sarasota P.D. It was because of guys like MacLaren who were part of that clique that Frank would never break into. Didn't want to. Didn't like the politics.

The Medical Examiner's briefcase was opened wide on the end of the bed so that both sides were laid flat. To MacLaren the contents looked ominous, a cross between a mechanics toolbox and a mad chemist's workbench. The M.E. stood at the edge of the bed with a long collapsible pointer in his hands, like he was going to give a presentation with flip charts.

"Preliminarily and off the record," he pointed at the model's chest, "entry wound here," he moved the pointer to the letter opener, "from this sharp instrument here. Probably a standard item found in all desk drawers in the Ritz, accompanying their stationary. You'll have to check that. Judging from the bloodstain on the blade itself, I'd say it was deep enough to enter the heart and cause instant trauma resulting in immediate unconsciousness with imminent death soon to follow."

"Time?"

"Hard to tell."

"Why do you always say that? You're like a weatherman for chrissake. Give me your best guess."

"Well, with the humidity, rigor mortis wouldn't set in for up to twelve hours. I won't be positive until I get her to the lab."

"Just give me an idea, I won't hold you to it."

The M.E. scratched his chin. He hated this part of it. Homicide always wanted to know right away. They had no idea how complicated death could be. How conniving it is in trying to hide its footsteps. "Probably somewhere between midnight and six a.m."

"Big window."

"Need to get her to the lab."

"Okay, okay. Thanks." The Lieutenant made for the doorway.

"You might want to check this out." The M.E. used his pointer to lift the sheets covering the bottom half of the body. MacLaren moved to the side of the bed. Lying next to her right thigh was Dana's tiny cell phone. The lieutenant reached into the M.E.'s briefcase and pulled on a pair of rubber gloves. Carefully he retrieved the phone.

"I'd say that would be state's exhibit B," the M.E. said, "after the letter opener, of course."

TEN

A Nor'easter is a storm indigenous to the northeast, and in particular, Boston. It's like a winter hurricane. Two systems. One spawns from the warm waters of the Gulf Stream traveling up the eastern seaboard, and then mixes with the other, a frigid arctic high dropping down from Canada. One churning clockwise and the other twisting counter-clockwise. When they collide, vast amounts of snow can drop from the sky in a short period of time. Winds blow frantically out of control, visibility is nil, and major cities like Beantown grind to a halt and seemingly disappear.

By nightfall, west of the city, Bryce Corner was already blanketed with a foot of snow, and it was still coming down. Big Ben had just hung up from his wife. She'd gotten home okay from her job at the veterinarian's, the kids were upstairs in their rooms, and the dog was curled up on the braided rug in front of the fireplace. He told her he was leaving the station and would be home in five minutes. The phone rang again.

"Yes, Sugarplum," Ben answered.

"Bennie, it's Dodge."

"Hey Buddie, how's it goin'? You gotta be doing better than we are up here. Got a Nor'easter blowing like a bastard. Over a foot already. You're probably sweating your ass off sipping on a margarita right now, huh?"

"Bennie ..." there was a solemn tone in Dodge's voice.

Ben could sense the gravity of it, "What's the matter, Dodge?"

"Dana was found dead this morning."

Big Ben was quiet. Dodge knew he was inputting that info into his cop brain. Analyzing it, setting thoughts into motion in a calculated, structured manner. Ben was very good at things like that.

"I'm sorry to hear that, my friend. Are you all right?"

"Yeah, I guess so."

"Give me some basics. What do you mean found?"

"We were on the beach doing the photo shoot. Dana was late. I went to her room to see what the holdup was and I found her."

"When?"

"This morning."

It was evening now. Ben factored that in.

"How?"

"They're calling it a suicide."

"Suicide? Why the hell would she kill herself?"

"She wouldn't. I think she was murdered."

"What makes you think that?"

"I knew her, Bennie. She wasn't of that mold. She was very strong willed. Nothing could get her down. She wasn't the world's top fashion model by chance. She was smart and determined. A self-made achiever. She was young in years but very mature in drive and business acumen. She had far too much going for her to end it all now."

"So how's the suicide connection come in?"

"The investigating officer thinks ..."

"Wait," he said. He took a moment to think. "Were you alone when you found her?"

"No, my assistant Fletcher Ross was with me."

"Where did you find her?"

"On the bed."

"How?"

"How? You mean how did I find her?"

"No. How was she? Position, clothing, etc."

Dodge knew Ben wasn't taking any notes. He was cataloguing everything in his mind. He was remarkable like that. He could tell you in minute detail about any case he'd ever had.

But don't ask him what he had for dinner last night, or what color socks he put on this morning.

"She was just … laying …there …"

"Dodge, I know this is hard, but you need to give me a visual. Try."

Dodge closed his eyes and relived the moment when he had walked in on Dana. "She was laying in the bed. Sort of propped up on the pillows. She was naked, the covers were drawn up to her waist."

"How did you know she was dead?"

"There was a … a knife sticking out of her chest. A letter opener actually."

"Were her eyes open or shut?"

"I don't remember. I don't think I noticed. What difference does that make?"

"It does. What else can you remember?"

"I went to her and sat next to her. I couldn't believe what I was seeing. I pulled her up to me and hugged her."

"How did you hug her? What about the knife?"

"I pulled it out." Dodge could hear Ben catching his breath, readying himself to chastise him. "I know, I know. Stupid. But Bennie, she was there, so helpless. It was awful."

"Okay. Who called the police? You or Fletcher?"

"Neither of us."

"Neither? How the hell'd the cops get there?"

"The security officer came in." Dodge told him how he had gotten the passkey from the front desk. "I was upset. The clerk must have called security."

"So security called the police?"

"I guess so."

"Then what happened?"

Dodge recounted the events as best as he could.

"How'd it get from murder to suicide?"

"My cell phone."

"You're not making any sense to me. Make sense to me."

Big Ben was the analyst. Even as kids, Dodge was the creative one, but Bennie had to analyze everything until it made sense to him. He needed to know what made things happen. One time there was a car accident on the common. Old man Pendleton had run his pick-up into a big tree. He was all right. Dodge and Bennie had watched from the seats of their bicycles as the truck was towed away. Then Bennie had to go over and check everything out. Why weren't there any skid marks on the road? Why had the truck jumped the curb and plowed into the tree? Was the old man drunk as they'd heard passersby say? It was Bennie who walked the entire scene down the street where he found the skid marks on the curbing, just after the trail of liquid in the street that turned out to be brake fluid. Bennie was the one, a kid, who figured it out on his own. The brakes had let go. A broken brake line had spit out the fluid on the road. The truck couldn't slow down to make the curve and had plowed into the tree on the common. Ben was like that. He had always exhibited strong powers of deductive reasoning. That's why Dodge had called him.

"Lieutenant MacLaren found Dana's cell phone. She had sent me a text message last night."

"What time did you get it?"

"I didn't. I'd left my phone back in the room when I went out to dinner last night. I had it turned off. Then we got back so late, I just went right to bed. This morning I got up and went straight down to the beach without checking for messages."

"You take it with you?"

"No, it was still back in the room."

"Who'd you go to dinner with?"

"Andre, the photographer; my design assistant, Fletcher Ross; and my business manager, Harlow."

"Harlow's there?"

"Of course."

"What time did you get back to your room?"

"Somewhere around two o'clock."

"Okay, so how did you finally get the message?"

"Bennie, aren't you interested in what the message says?"

41

"One thing at a time. How did you get the message?"

"Lieutenant MacLaren asked me about it. I told him I hadn't received it. He asked why. I told him. We went to my suite to get my phone. He asked me to retrieve the message."

"Who was present when he did this?"

"Just he and I."

"Hmm. Okay, what did it say?"

"I thought I was doing okay, but I am not. All the good times we had, all the memories we shared. Now, the heartache is too great. You have decided to move on with your life with someone else. I cannot. This heart was made for only you. Forgive me, my love."

"That verbatim?"

"Yes."

"What time was the message sent to you?"

"I don't know."

"Look it up on your phone."

"I don't have it, MacLaren took it."

"What?! When?"

"This morning after I had read the message and he had found out it's content."

"He already knew. I'm sure he'd read her outbox before he took you to get your phone. He just wanted to see your reaction." Ben got quiet. "Give me a minute," he said.

Dodge was standing outside on the balcony of his suite at the Ritz-Carlton. It was past dusk but the sky was still luminous on the edge of the ocean that could lead you to Mexico. While Big Ben thought things out, the designer paced around his balcony, the cordless phone pressed to his ear. On the eastern side, he stopped and rested his elbows on the railing. He could see the lights of downtown Sarasota sparkling just beyond the bay. Andre had taken the crew to dinner at Marina Jack. Harlow and Fletcher had gone with them. Dodge stayed behind. He wanted some time alone. It had been a hard day for everyone. MacLaren had taken statements from each model and crewmember individually. Not much came from that. Everyone was stunned. No one could offer any insight as to why Dana would commit suicide. There were a few references to her relationship with Dodge Maddison, but all of them had thought that to be over with. All of them except Isabella. She was angry, and excited, at the same time. Angry that Dana had risen to super model status due to her involvement with the designer. She was sure the relationship had never ended and that Dana was using her feminine wiles to hold onto her envied position. She felt that there were others, especially herself, that were more qualified (a.k.a. more beautiful) than Maddison's pet. Isabella exhibited little sadness and actually appeared excited that there would now be an opening for the cover model. MacLaren had shaken his head at this, thinking, she's not even cold and the vultures are circling.

The only other one of any interest to MacLaren was Santiago. The videographer denied any relationship with Dana, but did however confirm being in London with her at the time Maddison had bumped into them. Santiago claimed he and the model were just close friends. He too felt that Maddison and Dana were still an item. Even though he claimed that Dana told him that wasn't so, that she had been dumped for another woman, some woman, he said, who owned an Inn or something like that somewhere in Connecticut. When MacLaren asked him about the Band-Aid on his left cheek, Santiago said he'd bumped into a piece of equipment while setting up that morning. The lieutenant asked to see it. Santiago obliged and took the Band-Aid off. Looks nasty, the lieutenant said, should be more careful. It was dark, Santiago replied. The cut was later collaborated by another crewmember that said he had seen it happen. When MacLaren asked Santiago if he had been, or was currently, involved with any of the other models, Santiago had smiled and said no comment. MacLaren thought Santiago appeared too confident. And in MacLaren's mind, too confident equaled too nervous. There was something there. He was probably lying about his relationship with the dead model, but MacLaren figured that was his only involvement in the case. He had the cell-phone suicide note; had several statements concurring the designer/model affair; knew from experience that young girls flirted with suicide at the age Dana was at; and also knew that huge monetary success made people crazy enough to do crazy things.

To MacLaren, it was a no-brainer. Dana was still in love with Maddison. She was distraught over his new love affair and unable to handle the rejection. Maybe they'd had an argument earlier in the evening, who knows. Probably drunk, judging from the empty champagne bottle with the single flute in her room, and maybe drugged up too (although he'd wait for the coroner's report on those two items). Distraught, drunk, dejected; she opted to end it all by jamming a knife into her broken heart. At any rate, he felt confident that that was the extent of it. He didn't suspect foul play, but he would, as a matter of routine, follow through on the few i's that needed dotting and the t's that needed crossing. Then he could quickly wrap up the investigation and get these mad people out of his paradise town and back to the lunatic asylum of New York City where they belonged.

The snow was falling heavier and thicker. Ben could see it outside the window beyond his boots, crossed atop his desk in the police station in Bryce Corner. He was leaning precariously too far back in his big, worn out swivel chair.

"Why are you calling me," Big Ben asked.

"Besides the obvious?"

"Why do I feel there's something beneath the surface of this phone call?"

"I need your help."

"I can offer that."

"Here."

"Here?"

"In Sarasota."

Ben released himself from his reclined position, planted his big boots on the floor and got up, pushing the swivel chair against the wall. "What? Are you nuts? I've got a town to run."

"There's something going on here that I know you can solve."

"Yeah, like a suicide that the police must feel confident of."

"No, like a murder that the police are going to gloss over."

"Dodge, you're too close to it. You're hurt, over-whelmed with emotion, not thinking straight. Let the cops handle it."

"MacLaren thinks it's an open and shut case. He's going to write it off to suicide."

"Maybe it is. Did you think of that?"

"Yes, and it's not. The text message is false. Dana never spoke like that. I know she didn't write it."

"So, let's just say you're right. Just say. Then we're back to *why* and *who* would want her dead. Do you have any ideas?"

The designer was still. The night breeze rolling off the sea reached the top of the hotel. It had a salty smell to it. Pleasant and tangy. Like Dana's hair when she came out of the ocean that time she and Dodge had vacationed in Cancun. She was so innocent, so beautiful, and so full of fun and laughter. Who would want to put an end to something like that?

"No," he said almost inaudibly, "I have no idea."

Ben was sifting through the information his friend had given him. He was also thinking about Dodge's request. He knew he wouldn't ask something like that of him if he weren't desperate. It wasn't just emotion, Dodge was too pragmatic. If he believed someone had killed Dana, then maybe someone had.

"How did you leave it with MacLaren?"

"I told him the message had to be bogus. That she would never commit suicide. Someone, for God only knows what reason, has killed her."

"What was his response?"

"Told me to go have a stiff drink and let it all sink in."

"May not have been bad advice."

"Bennie, all the people are here. They're all going to stay here, the models, Andre's film crew, all of them. Whoever did this is here right now. If we don't get them before they leave, it'll be that much harder. This is the perfect time to catch them."

"What do you mean they're all going to stay there?"

"I spoke with Dana's family. They're flying down tomorrow morning. They want to do a memorial service for her here in Sarasota, probably Thursday or Friday."

45

"You realize I can't just pick up and leave on a moments notice, don't you?"

"Of course you can, you're the Chief of Police."

"Doesn't work that way, its not that easy."

"Bennie, how many times have I asked for your help?"

"Since kindergarten? I've lost count. What would I tell Carlene?"

"Tell her exactly what happened. It'll only be for a couple of days. That may be all the time we have. I really need you on this, Bennie."

"You're a pain in my ass, you know that?"

"Thanks Bennie. I knew I could count on you."

"I'm not sure what I can do for flights with this blizzard going on. I think Logan is closed. Let me work on it. I'll get back to you."

Dodge Maddison walked back into the suite, closing the sliding doors behind him. The room was cool with the air-conditioning. He placed the cordless phone onto its base on the desk in the corner and turned off the lamp. The room darkened, with only the twilight coming through the wide windows. He needed to call Annison, needed to tell her about Dana. She was probably wondering how the photo shoot was going and he should ask her how the renovations were coming along. Plus, he hoped she was hunkered down against the storm. But he suddenly realized he hadn't eaten all day. He was hungry. He'd call her later. He was burnt out from talking about it all day and didn't feel like going through it again right now. He thought of joining everyone at dinner, but his desire to be alone was too strong.

A half-hour north in a small fishing village on the Manatee River there was an old pub. Rusty's Anchor had been there for over a century and was renowned for its fresh fish sandwich. That sounded good to him. Sandwich and a beer and the type of noisy solitude you could only find in a bar filled with generations of colorful locals.

ELEVEN

The crime scene tape wasn't difficult to peel back from the doorjamb. Even with the air controlled by a powerful HVAC unit located on top of the hotel, the Florida humidity could still permeate the environment enough to keep the adhesive tack pliable. And the door opened inward. So only a short portion of the fluorescent yellow tape needed to be temporarily removed from one side of the doorway. The large 8½ x 11 sticker positioned in the corner, half on the door and half on the jamb, with the blazing message; OFFICIAL CRIME SCENE - DO NOT ENTER - UNDER PENALTY OF LAW, didn't pose much of a problem either. The magnetic card slid quietly in and out of the door receptacle, making the green light blink. An easy downward pressure on the handle released the latch and the door swung open noiselessly.

Inside, it was dark, but turning a light on was not an option. It took only a minute to place the champagne flute with both sets of prints in a discreet corner underneath the bed, behind the headboard leg, where it would look like it may have been missed in an initial search.

Back at the entrance, the empty hallway remained conducive to safely re-adhering the police tapes to the doorway. The penthouse suite inhabitants were still out dining in their small groups, probably in remorseful reminiscence or telling amusing anecdotes about the newly departed Dana. Or wondering why she would kill herself in such a manner. And what the immediate future meant to them. But none of that mattered anymore.

The hotel parking lot was on the edge of the beach and you could hear the surf in the dark distance, but not even the final sounds of the ocean could offer any comfort. The car was parked in the main lot near the beach. The salty night winds had covered it with a thin sheet of moisture that the wipers diligently removed from the windshield. Weather wise, it wasn't too hot this evening, but warm and sticky enough to keep the A/C activated and the cool air entered the cabin of the car quickly.

It took forty-five minutes to travel from Lido Key, down the Trail to Bee Ridge Road to I-75 south, to exit 205, which was State Road 72, then east along the lonely road to Myakka River State Park. The park had closed at sunset, but there was an access road, a narrow overgrown power-line path at the southern end of the 58 square mile preserve. They had been here once before and had gotten lost for hours in the interior amongst the wetlands and the reedy prairies. This remote spot in the thick flatwoods of the backcountry, beyond the hiking trails, may have been where it happened, if the time factor was correct.

Tonight was darker than the last time. Now there were scattered clouds drifting slowly from west to east allowing only brief glimpses of the moon and the few twinkling stars brave enough to pierce the deep blue Florida twilight. The smells were the same; tangy wetland smells mixed with pine scents from the surrounding trees. And the chorus of the night birds was still there chanting along with the grunts and hollow moans of the alligators and the other unknown prehistoric creatures of the inner lands.

The hose didn't fit snugly, but it slid far enough into the exhaust pipe to remain in position. The middle of it lay curled in a neat pile by the back door with the other end running through the back passenger-side window, rolled as close to the top as possible without pinching it.

It would have been easier with a few pictures to look at while the carbon monoxide quietly and odorously entered the cabin of the car, but then the light would have had to be on, and that would have attracted the mosquitoes, scouring the nocturnal prairies for warm, tasty blood. So, the mind's portfolio of pictures revolved round and round like a private slide show of the times they shared together, and the imagination played out the future that was lost forever to them, to the three of them.

An hour later the wind picked up and blew the clouds away, allowing the moonshine to illuminate the tranquil scene. Soft rippling water sparkled in the distant lake, little diamonds on a jeweler's velvet tray. The tall gray grasses of the wetlands turned bright yellow, and the shadows of the huge swamp trees, with their dangling Spanish moss, came alive and danced to the midnight music of the marsh. Tomorrow held the promise of a new glory.

TWELVE

"Nice outfit."

"What?" Big Ben wore a flannel plaid shirt over a thick Henley top. His over-sized Carharrt coat with the fur-lined hood and the quilted zip-in lining was over that. He carried a small gym bag in his left hand. His right hand was free. He always kept his right hand free. It was his gun hand. Dodge wondered if he was carrying.

"Glad you dressed appropriately."

"Hey, I just left a fucking blizzard. Don't give me any shit."

The two men embraced.

"Glad you came, Bennie."

"Carlene's pissed. I got an ultimatum with a forty-eight-hour time limit to wrap this thing up and get back home."

"Seriously?"

"Naw, she's cool. Said to give you a hug, so that was the hug."

"Got any luggage?"

"This is it."

"Great. Harlow's double-parked out front."

"Lead the way."

The two of them were the same six-foot height, but Ben had a hundred-pound advantage over Dodge. Walking through the Sarasota airport in lightweight slacks and a short-sleeved cotton shirt, Dodge looked like the tropical Thin Man escorting the Abominable Snowman.

Outside terminal A of Sarasota's regional airport, Harlow sat behind the steering wheel of the rental car, a slate blue Jaguar convertible. She saw the two men exit the small building and popped the trunk open. She got out of the car.

"Hello Ben," she gave the big man a hug, struggling to get her arms around all the heavy clothing.

"Hi, how are you?"

"Fine, you?"

"Good. Damn it's hot out." Ben threw his bag into the trunk and then took his coat off and threw that in too.

"Is your lighter clothing in your bag?"

"Sort of. I packed in a hurry."

Ben unbuttoned his flannel shirt and took it off to toss into the trunk. A leather shoulder holster swung on his left side. There was a black snub-nose Smith&Wesson .38 in it.

"What? You brought a gun?"

"Part of the clothing. I'm accessorized, as you would call it."

"How the hell did you get that on the plane?"

"Handed the pilot an official form."

"What official form?"

"Letter of Guest Jurisdiction for Official Business, completed and signed by the Chief of Police."

"You *are* the Chief of Police."

"That's why it was so easy," Ben laughed, "Ah, the power of the cops." He took the holster off and put it in the front compartment of his carry bag. He closed the trunk. Now he had only the heavy weight long-sleeved Henley top over his jeans

Dodge shook his head, "Got any footwear besides those snow boots?" knowing the answer already.

"Well … I packed in a hurry, y'know?"

"Let's stop at Tommy Bahama's before we go to the hotel," Dodge said to Harlow. "The first thing we've got to do is get him some decent clothing."

Dodge opened the passenger door and folded the seatback forward and got into the back. "Here big guy, you ride in the front."

"Nice car," Ben said.

"Yes," Harlow said, "It's cute isn't it? Dodge rented us all Jag convertibles to get around in."

"Swell."

"I wanted a red one but all they had left was this color, so everyone's got a baby blue Jag for the week."

"Everyone?" Ben asked.

"Well no, just five really. Dodge has one, and Fletcher, Andre and me."

"That's only four, Harlow."

"Oh, yes, I forgot. Dana had one too."

"Come on," Dodge said, "We've got to get going."

Ben slid down into the front seat with a grunt, "What the hell? Could they build this thing any closer to the ground? I feel like I'm sitting in a slipper."

Harlow drove out of the airport, down University Parkway and took a left onto Tamiami Trail at the intersection in front of the Ca d'Zan mansion.

"Anything new come up in the past two days?" Ben asked. All flights at Logan Airport had been postponed thirty-six hours while Boston dug out of two feet of snow.

"Not from the police's point of view. They seem satisfied with calling it a suicide, although MacLaren did say that wasn't official yet."

Harlow's cell phone rang and she answered it.

"Just a minute," she said, handing the phone to Dodge. "Speak of the devil."

"Hello Lieutenant ... Oh? ... Sure ... When? ... Okay. I'll be bringing along a friend of mine, Police Chief Ben Benson, that okay? From the Boston area ... No, nothing official," he looked at Ben, "he's down here on vacation," Ben's eyebrow's raised. "How about an hour? Good, see you then."

"Says he might have something conclusive and has a few additional questions. We'll meet him at his office in an hour."

"I'm starving. Anybody else hungry?" Ben asked.

"We can eat at Bahama's Cafe. Harlow can get us a table while you and I do some quick shopping."

Harlow lucked out and found a parking spot on St. Armands Circle right in front of the boutique. The tourists weren't in Sarasota yet, but they soon would be. Then it would be jammed day and night and parking a nightmare.

The men went into the shop and Harlow went upstairs and got them a table on the front porch overlooking the sidewalks. She ordered herself a Pomegranate Margarita.

Twenty minutes later Dodge and a big man in a loud print shirt with parrots on it approached her.

"Verrry nice," she said.

Big Ben turned in a pirouette in front of her, "Tropical, right?"

"Very. What are those?"

"What?"

"Sticking out of the bottom of your shorts."

Ben wore khaki cargo shorts with the side cargo pockets puffed full of whatever he'd transferred from his other pants. The right side weighed heavier. "My legs!"

"Oh, I thought they were tree trunks," she laughed.

"Funny," he said and took a seat next to her.

"Love the hat."

"Thank you." Ben had purchased a yellow cap with RELAX embroidered on the front. "I think I fit right in now."

"I took the liberty of ordering three lunch specials for us," she said.

The waiter came around and they ordered three of the margaritas.

"How far away is the P.D.?" Ben asked.

"Downtown, just over the causeway. It'll only take five minutes to get there."

"What's this MacLaren like?"

"A local. Bit of a go-getter according to the security captain at the Ritz, an ex-cop named Eddie Frank. Guess they used to work together. Frank thinks MacLaren's too hasty in getting convictions. I could sense some friction between them when he was interviewing everyone the other day."

"I'd like to talk with Eddie Frank, after I meet MacLaren. Don't expect too much from me here, Dodge. I'm out of my element and way out of my jurisdiction. I'd be surprised if the Lieutenant gives me more than a courtesy handshake. Cops don't like other cops in their own back yard."

"Oh, I'm sure you'll dazzle him with your new tropical attire."

Their drinks arrived, and the sandwiches right behind them.

"I think I should get back to the beach after lunch," Harlow said. "You can drop me off on your way to see the Lieutenant."

"Got to work on your tan?" Ben asked.

"Not really, Andre is finishing the shoot while everyone is still here."

"Oh?" he addressed Dodge.

"Yeah. At first I was against it, but Andre was persistent and Harlow too thought it prudent."

"It just seemed to make sense," she said. "Everyone was staying to attend the service tomorrow and I thought it might bring a little closure for all of us. Dana would have done the same thing. We're going to keep her on the cover and dedicate the issue to her."

"The cover? I thought she never got to the shoot."

"She didn't," Dodge said. "When we get back to the City, Andre's going to look through his past work with Dana and find a good shot we can use for the cover."

"That kosher with the other models?"

"All except Isabella," Harlow said. "She's miffed that she won't be on the cover. Came right out and said that to me. Can you believe it?"

"Hmm," Ben took a mental note.

After lunch the three of them walked to the car. The day was sunny and pleasant. Harlow declined a ride back to the Ritz saying she'd rather walk back to the hotel along the shore. Ben got into the convertible and adjusted his hat against the sun. Dodge and Harlow stood on the sidewalk talking about the photo shoot. Above them a group of green parrots were squawking in a Coconut Palm. Big Ben watched them fluttering amongst the palm fronds. Harlow said good-bye to Ben and gave Dodge a squeeze on his forearm. Dodge returned that with a quick kiss on her cheek and got into the driver's seat. He pushed the seat back to accommodate his long legs.

"That still goin' on?"

"What? We're just friends, Bennie."

"You and I are friends, but you don't see me pecking you on the cheek."

"I have no comment."

"You don't need a comment. What's up with Annison?"

Dodge backed the car up and pulled around a beige Escalade and drove down the street lined with palm trees toward the causeway.

"She wanted to come down with you, but I didn't feel it necessary. She didn't know Dana. They'd only met once and that was an awkward meeting."

"The one in your apartment in New York?"

"Yeah. Did I tell you about that?"

"Yup."

"Well anyway, she's concentrating on the renovations at the house. Said you stopped in to see her the other day."

"Yeah." Ben took his new hat off and admired it. He'd never had a yellow hat before.

"What's up with you?" Dodge asked.

"Nothin'."

"Don't bullshit me."

Ben snapped the hat back onto his head and adjusted the bill. "I guess I can't figure out how you do it, the juggling. I mean, I know there's lots of women in your world, fashion designer and all, but if you're really serious about settling down with Annison, then why the thing with Harlow? And what was really going on with you and the model? Was it really over with Dana?"

"That's a lot of questions for a guy on vacation."

"Fuck you, Dodge. I'm here because you asked for my help. Pleaded. So if I'm gonna help you, then don't leave me in the dark. What was really going on down here?"

THIRTEEN

Lieutenant MacLaren's office was located on the second floor of the county courthouse complex on the corner of Main Street and First Avenue. The Spanish-Mediterranean style building had been built in the early nineteen hundreds and a complete facelift, sponsored by the Florida State Historical Commission, had been topped-off just this year. The two coral colored edifices were joined in the middle by a tall tower complete with an ornate belfry. Fronting that was a floral garden interspersed with a few metal tables with coordinating metal chairs and bright orange umbrellas, perfectly matching the colors of the barrel tiles on the roof. The tables were full of lunchtime employees and a tourist was setting up a picture of his family next to an elaborate plaque in the middle of the garden. Taking Big Ben in his new Florida regalia for a fellow tourist, the man asked Ben if he'd mind taking the picture. Ben obliged while Dodge stood chuckling near the entranceway.

They entered the building, took the elevator to the second floor, and were led to a small conference room by a young female cop. She offered to get them coffee but they declined.

"The lieutenant will be right in," she said, closing the door.

"I love a girl with a gun on her hip," Ben said.

"She looks too young to be a cop."

"Maybe she'd like to transfer up north."

"I'm sure Carlene would be in favor of that."

Dodge looked around the small windowless room. The walls were beige with colorful beach-themed artwork on them. The table they sat at had six chairs around it and a telephone at one end. There was no other furniture in the room. "Where's the one-way glass?"

"Looks like they just re-did the place. All the new interrogation rooms use hidden cameras now."

"You think this is an interrogation room?"

"Definitely."

"Why not his office?"

"The taping equipment is all set up in here."

"What?"

"Relax. His office is probably a desk in the middle of a big room full of cops. It's more private here. And if you convince him it's murder, you'd probably be his number one suspect. It'd be easier to get you to rollover in here," Ben grinned.

"Not even funny."

The door opened and MacLaren came through holding a file folder and a coffee mug that said 'Go Bucks' on it. He wore a tan linen blazer over a white cotton shirt above olive-drab slacks. There was a bulge at the belt line on the right side beneath the blazer.

"Thanks for coming down."

Dodge and Ben stood. MacLaren shook Dodge's hand and then extended it to Ben. "MacLaren," he said, "you must be Benson."

"That'd be me."

"Boston, right?"

"Outside. Small country town called Bryce Corner."

"Keep you busy?" MacLaren said as if he was addressing the Maytag Repair Man.

"Enough." Big Ben caught the mocking inference. He'd been right about not being welcomed.

MacLaren looked the big man up and down, scanning the over-done tropical outfit.

"Nice shirt. Vacation?"

"Just a few days. Too much snow up north."

"Should transfer down here. We can always use a big guy like you around."

"I'm sure I'd get bored."

MacLaren wouldn't grace that with an answer. The pseudo-pleasantries were over.

Dodge said, "Have you got anything further on the case, Lieutenant?"

"That's why I asked you to come in." He sat at the end near the phone. "I've been thinking about your, how should I say this, adamant suggestion that Dana's death was not suicidal, and I'm curious as to why you would advocate murder. But, before you reiterate what you've already told me, let me tell you what I've got. I've got the cause of death, the approximate time of death and the autopsy report. She had consumed a fair amount of alcohol, champagne actually. There were no drugs found in her system or in the hotel room, which would support your statement that she was not a drug taker."

"Could I see the letter opener, Lieutenant?" Big Ben asked.

MacLaren stared at him for a moment and then replied, "Sure." He picked up the phone and said, "Sergeant, would you bring in the box that's on my desk labeled 'Model'?"

MacLaren continued, "So, let's play out the murder scenario, shall we? Who do you think killed her?" He addressed this to Dodge, and he watched for a reaction from him. Ben got the feeling that the Lieutenant had something up his sleeve.

"I have no idea."

"So, you think someone just snuck in out of the blue and killed her?"

"I don't know what to think. Isn't that your job?"

The female cop returned with a cardboard box and placed it on the table at the Lieutenant's end. She smiled at Ben as she left the room. MacLaren took out a plastic bag with the letter opener in it and slid it down the table. He noticed that Dodge followed it with his eyes and stirred in his seat. He put the report file in the box and pushed the box towards Ben. "Here, may as well have all of it. I'd be interested in your input. Now, let's talk about some possible suspects. We have a beautiful young woman in an enviable career with the world at her fingertips that ends up dead in a tropical resort town. Surrounding her is a host of other beauties that would kill for her position. Is that fair to say, Mr. Maddison?"

He didn't wait for a reply. "Added to that is an affair with a world famous fashion designer with a reputation for affairs."

"I've told you, our relationship was over."

"Add into that a mix of jealousy from your business manager, Harlow, and a new recent love interest, an Annison Barrett, who seems to be the reason that the affair with Dana was terminated."

"That's preposterous. Neither of them had anything to do with this."

"Means, motive and opportunity. Jealousy is a very strong motive. Opportunity wise, Harlow was here and, according to my research, Annison Barrett was in Florida at the time of the murder, as you insist on calling it."

"Annison was nowhere near here. We were in Miami together and she flew back to Boston the day I flew into Sarasota."

Big Ben knew that Annison had been in Florida with Dodge. He also remembered that she had told him she'd rented a car and driven down to Key Largo to visit a friend. He wondered if Dodge knew of that. If MacLaren were good, he'd already have the rental car information at hand. He could see where he was going with the jealousy thing. He'd wondered about it himself. Not that he believed it, but his cop mind had presented the possibility to him.

"I think we can prove they were both here." He paused, gauging Dodge's reaction. "Two rivals. Envy is also a strong motive."

"I think you're barking up the wrong tree."

"There was no forced entry. Whoever it was gained easy access. She knew them."

"What about cameras," Big Ben said. "Aren't there security cameras at the Ritz-Carlton?"

"Yes, all over the place, except on the penthouse floor. Seems they accommodate their VIP guest's desires to be discreet."

"But the other locations, I'm assuming lobby, elevators, et cetera, would show anyone in the hotel, right?" Ben said.

"We've accounted for all the models, the production crew and Mr. Maddison's entourage. But there would still be the possibility of someone getting in and out of the hotel without being noticed."

"Are you referring to Annison, Lieutenant?" Dodge said.

"Only as a peripheral possibility."

Dodge shook his head, "That's crazy."

"No, nothing's crazy in a murder investigation, Mr. Maddison."

MacLaren was riling Dodge and Ben knew it, but he couldn't piece together why.

"Lieutenant …" Ben had been reading the report.

"Wait," Dodge said. "What has made you change your mind on the suicide, Lieutenant?"

"The fingerprints …" Big Ben offered.

MacLaren smiled, "Go on ..."

"The prints on the letter opener are backwards."

"Bennie, what are you talking about?"

Ben went to pick up the letter opener but MacLaren reached into the drawer at his end of the table and pulled out a similar one. "Here, pick this up," he shoved the opener over to Dodge. Instinctively he picked it up, holding it in his right hand the way you would if you were going to open a letter. "Stab yourself."

"What?"

"Amuse me. Pretend you're going to stab yourself in the chest. Like Dana would have if she was going to kill herself."

Dodge Maddison looked at the blade and then reversed it and brought it to his chest.

"Bingo," MacLaren said.

"Hari-kari," Ben said.

"What's going on?" Dodge asked.

"Ancient Japanese custom. If you dishonored your family you were expected to commit suicide by plunging a ceremonial knife into your heart. The strength to push a blade into your chest would come from holding it the way you are now. Instinctively, you flipped the letter opener around. What you've just exhibited my friend is the proper way to hold the knife if you're going to kill yourself. Dana's prints are not consistent with that."

"Very good, big man. You see Mr. Maddison, the only prints on the letter opener were yours and the deceased. Yours were consistent with the way you described you removed the blade from her chest, but Dana's were not positioned in such a way as to suggest she wanted to commit suicide. Her prints were upside down."

"Meaning?"

"Meaning someone stabbed her and then wiped the handle clean and then placed her fingerprints onto it."

"You're reaching, Lieutenant," Ben said.

"Am I," he was watching Dodge. "I've got a murder weapon with two sets of fingerprints on it, hers and her ex-lover's."

"You know how mine got on there. Fletcher Ross can verify that."

"Yes, and how convenient that your fashion assistant happened to be there to see you remove the blade from her chest."

"MacLaren, I did not kill Dana."

"You opened Pandora's box, Maddison, not me."

The two of them glared at each other.

"What about the cell phone message?" Ben said.

"That's also very interesting," MacLaren stood, came around the table and retrieved Dana's phone from the box. He carefully flipped it open and placed it facing Dodge and Ben. "The fingerprints on the keypad are those of Dana's right index finger. Perfect prints actually. Too perfect." He took out his own cell phone and began texting, "You see, when someone texts a message, they usually use their thumbs."

"That won't hold water," Ben said.

"Maybe not, but I think her fingernails will. Dana had long, natural, well-maintained fingernails. My wife has the same. Boy, you should have seen her trying to text a message on her cell phone last night when I asked her to do so using only her index finger or thumb."

62

Big Ben could now see where MacLaren was going and he didn't like it.

"I'm afraid you're confusing me, Lieutenant," Dodge said.

"I think what he's implying," Ben said, "is that women with long nails input text with their nails. The killer didn't think of that. He sent the bogus suicide message, wiped the phone clean and then pressed Dana's fingerprints onto the keypad."

"For a small town country cop you're pretty clever," MacLaren said.

"I grew up watching Perry Mason."

"Then there's the missing champagne flute," MacLaren went on. "Room service says they delivered a bottle of Dom Perignon with two champagne glasses to Dana's suite around midnight. When we retrieved the bottle the next morning, it was empty. And as I said before, autopsy shows half a bottle in her system."

"She could have dumped the rest down the sink," Ben was playing devil's advocate.

"No one dumps half a bottle of Dom."

"It's possible."

"Unlikely."

"But still possible."

"Unlikely," MacLaren said in a tone of finality. "But what is likely is that the killer was with her drinking champagne for a couple of hours, something happened, an argument maybe, and then the killer stabbed her and then tried to make the scene look like a suicide. The room was wiped clean of fingerprints, Dana was positioned on the bed with the cell phone and its suicide message by her side, and then the second champagne glass was taken out and disposed of, probably thrown into the ocean for all we know."

Big Ben sat silently with his analytical mind at work. Dodge felt numb. MacLaren paced around the table.

"For suspects," the Lieutenant continued, "we've got a slew of envious models, a production crew, and her ex-lover; who now has not one, but two new lovers of his own - they also being suspects."

"What about the boyfriend?" Ben said.

"Santiago? No, I don't think he's involved. I think he was exactly that, a boy friend," MacLaren smiled. "We have discerned the fact that Mr. Santiago is very happily gay."

An unsettling quiet filled the room. Ben shuffled the remaining papers back into the file folder. Dodge sat forward with his right elbow on the table and massaged his temple. MacLaren resumed his seat.

"Allow me to present two more compelling pieces of information," he said, extricating a folded piece of paper from his inside sportcoat pocket. "First, were you aware, Mr. Maddison, that Dana had an insurance policy with Lloyd's of London?"

Dodge sat up straight, "Yes, I was aware of that. That's standard procedure for a super model. Her appearance, her body, was her livelihood. She wanted to protect that."

"When did she take out the policy?"

"I have no idea."

"Less than a year ago. Not long after the two of you became an item."

Big Ben watched MacLaren's eyes. They were focused on Dodge Maddison's eyes. Ben knew he was reading the pupils.

"The policy includes a death benefit. Do you know who she named beneficiary?"

"Yes, Dana told me she listed her sister as beneficiary."

MacLaren took the paper and pushed it over to Dodge, still concentrating on his eyes.

Maddison perused the paper. His eyes stopped at the beneficiary box.

"That would make you five million dollars richer, Mr. Maddison."

"What! This can't be," Dodge slid the paper to Ben. "Are you trying to trick me, Lieutenant? Because if you are, I will have this policy verified by Lloyd's and when the proper beneficiary is found to be her sister, I will drop a very powerful law suit into your lap."

"It's verified and you know it."

Maddison and MacLaren locked eyes.

"You know it because you suggested she draw up the policy. You offered to be the beneficiary. You had her in your power. She was young and stargazed with you and you took advantage of that."

"Preposterous."

"Five million dollars isn't preposterous."

"I don't need five million dollars, MacLaren."

"Everybody needs five million dollars."

"This is bullshit and you know it." Dodge said.

"You had a nice thing going. Supermodel Dana, attractive assistant Harlow, and then a wild card - another woman, Annison Barrett to disrupt your cozy little triad ... or what is it called when it's a guy with three women? A quatro-ad?"

"Fuck you!"

"Dodge," Ben warned.

"You couldn't handle it could you? Too many women in your bed at the same time. Better to retreat to the comfort zone of the triad, something you'd been managing for quite some time I imagine. So, why not eliminate the one who puts the most bucks in your pocket? Break up with her, wait a couple months 'til the word is out, everyone gets acclimated to the idea that its over between the two of you, and then do the deed. Make it look like suicide. Get away clean."

Ben saw his friend getting hot. Dodge's face started to redden. MacLaren would probably think that was a sign of guilt, but Ben knew it was irritation coming to a boiling point. He knew Dodge. It took a lot to rile him and MacLaren had served him a lot.

The Lieutenant rose and, looking at Big Ben, said, "Means, opportunity, and motive."

Then abruptly he stopped directly behind Maddison, placed his hand on his shoulder, and said sternly, "Come on, make it easy for yourself, tell me why you did it!"

The lid blew off the steaming pot. Dodge swatted the Lieutenant's hand off his shoulder. He jumped up, pushing his chair back so violently that it tipped over and fell between them.

MacLaren grabbed Dodge's arm and twisted it behind him. "I'm placing you under arrest for the murder ..."

In a flash, Ben was up, around the table and grabbing the Lieutenant by the shoulders. He spun him around forcefully and pushed him against the wall. He leveled his beefy forearm into MacLaren's throat.

"Let him go."

MacLaren still had hold of Dodge's arm.

"Let him go!" he pushed harder against the Lieutenant's throat.

He released the designer. Dodge stepped away. Ben pushed MacLaren harder against the wall causing him to rise on his tiptoes. The door opened and three cops rushed in, guns drawn.

No one spoke. One cop had a gun on Dodge. The other two had theirs leveled at the big man in the tourist's outfit. Ben's face was so close to MacLaren's that their noses touched.

"I could arrest you right now for obstruction of justice," the Lieutenant said between clenched teeth, "assaulting a police officer, and a shit load of other offenses that I'm sure even a Police Chief from butt-fuck Massachusetts must be aware of."

Big Ben's face turned crimson with anger. He really wanted to punch MacLaren in his pudgy little gut but he knew the cops would not hesitate in shooting him. He released his hold and MacLaren came off his tiptoes and stood firmly on the floor. "But I won't," MacLaren continued, "because your friend here is going to need someone to contact his lawyer for him, and why not his good ole country pal down on vacation."

Ben was still in front of him, like the Incredible Hulk, blocking any movement.

"Lieutenant?" one of the uniforms said, his 9mm Glock at the ready and pointed at the big man. MacLaren held his opened palm out, telling them to stand firm. He reached into his sportcoat and pulled out another piece of paper. He held it in front of Ben's face.

"Addendum to the autopsy report. The model was pregnant. Wonder what the blood tests will show?"

Big Ben grabbed the paper and stood back to read it. MacLaren walked back to the front of the table, brushing the front of his sportcoat.

"Get him outta here and book him!"

Ben walked out of the building and stood on the sidewalk beneath swaying palm trees. The wind had picked up and was blowing into downtown Sarasota from across the bay. It was sunny, and with the sea breeze, the heat of the afternoon felt comfortable. The car was parked across the street in one of those slanted forty-five degree angle spots that the quaint old Florida main streets have. There were several small stores and boutiques crowded together along the street. Big Ben held the car keys in his hand, but didn't know where to go. He needed a game plan. Down the way he could see an awning shading several small tables on the sidewalk. The awning said *Sarasota News & Café*. He stuffed the keys into the cargo pocket of his shorts and crossed the street. He needed a strong cup of coffee and a phone book.

FOURTEEN

There weren't any seats available at any of the small tables crammed into the café side of the bookstore so Big Ben took a seat on the brown leather couch near the front window. He'd asked to borrow the Sarasota phone book and he laid that on the narrow table in front of the couch, opened to the yellow pages under Attorney's. He sipped his black coffee that he'd ordered as a regular and then, as the counter girl was halfway through pouring it, had changed his mind and asked her to top it off with black decaf. He could see his wife Carlene smiling at him and saying something witty like, oh, you're actually going to listen to my advice for once? He'd only been away from her not even a day and he missed her. He thought about it and couldn't think of the last time he'd been away from home without her. He hadn't seen much of Sarasota yet, but he liked it so far. It was a heck of a lot more pleasant than blizzardy Bryce Corner, Massachusetts. Maybe after he got things wrapped up here he could come back sometime with Carlene, just the two of them, without the kids. That'd be nice. When was the last time they had done that?

"May I?" an attractive woman dressed professionally in a gray suit stood at the table with a chilled coffee drink in one hand and a pastry in the other.

"Sure." Ben slid over to accommodate her, realizing he had been taking up the whole couch.

She sat and placed her purchases on the coffee table. She had a small purse over her shoulder that she took off and set beside her on the couch. When she leaned forward to open the pastry bag, her skirt rose up along her thigh.

Careful Big Boy, Ben heard Carlene say, remember how you miss me.

The table was narrow and short and Ben had moved the phone book over to his extreme end.

"Got enough room there?" he asked.

"Yes, thank you." She spread out the pastry on its thin wax paper and picked up her coffee drink with the oversize straw sticking out of the cover. She sipped and returned the cup to the table. There was a red lipstick imprint on the tip of the straw.

Ben flipped a page and ran his finger slowly down the column on the left. He was into the D's.

"Are you looking for an attorney?"

"Yes, actually I am."

"What type?"

"Criminal."

"Are you in trouble?"

"No, a friend of mine is."

"Anything serious?"

"Naw, he just got booked for murder."

She laughed. "Seriously?"

"Yup."

"Oh, that doesn't sound too good."

"It's not. He's innocent."

"Um hmmm."

"I know, that's what they all say, right?"

"Usually, yes."

She took a bite of her pastry and patted her lips with a paper napkin that she spread carefully on her lap. Ben was pleased that it was small and didn't cover too much of her thigh.

"Is that what you were doing at the courthouse complex?" she asked.

"What?"

"Bailing your friend out?"

"No, we went in there to square a few things away and he ended up in the hoosegow."

"Hoosegow?"

"Old New England word for jail."

"Never heard of that one."

"I'm a cop, Chief of Police, small town outside Boston. I've pretty much heard every form of connotation for jail."

"I saw you there, when you were leaving."

"Really?"

"You're hard to miss."

Ben didn't know if she was referring to his size or his outfit or both. He decided not to ask. Instead he said kiddingly, "Are you a stalker?"

"No," she laughed. "Well, that may be all in how you interpret my vocation." She turned more fully toward him to reach into her purse. When she did Ben noticed a scar on her left cheek. It was about three inches along her jawbone. It was an old scar that had healed fairly well. The scar tissue was thin and hardly noticeable. A clean cut, he surmised. Probably a knife or razor.

"Lydia Lawrence, Esq." Ben read, "of Lawrence & Lawrence, Attorneys-At-Law. So, you *were* stalking me," Ben smiled at her.

"No, I promise, I wasn't," she touched her fingertips to his arm. "I was at the courthouse. I got a continuance on a case and I realized I hadn't eaten yet today, so I came over here to grab a bite." She picked up her coffee drink and took another sip. "Honestly."

"Okay, I believe you." Ben offered his hand to her, "Ben Benson."

Lydia put her cup down and wiped the moisture off her fingers with the napkin. She accepted his handshake, "Nice to meet you."

"The other Lawrence your husband?"

"No, my dad."

"What kind of law do you practice?"

"You're not going to believe me."

"I'll try."

"Criminal Law."

They both hesitated for a second then burst out laughing at the same time.

"You're right, I don't believe you."

"I feel foolish. You probably do think I'm a stalker. Let me give you a few references for good attorneys in town."

"No, let me ask you a question first. How long have you been practicing?"

"About five years, my dad almost thirty."

"And your rate of success?"

"Seventy percent."

"Not bad. Why did you get into it?"

"Long story."

"The scar?"

Lydia Lawrence, Esq. broke off a piece of her pastry and chewed. When she finished she took another sip of coffee then leaned back into the worn softness of the leather couch. She wrapped the paper napkin around the coffee cup and held it in her hands.

"You're very perceptive Chief Benson."

"Comes in handy in my business."

"I was in college, in New York City. I used to jog early in the morning. Central Park. I thought it was safe. Guiliani had done a good job of cleaning up the City." She sipped. "One morning I got grabbed. Didn't even see him until it was too late. He had a knife. He held it to my throat. I could feel the cold sharpness of it pressing into my skin. I fought as best as I could until he cut me along my chin. He told me he would kill me if I resisted. I believed him. I could feel the blood running down my neck. It was hot. I let him do what he did. I couldn't move. I just lay there biting my lower lip trying not to give him the pleasure of my crying. And then, as quickly as he had grabbed me, it was over and he was gone. Then the tears came."

"I'm sorry."

Lydia sat up and placed her cup back onto the table. "They dragged all the known sex offenders in the neighborhood in for a line-up. I picked one out and they arrested him, tried him, convicted him and sent him off to jail. I was angry. I wanted someone punished for what had happened to me. I didn't care who it was. They were all the same to me. They were all criminals. Two years later another woman was attacked in the same place. Same M.O. Knife to the throat, cut jawbone, everything. They got the guy this time and he confessed to several other rapes."

"What happened to the first guy?"

"They let him go, but he had lost two years of his freedom because of me. He had a little boy. He had a good job and a nice wife. He'd turned himself around and I spun him right back into his old world without even a care."

"So you took up criminal law."

"Yes. It was too late to rectify what I had done to him, but I felt I owed it to somebody to make amends. I realized how easy it was for people to get convicted for things they didn't do. I want to change that."

"Interesting story Lydia Lawrence. You're a brave woman." Ben downed the rest of his coffee. "You could probably have that fixed if you went to a good plastic surgeon."

"I know."

Ben nodded his head. "Can I get you another drink?"

"No, I'm fine."

"I need another cup of joe. Be right back."

When he returned with a fresh cup of coffee, Lydia said, "So, what's your interesting story. How did you get involved in a murder in Sarasota?"

"My best friend called me the other night …" Ben filled Lydia in on the events of the past few days.

"I heard of it, but I thought it was a suicide."

"It was, until my good buddy Dodge insisted it was murder. Then the investigating officer dug deep and came up with some pretty incriminating evidence."

"I know MacLaren. He's tough. His philosophy is everyone's guilty. Period."

"Can you help us?"

"I'm not sure what I can do."

"First thing would be to get Dodge out of jail."

"That may not be that easy."

"Why not?"

"Judges don't like letting first degree murder suspects roam the streets."

"But he's innocent."

"Judges don't care about innocence. They care about being crucified by the media for letting a potential murderer go free. Double murderer. They'll charge him with the unborn child too."

"He's not a murderer, Lydia. He's a law-abiding guy who just happens to be a well-known fashion designer that's got wrapped up in a mess. You don't think they'll cut him any slack?"

"The more famous the person is, the more careful they'll be. The media will be a circus. The judge isn't going to take any chances."

Ben knew she was right. He had hoped to find a lawyer who'd be able to get Dodge out of jail. He'd promised him he would. But he knew it was a slim chance. MacLaren had done his homework.

"Well, I'm sure once the DNA results come back negative they'll let him go," Ben said.

"What makes you so sure they'll be negative?"

Big Ben hadn't thought of that.

"And anyway, that may be a moot point," Lydia said.

"How so?"

"I don't know if I can go any further without actually being Mr. Maddison's attorney."

"If you'll take the case, you're hired."

"You have the authority to do that?"

"Yes I do."

"Shake."

They shook hands.

"Good, I am now officially hired. So, what I was saying is, I don't think that the paternity of the child will matter to the court. It certainly won't matter to MacLaren. He'll figure either Maddison knew it was his, which would add more fuel to his

73

circumstantial fire, or that if it's not, Maddison wouldn't have known that, but may have still believed it to be his."

"Dodge says he didn't know she was pregnant and that it wouldn't be his anyway."

"Doesn't matter. With his fingerprints on the murder weapon, the five million dollar insurance policy and the romantic arena he is in, your friend has a lot stacked against him – with or without fatherhood."

"So where do we go from here?"

"Well, I need to meet my new client. But first I'll stop by the office and pick up the necessary paperwork to bring with me for him to sign. Once I meet with him we can draw up a game plan."

"He's going to think you're there to spring him, y'know."

"I'll talk to my dad. He's got an impeccable reputation and knows a lot of people. I'll see what we can do, but I can't promise anything. My gut feeling is he'll remain incarcerated for a few more days. We'll work on an arraignment for tomorrow morning and ask for a preliminary hearing as soon as possible."

"All right. Sounds like you've got a lot to do. You don't need me there with you, do you?"

"No." An odd question Lydia thought.

"Good. I've got to get dug in here. I think I need to meet the cast of characters and gather some information. They're all staying at the Ritz-Carlton. I'll check in there and start snooping around. If I get lucky maybe I can bring a quick resolve to this thing. Here's my cell phone number," Big Ben reached into a cargo pocket and retrieved his wallet. He passed Lydia his card. "Call me anytime 24/7."

Lydia said, "My cell number is on the back of my card. I'll keep you posted and you do the same."

"Deal."

They left the cool atmosphere of the bookstore café and walked along the sidewalk in the mid-afternoon heat. They decided to each go about their business for the balance of the day and compare notes later.

"I bet I can figure out who did it before you even get to the prelim," Ben said.

"For your friend's sake, I hope you do."

As they approached the rental car, Ben asked Lydia if he could give her a lift.

"No thanks, the office is just around the corner on Palm Avenue."

They shook hands again and parted. When Lydia saw him open the door to the Jaguar she said, "My God, can you fit into that thing?"

"Barely. Can you give me directions to the airport?"

"Are you leaving?"

"Nope. Gonna trade in this slipper for a bigger boot."

FIFTEEN

By the time Ben got to the Ritz in the big black Hummer it was late afternoon. The sun hovered leisurely on the Gulf of Mexico and the day had another two hours of light left in it. A white van waited at the edge of the drive with its blinker on. Ben motioned for it to pull out. He couldn't tell if the driver gave him a courtesy wave because the windows were tinted black. You couldn't go that dark in Massachusetts, he thought. He noticed the side of the van was muddy and realized he hadn't seen a dirty vehicle yet in the brief time he'd been in Florida. Up north they were all covered with snow and road salt. His rearview mirror caught the red duct tape patching the left taillight. A mangy looking truck to be at the Ritz.

The valet welcomed him and Ben asked him to park the machine as close to the front doors as possible, back it into its parking spot and to return the keys to him. Big Ben was a man of habit and he was used to having his police vehicle always at the ready for a speedy departure. In his business seconds were precious. Like a sheriff in the old west, Ben wanted to be able to jump on his horse and ride off after the bandits quickly and effortlessly. And having a good horse was not a luxury. It was a necessity. He felt much better about the Hummer. He checked in at the front desk and entrusted his meager luggage to the bellman to take to his room.

The word was out. Attorney Lydia Lawrence had met with designer Dodge Maddison and, upon his instructions, had contacted Harlow who in turn spread the ill news to Fletcher Ross, Andre Chateauguy and the rest of the crew. To say they were surprised would have been an understatement. The entire group was gathered at the Tiki Bar on the beach. They had finished the photo shoot and had been celebrating with flavorful umbrella drinks when Harlow had come over to make the announcement. The festive glow about them had quickly turned into an aura of confusion and disbelief. No one for a moment thought Dodge Maddison was guilty of murdering Dana.

Big Ben left the lobby and walked through the colorful garden with the exotic plants that wove a pathway to the beach. The grass roof of the tiki hut was just ahead and he could see the assembled entourage. The models weren't hard to miss, glistening in their bikinis in small groups around the tables in the sunshine. He spotted Harlow beneath the shade of the hut seated at the far end of the bar with a man on either side of her. One was standing. He was tall, athletic looking and well dressed and holding onto a rocks glass. The other man was shorter, bald, and not so well dressed. He was seated on one of the bamboo barstools and seemed to be, by his flagrant hand gesturing, in command of their conversation. His drink had a purple umbrella in it and was perched on the edge of the bar next to a straw hat.

Harlow's back was to him when Big Ben approached the trio and the conversation halted. The gentlemen looked at him as if he were an annoying tourist barging into their territory to order a drink from the bartender.

"Harlow," Ben said.

She turned around. "Ben! Oh my god," she hugged him, "what the hell is going on?"

"It's going to be all right," he consoled her. "There's just a little bit of confusion in the minds of the Sarasota P.D. but we're working on it and everything's going to be just fine."

"Confusion? I'd say insanity!" Andre bellowed. "I mean what the fuck are they doing? She kills herself? She doesn't kill herself? They think somebody else kills her and so they point the finger at Dodge? What the fuck is that all about? Are they fucking clueless?"

Harlow said, "This is Chief Ben Benson from Bryce Corner, Dodge's best friend. Andre Chateauguy, our photographer and producer, and Fletcher Ross, our chief designer and fashion coordinator."

They shook hands. Ben noticed Andre had a firm handshake while Fletcher's was languid. He hoped he hadn't broken his hand.

"I've heard Dodge talk good things about you, Fletcher Ross."

"Thanks. Dodge told me he'd asked you to come down and we're glad you did. Especially now."

"Yeah Chief, you've got to straighten these local yokels out," Andre said.

"Call me Ben. Chief makes me sound like an Indian."

"Big Ben, like the clock, right?" Andre laughed.

"That's what they call him," Harlow said.

"I can see why. Would you like a drink?"

Ben thought for a second. "Sure," he leaned against the bar, "what do you have on draft?"

The bartender responded, "Bass, Guinness, Bud, Bud Light …"

"What's that tap on the end?"

"Fleming's Scottish Ale."

"Any good?"

The bartender poured a sample. "It's a hoppy pale ale."

Ben tasted. "Perfect. I'll take a pint."

"So, Boston, eh?" Andre said.

"Close to."

"How do you like Sarasota so far?"

"Sarasota's looking pretty good right now. I just left two feet of fresh snow."

"Yeah," Fletcher said, "New York got a few inches out of that storm too, but not as bad as you."

Ben raised his beer and said, "To Florida, aptly named the sunshine state," and took a long swig.

"So what the fuck's up with that Lieutenant dick?" Andre continued his contemptuous tirade. "He took my fucking fingerprints! Can you believe that? He actually had the balls to have me fingerprinted. The bastard."

"He's a thorough guy, I guess," Ben was standing next to Harlow. He had one foot resting on the rung of her barstool. "When was the last time you saw Dana," he asked Andre.

"Sunday. We were on the beach setting up the shots. I was taking light readings on her. Matching profile to shadow, checking the effect of the winds on the fabrics, y'know, if the wind is blowing the wrong way against the sun then you're turned into shadow and you can't get a decent shot to save your ass."

"What mood was she in?"

"The usual. Chipper, upbeat," Andre reflected for a moment. "She's a pleasure to work with actually. She takes her work very seriously, when she's into it."

"What do you mean?"

"She's a perfectionist and sometimes, most times, she stretches my patience. But the end results are always worth it." Andre took a sip of his drink. "We had some creative differences, but I am going to miss her."

Harlow and Fletcher Ross nodded their heads in agreement.

Big Ben turned his attention to Fletcher. "When was the last time you saw her, Fletcher?"

"Besides that horrific morning with Dodge, I guess it was Sunday. We went over wardrobes in the hotel and then walked the beach checking locations."

"By *we*, I assume you mean you and Dana."

"No. I was with all the models. Andre and Harlow were there too."

"So it was an assembled group. But tell me, what was the exact time that you last saw her?"

Fletcher thought for a moment, "Probably around one or two o'clock in the afternoon. The sun was way too hot by then. We had completed our work for the day and the girls were restless. They wanted to go play."

"Play?"

"They wanted to go shopping. So we called it a day."

"Did she go with the group?"

"I believe so. They all left the beach together so I assumed they all went out together."

"Any idea where they went?"

Harlow answered this one, "The girls walked down the beach to the Circle."

"The Circle?"

"St. Armands Circle. Where we had lunch. That area with all the shops and restaurants."

"Oh."

"But I think Dana wasn't with them because I saw her talking with Isabella later in a corner of the lobby."

"Who's Isabella?"

"One of the models." Harlow filled Ben in on the rivalry between Isabella and Dana.

"So Dana, a model, was talking with Isabella, another model, after the other models were gone?"

"Yes."

"Why would those two hang back?"

"I have no idea."

"Another round?" the bartender interjected.

"Sure, sure," Andre answered for them all.

Ben downed his drink and placed his plastic pint glass on the bar. He stepped to the wooden railing addressing the beach and placed his big hands onto it. He looked at the rolling ocean. The sun was lowering and a lone pelican was flying low just above the water. Ben watched it swoop skyward, hover for a second and then dive in an awkward contorted shape full speed into the sea, capturing an unlucky fish in its pouch. Sea gulls screeched behind in hopeless hope that he'd drop his prey.

"Hello there." One of the models was beside him. She placed her drink cup on the railing but kept her hands wrapped around it, her fingertips playing with the dripping moisture beads. "I like your outfit."

"Nice, huh?"

"Quite fashionable."

"Are you enjoying the Florida sun?"

"Too hot. I can't wait to get back to the Riviera next week, it's so much more pleasant."

"Never been there. Closest to the French Riviera I ever got was sitting in a Riviera convertible eating French fries."

The model laughed, "You're funny."

"What's that?"

"A mango margarita."

"You old enough to drink it?"

"I'm twenty-two."

"I've got sneakers older than you."

"Bet they don't smell as nice."

Ben stood off the railing and took a stance directly in front of her. "Isabella, right?"

"How did you know who I was?"

"I've heard things about you."

"Mmm, bad things I hope," Isabella took a provocative sip from her drink.

"Things like you don't seem too heartbroken over Dana's death."

"Should I be?"

"A peer, a friend, fellow model, fellow human being?"

"None of the above?"

"So … what, at birth you opted to forego compassion for an extra dose of flirtatiousness?"

"Whatever gets you more ahead."

"Even if you …?"

"Hey, that's how she did it."

"Ever hear of love?"

"Hngh. Yeah right. Ever hear of gold digger?"

"Jealous?"

"Not now."

"You're quite the coquette aren't you?"

"If you're trying to use a big word to insult me, don't. I know what coquette means and I'm not the vamp you may think I am. Ours is a ruthless business. If you don't make your mark young, and I mean very young, then you're history. Unlike Hollywood stars or athletes who can carry their reputation into their thirties, fashion models have a verrry limited window of opportunity. I started modeling when I was five, I'm twenty-two now and I'm almost over the hill. "

"Survival of the fittest?"

"Survival of the most cunning."

"And that's what you think Dana was?"

"She just happened to woo Dodge first, that's all."

"And you wish it had been you?"

"Absolutely."

"No shame to it?"

"Shame? Now there's a word I do *not* know," she smiled coquettishly.

After only a two minute conversation Ben could see why Harlow had called her ruthless. She was smart all right.

"You're the cop from Dodge's hometown, right?"

"That's right."

"Down here to help Dodge out."

"Yup."

"Best friends and all that."

"We are."

"If the situation was reversed, you think he'd drop everything and rush to your aid?"

"Yes, I do."

"Hmmm."

"I take it you don't."

"Not sure, but if you were a woman I'm sure he would."

"Bitterness is not becoming."

"But it's a great survival tool."

"Friendship is a stronger one," Big Ben could feel the abrasion from the wall Isabella kept around her and wondered what malaise from her past had erected it. "Maybe someday you'll appreciate that."

"Someday."

"What were you discussing with Dana in the lobby Sunday afternoon?"

"Wow, investigating already. Why don't you buy me another drink and we'll talk about it?"

He could see that she wasn't happy that her wiles were having no effect on him. But she was persistent, probably, he surmised, very used to getting her way ever since she was a cutesy little girl.

Ben had met Dana only once before, he had been in New York City on a police chief's conference and had visited the Maddison design studio one afternoon. He'd had lunch with Dodge and Dana and had found her to be pleasant, sophisticated and at ease with herself. Besides the physical attraction of a twenty-year-old super model, Ben could see where Dodge would have been attracted to her. Isabella, on the other hand was too blatantly shallow, a beautiful façade with a black widow snare behind it. Ben didn't think that approach would have worked on his best friend, and it certainly wasn't going to work on him."

"Are you avoiding my question?" Ben said.

"Not at all. We were discussing model things."

"Like?"

"Like clothes, make-up, favorite locales, stuff like that."

"Harlow said it looked like the two of you were having a heated discussion."

"Not at all. We got along fine."

Ben doubted that.

"When was the last time you saw her?"

"Then, in the lobby. I left to go meet the girls and she took the elevator."

"Did she join you later?"

"That's a laugh."

"Why?"

"Because she was *too good* to hang out with the peons. She was *upper echelon*, don't you know." She raised her pinky finger as she said this. "Her crowd was wherever Dodge Maddison and his clique were."

Andre drew near them with two drinks in his hands, "Here ya go Big Ben." Ben accepted the frothy beer.

Isabella said, "Ou, Big Ben, I like the sound of *that*."

"I see you've met our resident vixen and wannabe successor to the throne," Andre said to Ben.

"Yes, Isabella's been enlightening me on the cutthroatedness of the fashion model business."

"Well, she's certainly an expert."

"Fuck you Andre."

"In your dreams."

"In my nightmares."

"Now, now," Harlow had joined them, "let's behave, children."

Isabella offered her hand to Big Ben, "So very nice to meet you. I hope to be seeing *more* of you. Let me know if I can be of further assistance ..." and she turned and gave her sexiest runway exit.

"Very coy," Ben laughed.

"Yeah," Andre said, "she's about as coy as a prostitute."

"Andre," Harlow said, "would you be so kind as to give me a minute alone with Ben?"

"Sure, sure." He retreated to the bar and joined Fletcher Ross.

A zephyr rolled in from the Gulf lending a soft breeze to the approaching sunset. The tall sea oats swayed back and forth to the rhythm of the waves.

"Ben," Harlow said, "how serious is this?"

He knew what she was talking about. "Serious enough."

Harlow stood beside him. They gazed at the horizon with the sun dropping behind a thick cloud mass. If the clouds were lifting up from the west, there'd still be a chance that the sun would peek through in time for another spectacular Florida sunset. Ben was hoping so. It had been weeks, maybe months, since he'd seen the sun actually set.

Ben could feel Harlow's concern standing beside him. She knew this man, knew his wife, Carlene. She had been to their house with Dodge many times during her ten years with Maddison Designs. They had had dinners together, played cards, laughed, and even gotten drunk together. Big Ben was no stranger. She wanted to wrap her arms around his waist and tuck her head into his chest, the comforting big brother.

"I'm afraid Ben."

"Don't worry," he placed an arm over her shoulder, "It'll be all right. We've got a pretty sharp attorney with solid local connections. He'll be out in no time and we'll be back in Bryce Corner sipping eggnog with our Christmas dinner before you know it."

"I wish I could be with you."

"Sorry," he said. Ben had temporarily forgotten about Annison Barrett. She was so new in their lives. It had always been Harlow that Dodge had brought with him when he visited home. He never missed a holiday or a birthday party for the kids. He loved being Uncle Dodge. Even when he had been involved with Dana, he'd never brought her to Bryce Corner. Still it had been Harlow. Something Ben found odd and had questioned his good friend about. Ben, Dodge had said, you'll never understand Harlow and I, we're just close friends in a professional relationship. That's all there is to it. Why can't you see how simple it is. We work hard together, so it's nice to bring Harlow up here to relax. And she and Carlene have become such great friends.

But Ben didn't buy it. Not even after the Annison thing emerged. And that had been so sudden. And now they were planning a Bed & Breakfast together? And a marriage? And Dana was dead? What the fuck was going on?

SIXTEEN

"Hey, slow down! We don't wanna get stopped."

The white van tilted to one side as it sped around the rotary of St. Armands Circle. A shiny new Cadillac with Michigan plates pulled away from the curb and into the traffic at a snails pace. The driver of the van pumped his brakes and laid heavily on the horn. "Fuckin' fossils! Get the fuck off the road!"

"Stop attracting attention, Roger. I don't wanna blow this. This is the easiest ten grand we've ever made. Cool it, for chrissake."

"All right, all right. Get off my ass." Roger swung around the Caddy and took the road toward Longboat Key.

"Where are you going?"

"For a cold one."

"Roger, we don't have time for a cold one."

Roger ignored him. He saw a cop car in his rearview. When the blue lights came on he reached under his seat.

"Oh shit." Mikey said.

Roger slowed and pulled cautiously over to the right. The cop car sped by them, racing down the road.

"Fuck! I almost had a fucking heart attack."

"Now I really need a fucking cold one."

Two minutes later the van pulled onto the access road to Mote Marine and Aquarium. Next to that, on the channel connecting Sarasota Bay to the Gulf, sits The Old Salty Dog, a local watering hole on the wharf. Roger parked alongside the marina and jumped out. He didn't bother to lock the van. Mikey did though. He was nervous about the cargo and didn't want to chance anyone snooping around.

Three beers and three shots later Mikey went to the men's room. When he got back to the bar, Roger was missing. He looked around and saw him standing at a table dockside talking with the two girls they'd been ogling since their arrival ten minutes earlier. He wondered about Roger. Just by looking at him you could tell he'd done his share of being bad. He wore long, scraggly hair, uncombed and hanging from a dirty baseball cap and had rough-hewn leathery skin from too much salt-water sun. A glint in his eye that looked the same whether it was treacherous or endearing. When he grinned you could see his teeth weren't properly aligned and he had ink on both his arms that had been colorful once upon a time, but was now running down his arms, indistinctive, faded and blue like the trail of his life he'd left behind him.

He went over. Roger had helped himself to a chair. "Hey, Mikey! Pull up a chair. This here's ... what you'd say yur name was darlin'?"

"Fiona, and this is my sister Franny."

"Yeah, Fie-own-ah and Franny. This is my bro, Mikey."

"Hi," Mikey said. "Ah, Roger, can I talk to you for a sec?"

Roger ignored him and took a draw on his beer. "The girls tell me they're here visitin' dear ole gramma down on Longboat, ain't that right ladies?"

The sisters snickered.

"And they say they come down a lot, but have never been out on the water fishin'. Can you believe that? So I told 'em we'd take 'em out." Roger winked at the sisters and lifted his beer bottle back.

The girls laughed again. "Are you really fishermen?"

"Sure are."

"Where's your boat?"

"Gottit stuck over there at the marina. See that purty white one down in the slip?"

The girls twisted in their seats, "They're all white ones."

Roger laughed.

Mikey, still standing, said, "Really need to talk to you right now, Roger."

"Okay, okay," he stood up, took off his cap and bowed, "I'll only be a moment, ladies, don't yew go away." He made a foolish grin and replaced his cap back onto his head, backwards. The girls snickered some more.

Mikey didn't know Roger that well, nor Roger he. They'd met about a year ago up in northern Florida, crating oranges until a freak frost had ended their employment. Roger had said they could find work further south and Mikey had joined him in a run to Palmetto, Tropicana territory. They'd worked there long enough for Roger to get into his third fight with the migrants before the boss threw him out. And Mikey with him, although he'd never been any more involved in the fights than trying to break them up peacefully. He was the cleaner looking, calmer one. Always shaved, his hair buzz cut and his perfect teeth glistening white, he could pass as a respectable guy; a banker, a store clerk, or a car salesman. None of which he was, ever had been, nor ever would be. The two bad seeds shared an apartment, a hotel room really, in a shoddy hotel on the Manatee River behind the marina next to Rusty's Anchor. They found jobs on the dock; filleting fish, repairing boats, cleaning the docks, whatever to keep them housed, fed and in beer money.

At the side of the bar Mikey said, "We don't have time for this, man."

"Whoa, whoa," Roger held up his hands, the bottle of Bud swinging precariously with his drunken swaggering. "First yew said we didn't have time fur a cold one, but we've had two tree a doze already. Then you said ..."

"We've gotta take care of that shit in the van," Mikey cut in, "and then go collect the rest of the dough. All you're doing is getting drunk and horny."

"First a all, I ain't drunk. And second a all, I'm always horny," Roger laughed as if he was really funny, which Mikey knew he was not. "Besides, yur the one who ain't thinking straight, bro. It ain't even dark yet. We can't burn that shit 'til it's fuckin' dark."

True, Mikey thought. "But we're only five minutes from the Ritz for chrissake. We gotta travel someplace farther inland. Way inland so nobody'll suspect anything."

"Mikey, my man, you're too nervous. You gotta relax. Ain't nobody looking for us." Roger wrapped his arm around Mikey's shoulder, the beer bottle swaying in front of his face, "You gotta trust in ole Roger." He looked around to make sure nobody was within earshot. "Here's what we're gonna do. We ain't gotta go wasting gas driving way out to no Arcadia just to burn up a few bags. We can do that right here. We wait 'til the sun's down and drive over to South Lido Key. The park closes at sunset, but there ain't no gate or nothing so we can just drive in to the pines there to one of them picnic sights with the fireplace grills and burn the shit. If anyone comes by we'll say we're just puttin' out our grill. Just roasted a few weenies for supper that's all."

Roger had a good point. That park was pretty desolate at night. And the pines were thick there so if they kept the fire low it wouldn't be seen. Besides, he'd rather not chance driving an hour inland when they'd had so much to drink. The cops always scouted the county roads.

Roger could tell by Mikey's silence that he'd gotten through to him. "Good then. Now, let's just relax and have some fun with these two chicks. I need to get laid, man."

Mikey looked at the sisters. They were dressed casually and appeared relaxed, but even he could sense an air of sophistication in their attire and mannerisms that only came with blue blood. They said they were vacationing at their grandmother's on Longboat Key, an elegant stretch of island with sandy private beaches and hidden hush-hush residences that only the insanely rich could afford. Movie stars, rock stars, and international tycoons kept million dollar getaways there. Grammy had dough. Her granddaughters had probably been spoiled since day one. Mikey saw trouble in their eyes. He didn't like it.

"I don't like it, Roger. Let's not push our luck. These two look like trouble."

"They look like candy to me, Bro."

"Roger, they're in a whole different class."

"Fuckin' A. That's why it'll be easy. They wanna get down and dirty. They're looking for a taste of the local flavorin' – if you know what I mean," he poked Mikey with his elbow. "Besides, just the fact they're talking to us has cunt-siderably up'd our chances." Roger laughed at his sick humor again. "Go sit down, I'm gonna liven things up a bit." Then he yelled, "Barkeep! Four shots a tequila!"

SEVENTEEN

Big Ben's cell phone rang. He didn't recognize the number. "Hello."

"Ben, it's Lydia Lawrence."

"Oh, hello."

"I've just left the jail. I had a long talk with Mr. Maddison. I think it went well."

"Any chance of getting him released?"

"Not yet, but we're working on it."

"I was afraid of that."

"He'll be okay for the time being. He wants you to contact him as soon as you can. Where are you?"

"I'm at the Ritz-Carlton's beachside bar talking with Dodge's people now."

"Anything?"

"Not much, but I've just started. You?"

"Well, he pretty much corroborated what you told me earlier about his relationship with Dana, that it had ended some time ago, how he found her that morning, et cetera. He's certainly not happy about his present circumstances. He thinks MacLaren has something personal against him and that he has incarcerated him just to piss him off and show him who's boss. He wants to initiate a lawsuit for wrongful arrest."

Ben laughed, "That sounds like Dodge. When do you think you can get him out?"

"Realistically, another day or two, if that. I spoke with the D.A. and she claims to have a substantial amount of evidence. She's readying disclosures now and promised to have them in my hands by tomorrow morning."

"Okay, I'll finish up here and then I'll drive over to see Dodge."

"Ben ..."

"What?"

"There's something else."

"Yeah?"

"I don't know how it got out, but the media's here."

"What?"

"I had to sneak out the back. The front of the courthouse complex is already becoming a circus. Someone inside must have alerted them – for a handsome fee I'm sure. 'World Famous Fashion Designer Accused of Murdering Super Model'."

"Shit. I knew that would happen. I just didn't think it would be this quick. Local or national?"

"Both. I saw the Sun News van *and* CNN."

"Dammit! ... Listen, why don't you come over here and we can put a game plan together?"

Lydia took a moment. "It's only a matter of time before they descend on the Ritz, you know. Maybe only minutes."

"We'll have to handle that as it comes."

"All right, I just need to stop by the office for a minute, then I'll drive over."

"Good. I need to make a couple quick calls back home. I don't want my wife, and especially Annison Barrett, to find out on the news before I alert them."

"See you in about twenty minutes."

"That's fine. That'll give me time to check into my room and make the calls. I'll meet you at the outside Tiki Bar."

They hung up from each other.

Harlow had been close enough to catch bits and pieces of the conversation. "What's up?" she asked.

"The media's got a hold of it."

"Oh no."

"Exactly. Now the crucifying begins. This isn't going to be pretty."

"Is there something wrong?" Andre approached them.

Ben looked at Harlow and said, "You may as well tell them, I've got to go make some calls. I'll be back down in a few minutes."

Big Ben stopped at the registration desk to pick up his room key. A pleasant woman in a classy dress assisted him. She had a delightful smile and impeccable make-up. Her perennial bronze tan was accented with bright gold jewelry. Very Sarasota Ritz.

"Here you are, Chief Benson. Your luggage is already in your room. The elevators are at the far end of the lobby. Is there anything else I can be of assistance with?"

"Perhaps. There was a white van exiting the driveway as I came in about an hour ago. Would you know anything about that?"

"Yes, that was a FedEx pick up."

"It didn't appear to be a FedEx van."

"Nor was it our usual driver. In fact I was tempted to ask for identification because he wasn't wearing the customary FedEx uniform, but he did have the proper paperwork. He said he was an auxiliary carrier sub-contracted for the Christmas rush. I know they usually do that during their peak periods."

"Do you know what he picked up?"

"Several large pieces of luggage."

"Would you know who requested the pick-up?"

She reached to her left and retrieved a clipboard, "A Mister Andre Chateauguy."

"Thank you, Marlena," Ben had taken the liberty of reading her nametag.

"Will there be anything else? Dinner reservations?"

"No, thank you, you've been quite helpful."

"Enjoy your stay with us, Mr. Benson."

Dodge Maddison had made arrangements for Ben, who he knew had never stayed at a Ritz-Carlton before, to have one of the penthouse suites. As Ben exited the elevator and walked down the elegantly decored hallway he wished he were here under more pleasant circumstances. He had a feeling he wasn't going to enjoy this visit.

When he entered the room, he exclaimed, "Wow! Carlene would love this."

He crossed the expansive living room with the plush furniture and the deep carpeting and looked out the large windows. The setting sun was breaking through the horizon clouds and the view was spectacular. Ben reached for his cell phone and it rang in his hand. Without checking to see who it was, he answered, "Hello."

"Ben," it was his wife Carlene.

"Hi sweetheart. I was just reaching for my phone to call you when it rang. How are you doing?"

"I'm doing fine. The question is, how are *you* doing?"

Quickly Ben told her about the easy flight, the beautiful weather, his new tropical clothes, lunch with Dodge and Harlow, being on the beach having a beer at the Tiki Bar, even the come-on from the bikinied model ...

"Get to the bad news," she said.

Carlene and Ben had been together since high school. They had two teenage kids, two cars, a mortgage, a dog, a cat and a lifetime of memories. There were few things they didn't know about each other, if any. And just by the enormity of pure time they had shared together, they were inextricably united. Even in thoughts. Often they knew what each other were going to say before they said it. Beyond all that, circling above them like an ever-present hawk was the bald fact that he was a cop and she a cop's wife. And by that nature, more so than normal couples, they were frighteningly aware that each time they kissed good-bye in the morning, could be their last. Thus there was a greater sense of love to their relationship, which was at the same time, coupled with a lesser tolerance for bullshitting. Carlene always knew when Ben was stalling, trying to dance around a situation.

"Dodge has been arrested."

"I know," she said.

"How did you ... oh shit. Is it on the news already?"

"All over it."

"Dammit! I was trying to get ahead of that. Lydia just told me about it minutes ago."

"Lydia?"

"Lydia Lawrence, a local attorney. I've retained her and her dad to represent Dodge. She just called me from the jailhouse to tell me CNN was onto it."

"They're onto it alright. They've even got footage of you and Dodge entering the building."

"You're kidding me."

"Not at all. By the way, I'm not sure about that shirt."

"Hey, what's wrong with my shirt?"

"But I do like the colorful hat."

It was already dark in Bryce Corner, Massachusetts. The two feet of snow plowed against the edges left the rural roads looking like a bobsled run. The frosty night air glimmered silently beneath the old-style streetlights. Carlene sat in the big leather swivel chair positioned in front of the large desk in 'Ben's Den'. It was his auxiliary command post, fully equipped with state of the art computers, radios, scanners and other necessary electronics of his trade. With all the monitors and blinking lights, the wall above the desk looked like the cockpit of a major airliner. The other walls were adorned with pictures, commendations, plaques and memorabilia of Ben's professional life. The wall surrounding the window with the winter outside had shelves of deep mahogany filled with mystery novels by Ben's favorite authors. A glass fronted gun rack stood in the corner. It was clearly a room for a man's man, but Carlene felt closer to Ben here.

In a solemn voice she asked, "Do you think he's involved in it?"

A sensible, pragmatic question. Carrying more weight to it because Carlene was genuinely concerned. Dodge Maddison was more than an internationally famous fashion designer to her. Carlene had known Dodge Maddison most of her life. She knew him as her husband's best friend, and felt in a real sense that Dodge was like a brother to her and an uncle to her children.

Ben knew that Carlene had wondered about Dodge lately. He had too. They had voiced their opinions over the dinner table. They were confused. They felt not that his success had gone to his head, but rather that he was having an emotional time dealing with the loss of the only family he had, in addition to the sustenance of his demanding business. They had hoped that he would have settled down by now, ideally marrying Harlow whom he had shared a ten year relationship with, albeit platonic according to Dodge and Harlow. Platonic until the funeral of Dodge's grandparents just last fall.

Carlene and Ben both knew of the consummation. Knew it had happened when Harlow had come up for the services. But then she had abruptly gone back to the City, with Dodge staying in Bryce Corner to attend to the estate. That was when he had met Annison Barrett and started on a whirlwind romance (or a whirlwind infatuation as Carlene called it) culminating in a marriage proposal and plans to convert the grandparent's farmhouse into a Bed and Breakfast. Way too fast, they thought. And let's not forget the fling with Dana going on for the past year. So, the current circumstances were bewildering to say the least. Certainly a justification for Carlene's question.

"I'd love to answer that with an emphatic no," Ben said to his wife, "but I don't know. I haven't had much time to talk to him solo yet."

"But the thing with Dana *was* over between them wasn't it?"

"He says it ended when he took up with Annison Barrett - who I've gotta call by the way, hopefully before she sees the news on TV."

"It all happened too fast, Ben. I mean it seems like everything was going okay for him until he got involved with Dana, and that wasn't even a year ago, was it? That was stupid. She's only twenty years old for chrissake, and was only nineteen then. I don't know how Harlow put up with it."

"Well they both told us their relationship was just a business friendship, right?"

"Bullshit. And you know that."

"I don't know what I know. But I do know something that doesn't make me happy."

Carlene waited for him to continue. "Dana was pregnant," he said.

"Oh my god."

"Yeah, and that puts a whole new spin on things."

"Do you think it's his?"

"He says it's not."

"But it could be."

"But I've gotta believe him."

"You *want* to believe him. Don't let your friendship get in the way of your job. You're there to help him. Letting the friendship taint your investigative intuition isn't going to help Dodge. You've got to give him your best effort. Carry out your investigating like you normally would. You've always said the only way to be a cop is to be a cop."

He knew she was right. He was glad he had Carlene to talk to, to bounce things off of, and to keep him steady and focused. She was the even keel to his divergent bow.

"Listen, Babe, I've got to call Annison. I don't want her to hear the news of his arrest through CNN."

"Okay, but please tell me, are you alright? I don't like the sound of things down there."

"I'm fine."

She trusted him. Trusted him enough to know that he would tell her if he wasn't. Trusted her instincts too. He hadn't hesitated in responding to her. If he had, even for a split second, she'd have known he wasn't answering truthfully, trying to cover his feelings in order to protect her. A male thing that she'd never let him know she could easily detect.

"I'll have it wrapped up in no time," Ben said. "Then maybe I'll hang out for a few days and enjoy the respite from the snow and cold," he teased her.

"Well, don't get too comfortable with all the sun and fun, *and the cutesy little half-naked fashion model*, because I may just have to take a flight down there to remind you what you're supposed to be focusing on."

"Darlin', if you were here, *you'd* be the only thing I'd be able to focus on."

"Oh … you're good."

Ben could see her beautiful smile on the other end of the line.

"I love you," he said.

"Ditto, Big Boy. Be careful."

"I will."

"And call me!"

"Yes Ma'am."

They hung up and Ben immediately called Annison Barrett.

EIGHTEEN

The sun sets faster in December. By the time Big Ben got back to the Tiki Bar it had already dropped below the horizon, leaving bright purple clouds stretching over the verdigris green water. The sky above was fading from royal to dusky blue and the constellations were appearing in their usual way as persistent white dots beneath the timeless sapphire umbrella of the universe.

Fire red bamboo torches sticking in the sand flickered around the perimeter of the beachside dining area. A server was seating a four top at one of the tables. The models had disappeared to their rooms to prep for their last evening in town. They'd be returning to New York tomorrow, directly after the memorial service for Dana. Attorney Lydia Lawrence had arrived ten minutes ago, found and introduced herself to the group at the bar and was seated next to Harlow sipping on a single-malt scotch.

"What's that?" Ben asked her.

"Dalwhinnie, sixteen year, neat."

"A lawyer after my own heart. I could use one of those right about now." He signaled to the bartender and pointed at Lydia's glass. "Anyone else need a drink?"

Harlow had a full one, Fletcher Ross declined and Andre, with half a glass full said, "Sure, what the hell," and downed the rest of his fruity colada.

"Have you met everyone?" Ben asked Lydia.

"Yes, thank you. Did you complete your phone calls?"

"Yeah. My wife had already seen it on CNN, but I managed to get hold of Annison to let her know first hand."

"Now forgive me but I'm not sure I know who's who yet. Annison would be Dodge's?"

"Ah ..." Ben kept his eyes on Lydia and away from Harlow, "fiancée, I guess." He could feel Harlow bristle at the word.

"Forgive me," Lydia said directly to Harlow, "but it's a little confusing."

"Tell me about it," Harlow replied with a slip of sarcasm.

"Well, I'm sure it hasn't been easy for you, being in love with this man for the past ... how long has it been?" Lydia's bluntness stunned Harlow and, like the waiter flipping a fresh linen tablecloth over the nearby table, instantly covered the group with a cloak of surprise. Everyone caught their breath.

Boy, she dives right in, Ben said to himself.

"Listen," Lydia said, "I don't mean to put anyone on the spot here, but I've got a high profile case staring me in the face, with very little time to prepare a battle. Lieutenant MacLaren and the D.A., a very tenuous and shark-like woman named Tanya Chisholm, will push for an early conviction. And I'm not talking about the judicial system; I'm talking about the real jury that Dodge Maddison will be facing, the media. This man's reputation, his livelihood, his very life as he knows it, is very much on the line. People of his magnitude do not share the anonymity of Mr. and Mrs. American - they have the ease of being innocent until proven guilty. Dodge does not. We need to understand just how much danger he is in. The media will descend upon us like a dark plague and like hyenas in a feeding frenzy, they will claw at each other to get to the finish line first with the biggest headline. They will have no regard for guilt or innocence. Whatever sells the most, whoever gets on the talk show circuits first, is the winner. Dodge Maddison isn't even in the race.

"So if some of my queries seem blunt, I ask for your forgiveness in advance. I need to be a quick study. I don't mean to embarrass anyone, but these type of questions are nothing compared to the ones the prosecutor will be asking."

"It's not like we don't all know," Andre said to Harlow. "I mean the only ones who think it's a secret are you and Dodge."

"I know … I know." Harlow had had a couple stiff drinks on top of a very harrowing day. Her lips were loosening. "It's probably been since the first damn day I saw him."

"When was that?" Lydia prompted.

"Ten years ago when he walked into the Giovanni showroom I was working in on Sixth Avenue. Dodge wasn't as famous then, but he was known. Giovanni was, still is, a piece goods manufacturer out of Milan. Dodge had worked with him almost exclusively and the two had become good friends. Unbeknownst to me, they had conferred about me joining Maddison Designs. My degree and background in textiles had earned me an enviable position with Giovanni and I'd been with him for five years. I knew the ins and outs of his business extremely well. What I didn't know was that he was downsizing his operation, essentially eliminating the New York offices and returning the focus back to his home city of Milan. At that point, Maddison Designs was accounting for over fifty percent of Giovanni's goods, and growing. I knew of Dodge, had spoken to him on the phone several times, but had never actually met him. He always did his business with Giovanni personally, most always in Milan. With the operation reverting back to Italy, I was to be offered relocation or, as the purpose of Dodge's visit outlined, I could remain in New York and join his business."

Harlow took a long sip on her drink, her eyes were off focus, peering back into time, reliving the moments that had changed her life and set into motion the events that would eventually bring her to this place and time.

"Maddison Designs is located in the City, in Soho, in a marvelously restored building with the retail shop at street level, Dodge's residence in the penthouse and the manufacturing and design facilities on the five floors in between. For the two of them it was a well-designed move. Maddison Designs was growing and Dodge needed someone to oversee his operations, Giovanni was devoting more and more of his piece goods to Dodge, I was well versed in Giovanni's textile operation, and it seemed to be a natural evolution for the two companies."

"So the two companies were doing more business together, Giovanni was leaving New York, returning to Milan, and you were the perfect fit for Maddison Designs?" Lydia summarized.

"Yes. I started with Dodge the week after he came to see me."

"How did the personal relationship unfold?"

Lydia was gathering background. Putting together a mental picture of the life of her high profile client. The questions for Harlow were significant, not only because she had been the woman closest to Dodge Maddison's life for the lengthiest time, but more importantly, she had been intricately woven into his character, his inner workings as a man, simply due to the fact that she was in love with him. A woman in love becomes an internal barometer to a man's heart, whether he knows it or not.

The men found their thoughts drifting away from the conversation, not that the topic was boring, but the three of them had heard it before, maybe not from the horse's mouth, but certainly in the hushed voices in their work-a-day world. Fletcher Ross worked with Harlow daily and was privy to the ongoing office gossip about Dodge and his women and witness to Harlow's rigid, motherly protectionism. But when Dodge had taken up with Dana a year ago, a pall had fallen over the building. Everyone, from the girls on the sales floor in the boutique, to the seamstresses on the manufacturing floors, to the designers in the design studio, could see the eggshells spread around Harlow whenever she walked by them. Everyone approached her with extreme caution. No one wanted to be around her when the lid blew. Then, when Annison Barrett came on the scene, the hot topic was about the speed of the relationship and the rumor of Dodge relocating to New England to open a Bed & Breakfast. The scuttlebutt was that he had been working too hard for too long and then taken aback by the death of his beloved grandparents; thence becoming ripe for any gold digger who happened along. There was a general consensus that he should really think about therapy. All the while, Dodge seemed oblivious to the tune playing on Harlow's heartstrings. At this point, no one wanted to even be near Harlow. Even Fletcher Ross, who as head designer and the second closest to Harlow after Dodge, relegated himself to the design studio as a refuge from the inevitable explosion of the simmering emotional time bomb.

Andre Chateauguy, although as an independent fashion photographer only a peripheral player in the world of Maddison Designs, could also see the hidden emotional tension in Harlow of late. Whenever they occasioned to be working on a catalogue shoot or a fashion show together, he had sensed it. He'd even broached the topic with her once, actually just last week when they, he and Harlow, had been packing up the line to ship down to Florida for the Sarasota shoot. But, true to form, she had adamantly denied any attachment to Dodge beyond a professional one. Andre didn't believe it for a moment and had told her so.

Big Ben, by virtue of being Dodge's best friend, harbored a special insight. He and his wife Carlene had been close to Dodge and Harlow as a couple over the years. They'd shared times and holidays together in Bryce Corner, Massachusetts when Dodge frequently visited his grandparents Jed and Emma. Harlow was a common companion. Everyone could see and feel the deeper connection beneath the surface. Everyone except Dodge who wrote it off as just a working weekend for he and Harlow away from the office. Also, for Ben and Carlene, they had been there when Dodge had met Annison Barrett. They had met her and had spent time with the new Dodge and Annison pairing, much to Carlene's chagrin. So, Ben was well versed in the romantic life of Dodge Maddison. Well versed and well confused. He too had questioned Dodge's sanity, although keeping it to himself, for he believed every man had to deal with his own problems independently. But now, in the present circumstance, with Dana dead, Big Ben wondered if he should have said more to his lost friend. He hoped it wasn't too late.

The night was moving on. The sky had surrendered the sun on one side of it and was resurrecting the waning full moon on the other. Ben was resurrecting something too, a waxing hunger. He felt like he needed a thick juicy steak to go with the scotch burning a hole in his stomach. He broke into the conversation between Lydia and Harlow and asked if they'd like to dine. They were so engrossed that they didn't even respond. Andre looked at his watch and excused himself and Fletcher, "I didn't realize the time. We're meeting the crew to go to dinner in town. It's our last night here and I promised to take them out. Would you like to join us?"

Ben thought not. He thought it more prudent to spend the time with Lydia Lawrence and Harlow. "No thanks Andre. You guys go on, I'll entertain the ladies. I'm going to see if I can get a table right here."

"Suit yourself, but if you're up for it, you could probably find us later this evening having a nightcap somewhere on the Circle. Call my cell, I'll let you know where we are and I'll buy you a drink."

"Could be a plan."

Andre gave Ben his cell number and then he and Fletcher excused themselves from the women. Ben shuffled through the beach sand to the hostess stand to procure a table. Then he went inside the hotel to the men's room. When he exited the revolving doors to return to the beach, he found Andre and Fletcher standing to the side having a conversation. The pathway went right by them and Ben could hear Fletcher say, "I have no idea where he is, Andre. You're his boss, not me. You should know."

"Well I don't! And I'm not fucking happy about it either."

"What's up?" Ben said.

"One of the cameramen didn't show up for the shoot today and Andre's still upset about it."

"Not one of the cameramen, *the* cameraman! Santiago's my head videographer."

"Santiago?" Ben remembered MacLaren talking about him earlier in the day. He was the supposed boyfriend to Dana that MacLaren had ruled out of the investigation because he discovered that he was gay. "Where do you think he is?"

"No fucking idea. He didn't show up this morning. He checked out of the hotel last night and the sonofabitch *knew* we were shooting in the morning."

"He probably went back to New York," Fletcher offered.

"Fucking high strung immigrant fag. I'll fire his ass the second I see him!"

"Has he done this sort of thing before?" Ben asked.

"Never. That's what I don't understand. It's out of character for him to just disappear." Andre removed his straw hat and scratched the top of his baldhead. "Whatever, no big loss. There are a hundred photographers in the city that'd kill to have his job. I'll have him replaced by next week. Come on," he motioned to Fletcher with his hat, "we've got to get going."

NINETEEN

They were seated at a table fronting the beach. The ocean was dark but you could still see the thin white of the waves as they crested in horizontal lines across the darkened sand, like wayward chalk lines scrawled across a blackboard. Ben had ordered a glass of water, opting to hold off on another scotch until after dinner. Harlow was on a fresh drink, that she certainly didn't need, and Lydia Lawrence had hardly touched her first one. She was too busy pumping Harlow for information.

"We all arrived Saturday afternoon from New York."

"We?" Lydia asked Harlow.

"Fletcher and myself, Andre and his crew, and all the models. Dodge was already here. After everyone got situated, we gathered on the beach for a welcoming Bar-B-Q."

"When had Dodge arrived?"

"Earlier in the day."

"From New York?" Lydia already knew the answer to this from her discussion with Dodge, but she wanted to see if Harlow's version jived.

"He flew in from Miami. He'd been working with a vendor there during the week."

"You didn't accompany him?"

Ben knew Annison had been with Dodge in Miami. So did Lydia. Ben knew that Lydia was testing Harlow.

"No, I stayed in New York to ready the line to ship to Sarasota." She hadn't the heart to mention Annison Barrett.

Lydia had hoped to illicit some kind of response from her, bitter or otherwise, but it hadn't come. She moved on.

"How long did the beach Bar-B-Q go on?"

"It probably would have gone on all night," Harlow laughed, "everyone was really unwinding."

"Unwinding as in inebriated?"

"Well, the photographers and the girls certainly weren't feeling any pain. They were pretty funny doing Karaoke."

"All the girls? Aren't several of the models under age?"

"Are you kidding? That doesn't matter. Those girls could get anything they wanted."

"Including Dana?"

"Especially Dana."

"Anything she wanted? Did that include Dodge Maddison?"

In a court of law the prosecutor would have objected to this line of questioning ... leading the witness, your Honor ... Sustained ... But at a dinner table with the witness half in the bag, Lydia Lawrence was unconscionably maneuvering Harlow to her benefit.

Harlow responded, "I know where you're going with this, so I'll just tell you what you want to know. Yes, I was jealous of Dana. With Dodge and I, the business always came first. Did he know my feelings for him? He's not dumb. We have had ample opportunity to have an affair. In New York, Milan, Bryce Corner, the West Coast, any number of places we've traveled together. But we always retired to separate rooms. We never talked about it, but I think we both knew it was there."

"Why do you think he got involved with Dana?"

"Besides the obvious?" Harlow gave Lydia a what-a-ridiculous-question look.

"Yes, besides the obvious."

Harlow reached for her glass and almost tipped it over. That little voice inside her told her she'd had too much to drink, but she took another long sip just the same. She hadn't been drinking at the Bar-B-Q Saturday night and had only had one glass of wine at dinner Sunday evening with Dodge, Fletcher, and Andre. But as the events unfolded during the week, she'd slipped back into it. She knew she should stop. She knew Lydia was getting the better of her.

"Maybe Dana was his way of putting a distance between us," she said.

"And you accepted that?"

"I guess I did."

Big Ben had been quiet, sitting at the table enjoying the light breeze coming in off the night Gulf. He was thinking of Carlene. Tonight would be the first night in how long since he'd slept without her. He didn't mind being away from her, his profession sometimes took him away from home, but he never liked it. He liked the feel of her warm body against his when he crawled into bed at night. Liked the way she pushed back against him when they were spooning. Liked the spontaneity of their lovemaking. Wondered what she had made for dinner for her and the kids. Missed his dog. Would like to go running along the beach with ole Joe, chasing after a tennis ball.

"When did you and Dodge consummate the relationship?" Lydia didn't know for sure if they had, but she made an educated guess.

Ben knew they had, but he was nonetheless surprised that Lydia would even broach the topic.

Harlow was too tired and/or too mellow to keep her defenses up. "Not too long ago," she said in a low voice, hardly audible over the low rhythm of the nearby waves.

Ben looked at Harlow who was looking into the darkness of the ocean. Then he looked at Lydia, but she had her attention riveted on Harlow.

"And when Annison Barrett came into the picture, how did you handle that?"

Harlow didn't respond. Lydia Lawrence continued, "Did you feel he was then substituting Annison for Dana? Yet another woman to keep a distance between the two of you?"

"Are you analyzing me? Is that what this shit is all about?" Anger in her voice.

She's got her agitated now, Ben thought.

"Don't think it has been easy for me. Yes, I'm hurt! Damn hurt. In some weird way I rationalized the fling with Dana. But with this new woman ... she's his own age. Our age. It's different. I didn't expect it. I didn't know what to expect. I was afraid. Afraid of us, of what would happen to the business if we allowed the relationship to grow. We'd always thought bringing sex into it could ruin the working rapport we have. But I was willing. Willing to let it happen around us. That night of lovemaking was so strong. So beautiful. I've never felt so wonderful in my life. And so confused. I over reacted. I pushed him away. I fled back to the security of the business like a teen-age girl running back to mama for false consolation, when what I should have done was realize that I had finally grown up. Finally allowed my true feelings to surface and to take control of my life." Tears started running down her cheeks. "And then ... Oh God, I made such a fool of myself. I should have realized ... I should have just ..." Abruptly, Harlow got up and left the table. She crossed the dining area and made her way to the beach. She was walking fast and it only took a moment for her image to get swallowed up into the blurry darkness of the shoreline with the soft murmuring of the surf behind it.

"Well that went well," Ben said.

"I didn't mean to upset her."

"Sure you did."

"I didn't know she had gotten sexually involved with Dodge, it was just a hunch. Seemed like a natural thing to happen." She looked at Ben. He was watching her. "But you knew, didn't you?" His eyes told her yes.

"Anyway," Lydia said, "You've known her a long time, think she's capable of bumping off the model?"

"Lydia, it's been my unpleasant experience to find out that anyone is capable of anything."

"I know you're right."

"Sit tight," Ben said, "I'll go get her. We really should eat."

"Yes."

Ben went into the night. Lydia picked up her menu and brought the table candle close so she could read it easier.

Harlow hadn't gotten too far. Ben found her silhouette standing beside the tall sea grass just to the side of the tiki hut.

"You okay?" he put his arm around her and she nestled her head into his shoulder.

"Such a beautiful locale to have such an awful time. I wish we could all enjoy it more," she said.

"We should eat."

"Yeah, we should."

They walked together through the sand, Ben kept his arm around her and Harlow took in deep breaths of the salty air. She was carrying her shoes in one hand, the other wrapped around Ben's waist. "What do you think will happen, Ben?"

"I don't know. If we catch the killer soon, that would help. The longer it takes, the more damage to Dodge's reputation. I think that's what Lydia is trying to get ahead of."

"Does she think I did it?"

"She's the defense attorney. She pretty much doesn't care who did it. Her job is to prove Dodge didn't do it. If she can find the person to pin it on, all the better. Right now she suspects everybody."

"Do you."

"I'm a cop, Harlow. I think differently than most. I'll reserve comment until I'm absolutely sure."

"I mean, do you think I did it?"

He hesitated. "No, I don't."

"But you hesitated."

"I'm a cop. I think differently than most."

When they got back to the table, Harlow apologized for her behavior and Lydia for hers.

"That's okay," Harlow said. "I just want this to be over with. You can ask me anything. I want Dodge to be exonerated as quickly as possible. I'll do whatever necessary to help."

The server came and took their order. Harlow asked for a cup of coffee and he brought that right away.

"If you don't mind, could you help me with the timeline?" Lydia said.

"Sure. Where were we?"

"Bar-B-Q, Saturday night. Everyone was drinking and having a good time."

"Not that it matters, but I wasn't drinking that night. And now that I think of it, neither was Dana."

"Was anyone out of control?"

"Andre, but that's not unusual for him. And Isabella. She was pretty lit."

"Who was Dodge with?"

"At the Bar-B-Q? He was making the rounds. He spent time with everyone."

"Dana?"

"Yeah, he chatted with her, but I don't think any more or less than with anyone else."

"What was the general mood," Ben asked.

"Frivolous. Everybody was happy to be away from the cold weather."

"But you said Andre and Isabella were out of control."

"Not crazy, just having a good time. They were actually dancing together, a rare sight."

"What?"

"The two of them actually getting along."

"What time did the party break up?"

"I don't know. I think I was the first one to leave."

"What time?"

"About ten o'clock. I was tired and I knew we were getting an early start the next day."

"Where was Dana when you left?"

"Sitting at a table with some of the girls."

"And Dodge?" Lydia said.

"Actually, he walked me back to my room."

"Did he go in?"

"No."

"Did you want him to?"

"I don't think I need to answer that."

"So it was business as usual?"

"Yes."

The server came with their food and brought a welcome pause to the conversation. The three of them ate quietly, indulged in their own thoughts.

It was Ben who broke the quietude. "Okay, so everybody got here Saturday." He pushed his empty plate to the side, placing his napkin on top and then rested his elbows on the table. The ladies weren't even half done with their meals. "Sunday you all got the clothes together, scouted locations on the beach in preparation for the next day's shooting, and the girls went shopping. Then you went out to dinner with Dodge, Fletcher and Andre. Have I got it so far?"

"Yes," Harlow answered.

"What did Dana do Sunday night?"

"I don't know. She wasn't with us and she didn't go out to dinner with the models. I think she stayed in her hotel suite."

Lydia asked, "Was everyone else accounted for?"

"I believe so."

"Why would she stay alone in her room?" Lydia addressed this question to Ben to see if he was thinking what she was.

"To wait for her rendezvous," Ben said. They were on the same page.

The server removed Ben's plate. Harlow placed her fork and knife onto her plate and handed it up to the server. She'd eaten less than half.

"Would you like this in a to-go container, ma'am?"

"No thank you, but I would like another cup of coffee please."

"Sure thing."

Lydia asked Ben, "When did Dodge call you?"

"Monday night."

"And you got here today, Wednesday?"

"Yup. I'd have come Tuesday, but I had to settle a couple things at the station first. Besides, Logan was closed due to the snowstorm and didn't reopen until this morning."

"Dana was found Monday morning," Lydia said. "What happened to the photo shoot from that point?"

Harlow stirred cream into her fresh cup of coffee. "The day was pretty much spent in shock. The lieutenant spoke with all of us individually, which took quite a bit of time. That evening we all went out to dinner as a group to Marina Jack."

"All except Dodge," Ben said.

"Yes," Harlow said.

"How did you know that?" Lydia asked Ben.

"Because Dodge called me from his room that night. He told me they had all gone out to dinner. He said he stayed behind to gather his thoughts and make some phone calls."

"Did he go out?" she asked Harlow.

"At breakfast the next morning he said he had driven up to a waterside restaurant somewhere for a sandwich and a beer."

Lydia reached into her purse and jotted a note on a small leather bound pad. She flipped through it making further notes on some of the pages. Then she read through them and flipped to a fresh page. "Okay, so what was the conversation at breakfast on Tuesday morning?"

"Andre persuaded Dodge to go ahead with the shoot."

"Wasn't that kind of odd?"

"At first we thought so, but Andre seemed to make sense. The models were here, the photographers were here and Dodge was here. Either we did it or we side-lined the catalogue for the season."

"Couldn't you have rescheduled?"

"Not with everyone's itinerary. Plus, budget wise, it made the most sense to continue as planned. So we decided to do the apparel shots Tuesday and the swimwear today."

"Everyone was okay with that?"

"Yes. Probably relieved to be working. We knew the services were going to be Thursday and that was weighing on everyone's mind. The family was coming down and we knew it was going to be hard for them, and for all of us. We worked together as a close-knit family and at that time we still believed

Dana's death to be a suicide. Some of us felt guilty that we hadn't seen it coming."

Lydia looked at Ben and he returned her gaze. He didn't say anything, so she continued. "When did the photo shoot get completed?"

"It was wrapped this afternoon. We packed up the clothing and the film and Andre FedEx'd it all to New York."

"I guess that's all I have for now," Lydia said going over her notes. "Oh, one more question. What did everyone do last night?"

"I heard that everyone sort of broke off into their own little groups and went separate ways. I was exhausted. I stayed in. I napped, showered, ordered room service and then went for a walk on the beach."

"Alone?"

"Yes," Harlow smiled to Lydia, "unfortunately alone."

The server came and offered dessert, which they all declined. Ben asked for the check and the server said, "I'll be happy to put that on your room Mr. Benson."

"That'll be fine. And please add a twenty percent gratuity."

"Thank you sir." He cleared the rest of the dishes and went his way.

"How did he know who I was?"

"Ben," Harlow laughed, "you're at the Ritz." It was the first time she had smiled all evening.

They walked along the sandy pathway through the small grassy dunes. Single file with Lydia in front followed by Harlow and Big Ben bringing up the rear. When they got to the spot where Ben had spoken with Andre and Fletcher, Ben said to Harlow, "Did you know that Santiago was missing?"

"Yes. They were talking about it this morning."

"Do you know where he is?"

"Haven't the foggiest."

"What was his role?" Lydia asked.

"As head videographer he'd be in charge of all the equipment. And the film."

"Who's responsibility would that be with him missing?"

"Andre's. And he's not at all happy about it."

"Wasn't Santiago the one rumored to be involved with Dana?" Lydia said.

Harlow laughed, "They were close, but not involved."

"Close like in a professional way or more like brother and sister?" Lydia said.

"More like sister and sister. Those two were always seen together giggling to each other."

"Would you say then that they were exceptionally close in a friendship kind of way?"

"Yes, definitely."

"Would it stand to reason that Santiago was Dana's confidant?"

They had reached the brick roundabout facing the entranceway. The three of them stood facing each other. The ambient glow from the Ritz's exterior lighting washed over majestic royal palms, surrounding them like steadfast sentinels in the tropical night.

"Yes, I guess so."

"Would it be safe to assume that of all the people here, Santiago was the closest to Dana?"

Harlow nodded.

"As a close friend and confidant would he not be privy to her state of mind? Her life? Her emotions, demons, secrets?"

Harlow did not speak. Ben's mind was racing. Lydia continued. "Does it not seem extremely odd that Dana is murdered and now Santiago has disappeared?" Lydia's courtroom persona let the weight of her questions sink in. In a lower voice she said to Ben, "I think we need to find Mr. Santiago and have a chat."

"I think you're absolutely right."

TWENTY

The familiar double knock echoed from the door. Dana rose naked from her bed and ran to answer it with anticipation springing from her tiptoes. She opened the door and jumped onto him, locking her legs around his waist.

"Whoa!" he said, "don't knock me over." He walked her into the suite, kicking the door shut with his heel. He pressed her against the wall in the foyer and kissed her hard on the lips.

"What took you sooo long?"

"I couldn't break away any sooner."

She kissed him and squeezed her legs tight around his waist. "Don't put me down, don't ever put me down."

"I know where I can put you down ..."

"Mmmm."

The suite was dark save for the moon glow coming through the balcony doors, like a wispy white curtain blown in by a gentle sea wind. The bedroom was seductively lit with two candle tapers on either side of the bed. A silver champagne bucket rested atop an ornate serving cart. Two champagne flutes with the Ritz-Carlton logo stood next to it. One was half full.

"Wow." he said. "This is fantastic."

"It's a special occasion."

"Every time with you is a special occasion."

"Mmmm," she kissed him again.

Gently he laid her onto the bed and pressed his body full upon her.

"Wait, wait ..." she said crawling out from beneath him and hiking herself against the array of fluffy pillows. "I want to make a toast first." Dana reached for her champagne glass but he placed his fingers over hers making her raise the glass to his lips to feed him the bubbly elixir.

"I *can't* wait," he spread her legs and ran his fingers along the inside of her thighs.

Her legs began to tingle.

Quickly he took his shirt off and then stood to remove his pants and underwear. She watched his every motion.

"I love your body," she whispered.

"Good, because I love yours too."

He knelt on the floor and pulled her by the waist to the edge of the bed keeping her legs raised and the inside of her thighs quivering before him. Slowly he moved his head toward her, running his tongue along the smooth inner length of her leg.

She watched him.

She could feel the pulsing begin deep inside her.

Her nipples were aching. She squeezed them between her fingers.

He looked at her and smiled that provocative grin of his and then buried his face into her.

Dana moaned, "Oh, you are *so* evil." She leaned back onto the mattress, giving in to him, allowing him to please her with his every whim. The toasting could wait. Now, she only wanted him. Wanted him deep inside of her.

Their lovemaking was invigorating, and exhausting. She always wanted more, I can't get enough of you, she'd say. And he would smile and say, let me rest darling. And she would snuggle into him and play with his chest hairs until he fell asleep. But tonight was different.

"I really want to make a toast."

He was on his back without the covers. The ceiling fan was cooling the waning heat of his body.

"What is it my love? Did you get the contract for Rio de Janeiro?"

"Better than that." She sat up and took the champagne bottle from the bucket and poured some into the glasses. White foam swelled over the tops of the flutes like the gush of a geyser, and then settled into a rich golden sheen imbued with popping effervescence.

She took up her glass and handed the other to him. "To us," they clinked glasses, "to the three of us."

He drank of the cool champagne and watched her eyes twinkle in the candlelight. It took a second, but then it dawned on him. "The three of us?"

She put her glass back onto the serving tray. She was clearly excited, sitting on the bed, flexing her legs back and forth like the wings of a butterfly drinking nectar from a beautiful flower. "I'm pregnant," she said with a bright smile. "*We're* pregnant! I couldn't *wait* to tell you!" She threw her arms around his neck in childlike jubilation.

A knock came upon the door. It had to travel through the foyer, along the hallway and across the expansive great room of the suite to get to the royal bedroom. So it was soft at the end of its journey. A knock whispered.

"What was that?" he said.

"I think there's someone at the door."

"This late? Did you order room service?"

"No."

It came again. Faint.

"Who could it be?" he asked.

"I have no idea. Let it be. Hold me."

It came again. He sat up on the edge of the bed. "Does anyone know I'm here?"

"Of course not darling."

He pulled on his pants, put his arms through his shirtsleeves.

"What are you doing?"

"I'm just going to look through the peephole."

"No," she reached for him. "They'll go away. Please come back to bed."

118

"I want to see who it is."

The knock returned. No louder, but longer. Persistent.

"Why would anyone be here now?"

"It's someone drunk. One of the girls on the way to her room. Probably Isabella. She's been hounding me lately. She gets drunk and she wants to talk my ear off. She'll go away."

Again.

"Please," she implored him, but he was already out of the room walking toward the door in his bare feet.

Quietly, stealthily, he reached the door and brought an eye to the peephole. He saw who it was and stood back, staring at the door.

The knock again, louder now that he was closer to it. He looked back to the bedroom. Saw Dana cross the room, a delicate form in the candlelight. Heard the door to the master bath close.

He looked into the peephole again. Still there.

He buttoned his shirt, flipped the light switch illuminating the foyer and opened the door.

TWENTY-ONE

"What da Fuck?" Mikey's head bounced off the roof of the van.

The two sisters screamed in unison, tumbling against the side of the van's interior, lucky to be cushioned by the overstuffed garment bags.

The van had bottomed out hard onto a speed bump at the entrance to South Lido Park. Roger had ignored the "bump" sign with the red caution flag. He also ignored the ten mile-per-hour speed limit.

"What's the matter with you man?"

"Hold on Buckos," Roger laughed.

The parking lot was deserted and absent of lighting. Roger swerved the van, tires spitting sand and crushed shells, to the further end of the park. He squeezed into a narrow pathway marked "Nature Trail", knocking the sign over as he careened by. Pygmy palm fronds and mangrove branches scratched the sides of the van in eerie screeches sounding like sharp-nailed monsters clawing to get in.

In the path of the headlights a clearing appeared and Roger spun the steering wheel all the way to the left, the van sliding to a welcomed stop just shy of a reedy marsh. Mikey flung his door open and jumped out, happy to be on the ground. He slid open the side door and a large garment bag fell at his feet. The two sisters clambered over it like they were escaping from a madman. Fiona tripped and fell into Mikey's arms. "Oh my god, he's crazy!"

Roger came around the van holding an outstretched bottle of tequila, "All right! Let's get this party started!" The party was already well on its way, merely being relocated from the Salty Dog where Roger and crew had been shut off.

The setting was a small clearing in the backcountry of the park. Canopied by the dense foliage of palm trees and Australian Pines and surrounded by the lower outgrowth of thick mangroves with their tangly, spider-leg roots, the spot was dark and perfectly hidden from the high-rise condominiums across Sarasota Bay and the low-lying residential areas of Lido Key.

"Here, Darlin', hold onto this," Roger took a swig from the bottle and handed it to Franny. He jumped into the van and started throwing the ill-gotten contraband out the door. Mikey looked around, surveying the situation. There was a spot maybe twenty yards off that seemed open and flat. The earth was blackened and ashen. Someone had built a campfire there before. Perfect. He reached into the front of the van and drew out a flashlight from the glove box. "Follow me," he said to Fiona, and the two of them headed into the dark trail toward the sound of the tide crashing onto the shoreline.

"What are you doing with all this stuff?" Franny asked Roger.

"Never mind, just stand outta the way," and he continued throwing out the clothing bags and the boxes that he didn't know contained dozens of video films and photo discs.

He saw the spot that Mikey had been eyeing and started dragging the merchandise over to it. Franny stood silent, wondering where her sister had gone. She was becoming a little frightened. She lifted the bottle of tequila back and winced as it tore into her throat. She wavered a bit and then hiccupped. She was unsteady and she turned and sat in the open doorway of the van.

Roger came back for another of the garment bags. "You all right, Darlin'?" He took the bottle from her hand and lifted it back.

"Where did my sister go?"

"Don't worry, she'll be right back." He handed the bottle back to her and grabbed another bag to drag off.

Franny didn't know exactly where they were but she knew how they had gotten there. Her eyes strained through the darkness to find the trail behind where they had come in.

"Are there animals around here?"

Roger laughed, "Just me and Mikey."

Not funny, she said to herself. "No really. Are there panthers or something like that?"

Roger came back and leaned an arm against the side of the van. "Nah, panthers are further north, or south for that matter. But anyways, they'd be more inland, not near the shore. All we've got here are gators and snakes."

"Oh my god! Are you fucking serious?" Franny retreated into the van grabbing one of the garment bags for protection in front of her.

"Don't you worry, little darlin', Roger's here ta protect ya." He entered the van and closed the side door.

It didn't take long for the driftwood to catch and Mikey and Fiona stood back from the heat of it as it roared to life illuminating the trees and foliage around them. Fiona saw huge green monsters swaying to the rhythm of the flickering flames. Mikey unzipped one of the bags and began tossing clothing into the fire.

Fiona said, "I know I probably shouldn't ask this, but what are you doing?"

Mikey didn't answer her.

Fiona looked over to the van. She could hear her sister's giggling. She wondered about her sometimes. Franny was the promiscuous one, always looking for trouble, and always finding it. Fiona was okay with the drinks at the bar, but hadn't been too keen on going with these two guys in their van. But as always, Franny had talked her into it. They're harmless, she'd said, besides I want to have some fun on this vacation. Who wants to hang around Gramma and her old wrinkled friends going to museums and operas and shit like that? Huh? Come on, live a little! So, here they were, Franny in the van, cocked out of her mind, living it up, and Fiona outside in the middle of nowhere with some guy she'd just met only hours ago, watching him burn up a bunch of dresses.

"Where did you get all this stuff?"

Again, no answer from Mikey.

Fiona unzipped one of the bags and took out a dress. "Wow. This is nice."

"Don't get attached to it," Mikey took it from her and threw it into the flames, "it's got a very short season."

There were noises coming from the van. Fiona and Mikey looked over to it and then back at each other. Neither one said anything. Mikey resumed his task. "You could help, y'know. We'd get out of here quicker." Fiona looked over at the van again. Then she unzipped another bag and began handing clothing to Mikey who quickly fed them into the rising fire.

The smoke rose in a linear column above the blazing fire. An unusual odor permeated the air; a foul mix of burnt cotton, linen and polyester. When the garment bags were all gone, Mikey picked up a big cardboard box and threw that in without opening it. It lay like a huge brown block in the middle of scorching red and orange flames, refusing to give in to the heat and devastation all around it. And then it blew up, exploding into a huge blinding yellow light. The bubble wrap that had neatly packaged dozens of video film and discs started crackling into the quiet night like popcorn in a microwave. Fiona and Mikey shielded their eyes from the fire and took a few paces backward to escape the tremendous heat. Anxiously they watched from a distance. Mikey looked at the treetops, hoping the flames wouldn't reach that high. The whole area was awash with light and he was sure that someone could see the brightness emanating from the closed park and rising into the sky like one of those big spotlights they have at a carnival or a car dealership.

The side door of the van opened with a shrilling sound, dry metal forced against anodized rust. Roger leapt out shouting, "Whoo rah!" and came toward the fire, the near empty tequila bottle crooked in his arm as he buckled his pants.

"Oh MY god!" Fiona said loudly, crossing to the van.

Roger winked as they passed each other. "Your sister's a real sweet ..."

"Fuck you asshole!"

Franny was sitting cross-legged and topless in the van. Fiona said, "WHAT were you thinking?"

Franny hic-cupped.

"I am *so* disappointed in you."

"You're always disappointed in me, just because I don't act like you."

"That's bullshit."

"You're bullshit."

They eyed each other at a standoff.

Franny grinned mischievously, "He's got a really ..."

"I don't want to hear it!" Fiona put her hands over her ears.

Franny giggled and hic-cupped at the same time. "I can't get rid of these fucking hiccups."

Fiona looked over to the men standing by the fire. Mikey was tending to the blaze while Roger swayed beside him animating a story, no doubt about his sexual prowess.

"We've got to get out of here. Do you know what they're doing?"

Franny shrugged her shoulders.

"Here, look at this." Fiona stepped into the van closing the door behind her and opened the last remaining garment bag. She pulled out a bright red evening dress and held it against her.

Franny clicked on the interior lighting. "Wow, that's beautiful."

"And look," Fiona revealed the inside of the neckline, "It's a *Maddison*."

"Holy shit," Franny grabbed it from her hands and stared at the label. "All of this?"

Fiona rummaged through the garment bag. "Yes, all of it."

"Wow." Franny pulled the dress over her head and wriggled into it. "Ou, this feels heavenly."

"Fran, this shit is worth thousands and they're *burning* it!"

"Oh my god, feel this. This is pure silk." Franny smoothed the fabric over her naked breasts. The dress fit her perfectly.

"Are you listening to me? I don't know how they got this stuff but I'm sure it wasn't legally. They probably have no idea how valuable it is."

Franny was oblivious. She opened the door and stepped out. The lightweight silk fabric cascaded down her body like a soothing, sensual waterfall spilling from some forbidden tropical paradise. She spun around in a pirouette making the ruffles at the hemline fan out, cutting through the thick night air like a razor.

"Hey!" Roger grabbed her. "Gimme that." He reached for her and tore at the dress. Franny screamed, raising her arms across her breasts, clinging onto the ripped fabric.

Roger clutched her body from behind and began savagely pulling at the shoulder straps. "Gimme this fucking thing."

Franny's screaming became hysterical. Roger picked her up by one arm and started walking toward the fire, still trying to tear the dress from her. Franny fought to wriggle herself free, kicking her airborne legs and twisting and turning her body in a frenzy.

From behind him, Fiona jumped onto Roger's back and started clawing at his face. "Let her go! Let her go, you fucking asshole!"

Her fingernails ripped into the side of his face. Roger grunted and slapped at her. He was holding one sister on his hip with one arm and trying to reach the other sister, riding his back, with his other arm. He couldn't do both. He spun around wildly in a vicious circle and Franny fell to the ground, clutching the torn neckline of the designer dress to her breast. Roger reached both arms behind him and, by her hair, yanked Fiona up and over him and threw her hard onto the ground. Her nails had cut four symmetrical red lines into his left cheek. He looked like he was wearing war paint.

Roger ran his hand over the side of his face. The red lines smeared into a bloody blotch. His palm came away looking like a red mitten. "You Fucking Bitch!" He backhanded Fiona brutally across the face and raised his hand to hit her again.

Mikey grabbed Roger's raised wrist with his left hand, twisted him around and drove his right fist squarely into Roger's nose. Blood flowed instantly. Roger froze. He stared at Mikey.

There was really no match between them. Mikey was clearly more muscle bound. His hard body was fit and toned. His arms were strong and powerful. Roger was taller, but rather gangly. Spidery. Of the two of them, he was the one who liked to fight, but Mikey was the one who knew how to fight.

"Don't do it," Mikey warned.

Roger did have one advantage over Mikey; he was the crazier one. He stood firm with his feet placed apart, stanced directly below his shoulders. With the blood running off his upper lip, Mikey couldn't tell if Roger was grimacing or grinning at him. Roger leapt at Mikey with a fierce, imposing grunt.

Mikey stepped to his right, pushing all his weight onto his right leg. He cocked his left arm low, at the beltline, and slammed his fist into Roger's solar plexus. Buoyed by the forward motion, Roger's feet came off the ground and then slowly staggered back to earth. Mikey re-cocked his left arm and attacked the solar plexus again. While Roger was bent over at the waist, Mikey hammered him with a hard right to the jaw. He went down, gasping for breath. Mikey stood over him for a minute until he felt certain that it was over. He turned to go back to the fire.

His feet came out from under him and he went down. Roger tackled him and rammed his leg into Mikey's groin. He straddled him, sitting on his chest and pinning his arms beneath his legs and started pummeling his face, the classic bully in the schoolyard fighter. It only took a moment for Mikey to heave the scrawny Roger off him and they both got quickly to their feet.

"Come on you mother fucker!" Roger taunted him.

Again the two men stood facing each other, like jousting knights at either end of the stadium. Mikey knew now that Roger wasn't going to give it up. There was only one way to deal with him. Like a football player practicing his tackles, Mikey ran shoulder-first into his opponent and drove him back into the front metal fender of the van. It was a hard hit. Roger felt it in the back and Mikey had hit his knee on the corner of the front bumper. But neither of them relinquished. They tussled against the unrelenting surface of the van, locked in a bear hug, one trying to earn the advantage over the other. Strength won out and Mikey got Roger pinned against the grill and kept kneeing him between the legs. Finally, Roger went down with his hands raised in surrender. He rolled onto his side, moaning in a fetal position. Mikey's legs collapsed in exhaustion and he leaned against the front tire catching his breath.

The fire had died down. The cardboard box was no longer discernable. The foliage wasn't as bright or foreboding as it had been. Mikey's chest was heaving with the intake of oxygen and his adrenaline rush was subsiding. He thought he'd go stir the embers and get the fire out so they could leave. He felt something cold against his left temple.

"Get up you cocksucker!"

Mikey didn't move. He sat there catching his breath.

"Get up!"

"Oh, now what, Roger? You're going to shoot me? That won't make any noise. You may as well shoot yourself too. Save the cops the trouble."

Roger pulled the hammer back and pressed the gun harder into Mikey's temple. Mikey turned his head so he could look up and see Roger's eyes. "Well?" he said.

"Fuck you," Roger said and took the gun away.

"Fuck you too." Mikey stretched his arm up and Roger grabbed it helping him up. They leaned against the grill together. After awhile Roger said, "Let's get the fuck outta here and go get a beer."

"Smartest idea you've had all night."

"I think there's one more bag in there."

"All right, go get it. I'll fix the fire, but let's make it quick."

Mikey took a branch and stoked the fire. The embers were low. Fabric burns fast and doesn't leave much bulk to work with and the plastic of the videos and discs had melted into a stinky black pool in the center. Mikey found a piece of driftwood and threw that in. He crouched down and blew into the fire.

Roger dragged the last garment bag over. He emptied out the clothing and took a lighter to the black cotton garment bag. It caught right away and he threw it into the embers.

"The girls are gone."

"What?" Mikey stood up and looked around.

"Gonzo. They're not in the van, they're not in the bushes takin' a piss, they're long gone."

"We've got to find them."

"No we don't. Fuck 'em! They're on their own. They're probably back to the road by now anyway."

"But what if they go to the cops?"

"What, and embarrass their dear ole rich Gramma? I doubt it. Besides, there ain't gonna be nothing here but ashes. Don't worry about it. Let's get it done and get outta here. We gotta get back to the phone booth by midnight."

TWENTY-TWO

Big Ben's internal clock went off at six-fifteen a.m. For a second he didn't realize where he was. It was cool. He wondered why the heat wasn't working. Maybe Carlene had turned the thermostat down too far. Or maybe the pilot had blown out. It did that sometimes when a strong, non-prevailing wind came in from the northeast. He never could figure out why. It was a propane heating system vented to the roof. He thought maybe if the wind was just right it would blow down through the vent and extinguish the pilot light. Once or twice a winter he had to go down into the cellar and restart it. Ben rolled out of bed to do so. When he stood up he realized he wasn't home. Carlene wasn't in the kitchen making coffee. He was in Florida. The coolness was the air conditioning. Dodge was in jail.

By six-thirty he was outside. The sun was brightening the central prairies of the state and rolling up behind the muted architecture of downtown Sarasota, yawning in the blue waters across the causeway. At home, he'd be on the treadmill now. It felt real good to be walking along the beach in December in a T-shirt, shorts and sandals. His cell phone rang. It was Carlene.

"I finally got a good night's sleep," she said. "It's amazing how much room is in this bed without that big fidgety teddy-bear next to me."

"Funny, I got a great night's sleep too without that horny sex-pot pestering me all night." Ben smiled.

"I bet you missed her."

"You bet right."

He could hear her take a sip of coffee. "I miss that too."

"I made a full pot. I don't know why. Habit I guess."

"You are *my* habit."

"Are we going to have phone sex?"

"Okay, what are you wearing?"

"Ugly flannel pajamas, oversized ridiculous looking slippers, yours actually, and a terry-cloth bathrobe with a horrendously awful abstract pattern. Oh, and no make-up. And you?"

"I'm naked walking down the beach in flip-flops."

"Scaring anybody?"

"Must have. There's no one on the beach but me. Although some of the seagulls are giving me an amorous look."

"Careful, I've heard about those Florida seagulls. They're shallow, not into long term relationships."

"And they can't cook for shit."

"Ah, the real reason you miss me."

Ben smiled. The tide washed over his flip-flops. The water was warm on his feet.

"Is that the ocean I hear?"

"Yes."

"Let me hear it, Baby."

He held the cell phone to the rolling waves.

"Mmm, what a beautiful sound. I wish I was there with you."

"Me too. Maybe we'll come down sometime."

"That would be really nice."

Ben turned and walked up the shore into the white sand.

"Kids up yet?" he asked his wife.

"'Course not, it's not noon."

"How's my dog?"

"Joe Cocker misses you. He slept on your slippers last night."

"Wish I'd brought him with me. He'd love the beach."

"How's Dodge doing?"

"Still in. I'm going over this morning to talk with him. The memorial service is today, noontime."

There was a lifeguard tower. He climbed the three-tiered ladder and sat in the chair overlooking the morning sea turning from blue to emerald green with the filtrating sun rising behind his back. Ben filled Carlene in on the events and conversations of the previous evening. She listened attentively. Told him to be careful. Told him she loved him.

"Come home soon."

"I will."

She had to go. She was due at her job as a veterinary assistant at seven. They had minor surgery and a dental on a black Lab this morning. She smacked him a kiss through the phone and they hung up. Big Ben sat aligning his day with the pure, incessant timing of the new day rolling in with the waves.

Minutes later, as he lumbered his way back to the hotel, he was thinking about the upcoming memorial service for Dana and one thing bothered him. He didn't know what to wear. The only long pants he had with him were the jeans he'd worn down on the flight and he didn't think they'd be proper. Carlene had offered to help him pack but he'd declined. He should have said yes. She'd have thought out a better wardrobe for him. He scolded his male ego and wondered what time that Tommy place opened. He'd stop by on his way over to see Dodge.

MacLaren was seated at his desk in his office. Behind him the art-deco façade of the Hollywood Twenty loomed outside his second story window. In front of him sat Lydia Lawrence. They were silent. He was stirring a cup of coffee; she was entering data into her Blackberry. Big Ben tapped on the glass window. MacLaren motioned him inside.

"Coffee?" he asked.

"Sure."

MacLaren pointed to the coffee machine on top of the file cabinet. "Almost didn't recognize you."

"Good morning," Lydia said.

"Morning." Ben pulled a Styrofoam cup off the stack and poured his coffee. Black. No sugar. He wore tan British-khaki slacks above dark brown loafers, a blue chambray shirt, collar open, and a navy cotton sportcoat that fit him comfortably over his shoulder holster. He'd left the yellow "RELAX" hat on the

131

dashboard of the Hummer. He had a full head of brown hair that looked like it had missed a barber appointment two weeks ago. That annoyed MacLaren. Lydia liked the look.

"You missed the show," MacLaren said.

"Can't wait for your recap." Ben pulled a chair next to Lydia and sat.

"Counselor?" MacLaren said to Lydia.

"No bail. He's to remain in custody. The judge doesn't like the media swarming all over and doesn't want him talking to anyone."

"That doesn't justify indefinite incarceration," Ben said.

"No, it doesn't. But fear of flight does and the judge thinks he's a risk due to his international flexibility."

Ben was clearly upset with this news. He had felt that Lydia Lawrence and her father would have been able to get bail. He wondered if he'd been duped. After all, they, the Lawrence's, MacLaren, the prosecutor, judge, et al, were from the same town. He and Dodge Maddison were the outsiders.

As if she was reading his mind, Lydia said, "Look, even though the pre-lim didn't go our way, we've got a good chance, due to Dodge's notoriety, to get an early trial date. The judge doesn't want this to become a lengthy media event. He abhors attention like that. He even said something like, 'This trial will be conducted in Sarasota, Florida … not on Fashion Avenue … not in Hollywood.' He's a tough but honest judge. Still wishes cameras were banned in courtrooms. And may very well ban them in this case."

"Hollywood?"

"He's already been approached by script writers for an exclusive."

"Whatever happened to good, clean justice?"

"The media," MacLaren chimed in.

The door opened and a well-dressed woman in an impeccably crisp navy blue business suit strode in. She handed a file to Lydia Lawrence, "As promised," she said and then turned to face Ben. "Chief Benson, I presume."

Ben rose from his seat to shake her hand.

"Tanya Chisholm," she said, "D.A."

"Nice to meet you."

"Please, reclaim your seat," Tanya Chisholm said, "I didn't mean to barge in on you all," MacLaren snickered in the background, "but I wanted to drop off the disclosures to Ms. Lawrence." She was at the row of vertical filing cabinets where the Mr. Coffee machine was set up. She spoke with her back to them.

"Christ, MacLaren, don't you have any tea bags?" The D.A. turned and leaned her backside against the cabinet, crossing her ankles and placing her hands on the shelf behind her. "Here's where we're at," she tapped her fingernails against the polished wood veneer. Her bleached red hair was cropped short, gelled and combed straight back like she had just come out of the shower, or a swim in the ocean. Her physique was strong and lean. She definitely worked out. Ben thought she could bench press one-fifty. A yellow number two pencil was perched on her left ear, the sharpened end out. Oddly, it didn't look out of place, but rather seemed to punctuate her chiseled demeanor.   Everything about her - her attire, her appearance, her attitude - was hard and cold. If her goal was to appear tough, she had succeeded.

"The M.E. has released the body to the family who wishes to have it cremated," Tanya Chisholm looked at her gold-banded wristwatch, "probably as we speak. The service will be at Selby Gardens at noon. We've taken blood and cell samples from both the deceased and the fetus and sent them to CODEX for DNA testing and verification." She looked at Ben, "That's the main storage house for DNA held by the F.B.I."

"Oh, thank you," he said in his best country-bumpkin inflection. Big Ben was well aware of CODEX.

Tanya Chisholm, D.A. gave him a controlled sneer. Ben thought he could hear her hiss.

"But, as we well know," she held her snare at him, "because of the back log and even with a high priority on it, results could take up to a month."

Ben smiled.

"We've also sent along samples from Mr. Maddison."

"Good job," Ben said. "Very thorough."

Tanya Chisholm didn't miss a beat. "We will proceed as outlined in my report and as instructed by the court." She straightened and took a step toward Ben. "I anticipate a swift resolve." Extending her hand, she said, "I hope you enjoy our clime, Chief Benson."

"Thank you, I already am." He remained seated as he shook her hand.

The D.A. nodded good-bye to Lydia and strode to the door. "MacLaren, may I see you for a moment?"

MacLaren puffed his cheeks and blew out a stream of air. He picked up his coffee cup and exited his office, closing the door behind him.

Andre threw the sheets off him and sat on the edge of the bed rubbing his temples. "Ohh ... I've got a fucking headache," he moaned. "Do you have any aspirin?"

"Ibuprofin."

"Naw, that shit doesn't work for me." He turned and looked at her. "How do you feel?"

"I feel fine. Come here, I can make you forget about your headache." She lifted the sheets, exposing her exquisite body to him. Her long raven-black hair lay in curls across her breasts. Andre saw the hardness of her nipples, his eyes tracing a hungry line down her creamy, cappuccino-toned stomach, across her navel and marveling at the smooth, clean-shaven pubic area. His heart rate rose and beads of sweat formed on his brow and upper lip. She reached for him. "Ou ... see? You're already forgetting about that headache, aren't you?"

She tugged on him, "Put this in my pussy and it'll go away."

Andre crawled on top of Isabella and entered her. Quickly he reached that awkward rhythm that had brought him to orgasm twice during the previous night.

Isabella drew her French-manicured nails up Andre's back and over his shoulders. She saw that one of her nails was chipped. She'd have to have that fixed this morning.

Someone knocked on the glass of MacLaren's office. Ben and Lydia turned to see a distinguished looking gentleman motioning to them. He had white hair and a narrow white mustache that matched the white chalk-stripe in his charcoal gray suit. A starched white shirt held a red-striped tie in a perfect Windsor knot.

"It's my dad. Come on."

Lydia gathered her things and opened the door. Big Ben held onto his coffee cup and followed her. They fell into step behind Conrad Blake Lawrence, Esq. and made their way to a quiet spot down the corridor.

Lydia did the introductions.

"Nice to meet you Chief Benson," Mr. Lawrence said.

"Please, just call me Ben," he shook the lawyer's hand.

"Will do, and you may call me Connie. Now," he handed a folded piece of paper to Lydia, "I think this will do nicely."

Lydia unfolded the paper and read. "Perfect." She handed it to Ben. "This is a statement from Dodge we're releasing to the media."

The statement was written in first person from Dodge Maddison. It was brief and to the point, establishing sorrow for the deceased and her family, reiterating his unquestionable credibility, and vowing to aid the investigation in all ways prudent and expeditious to conclude this travesty and administer swift justice. The closing line was heartfelt, 'I was fortunate to have had my life brightened by the friendship and love of this beautiful, charismatic woman. Dana will truly be missed and I will carry her spirit in my heart forever'.

"This seems okay, but shouldn't he proclaim his innocence?" Ben asked.

"Never," Connie Lawrence said. "That would be misconstrued as an admission of guilt. The media would play upon that and only that. We do not want to feed them pliant fodder for their iniquitous ways. The media has an advantage and a mission. The advantage is their ability to influence millions of people instantly – and those people are the *real* judge and jury of Dodge Maddison. The mission is to satisfy their blood thirst. They will portray guilt over innocence, fabrication over evidence, and by all means, sales above justice. That is their mantra. They need to slaughter this icon and get onto the next."

Ben slowly nodded his head. He gave the paper back to Conrad Lawrence.

"I'm going to read this on the front steps," Lydia's father said. "Care to come along?"

"No thanks. I'd better go see Dodge. I think he could use a friendly face right about now."

"Good idea. Lydia, shall we?" The two attorneys fell into step beside each other and made for the front door.

TWENTY-THREE

The committee created to oversee the restoration of the Sarasota Courthouse Complex was membered by an eclectic group of citizens and professionals whose chief goal was the acquisition of local funds to match the state contribution doled out by the Florida Historical and Preservation Society. Their selected chairperson was not only a well-known and well-admired native son, but he was also an extremely successful attorney who happened to preside over an influential group of lawyers known as the Knights of The Court. Conrad Blake Lawrence, Esc. was King Arthur of the prestigious gentlemen's club that gathered once a week to hob-nob, smoke Cuban cigars, and drink expensive cognac. They appeared a bit pompous to other professional groups, but the Knights were nonetheless admired by the community for their charity and involvement in just causes ranging from Little League sponsorships and urban development, to protection of South Florida's wildlife and fragile eco-systems. The noble group prided itself in being champions of the underdog. In that vein, each member was required to retain a pro bono client at all times. The Knights had power and money and a collective conscience to use those attributes for the common good. What they did not have however, was a table. More precisely, a round table.

The restoration project provided them with that. The twin Spanish-Mediterranean style buildings, used as the County Courthouse and the Police Department Complex, were joined in the center by a grand tower with an elaborate belfry, the interior of which the Knights, due to their sizeable contribution, were allowed to design to their liking. The bells were removed and the long, vertical open-arches circling the tower were glassed in and became tinted windows with a spectacular panoramic view of the city of Sarasota, the thin keys of Siesta, Lido and Longboat, and the vast emerald carpet called the Gulf of Mexico. The marbled floor supported a weighty, custom-made round table with matching custom carved hi-back chairs. Connie Lawrence and company couldn't have been more thrilled with their new meeting room.

The private access was a windy narrow wooden staircase behind a heavy door of dark mahogany with large wrought-iron hinges and a huge iron padlock. This morning a uniformed police officer stood outside of it with the key in his hand. Locked inside were Dodge Maddison and Chief Ben Benson. For the purpose of privacy Attorney Lawrence had granted them special access to the tower.

"I can't deal with this, Bennie." Dodge Maddison had an angry tone in his voice. "I think we need to contact my business attorneys in New York and have them put us in touch with a firm that handles this type of thing. I need a fucking New York lawyer."

"I'll tell you what you're going to have to deal with, you need to chill and start thinking about how serious this is. No attorney is going to be able to get past this judge. He's a hard-ass. And the D.A. has an even harder-ass. The media's camped outside. They're at the Ritz. They're on the beach talking to tourists for chrissake. And you can bet your ass they'll be all over the memorial service. So, stop stomping around and let's get serious. Help me out here, Dodge. Give me something to go on. Give me something to look for. Who would want Dana dead? Who would benefit from her death?"

Ornately framed mirrors rested between all eight windows in the belfry. The mirrors enlarged the tiny room and married a striking view of the outside world with the inside domain. Seated at any one of the chairs circumfering the round table one could simultaneously enjoy a view of the entire room with an exquisite external panorama. Big Ben sat in one of the chairs. Dodge paced around the table. He stopped in front of one of the mirrors and looked at himself. He looked like shit. He hadn't slept at all last night. He needed a shower and a shave and some fresh clothes.

"I need some clothes, Bennie."

"Harlow's putting some things together for you. You're not listening to me are you?" He was, but he didn't answer.

"I just left Lydia Lawrence and her father Conrad. They've prepared a press release to help calm down the enemy."

"They're not the enemy. This fucking system is the enemy. I'm stuck in here because it's convenient to forget about law and order and blame the first person they see for a crime he didn't commit. Meanwhile, the real murderer is scot-free."

"Not if we figure out who that is."

Dodge pulled out a chair and sat at the table. "That's all I've been thinking about since Monday morning, and I just don't know. I can't think of anyone for any reason wanting to harm Dana."

"She wasn't harmed, Dodge, she was stabbed in the chest. Deeply, with a very sharp letter opener."

"When did you get so cruel?"

"I'm not cruel, I'm a cop. Someone, with a great amount of anger, killed that girl." Benjamin J. Benson, Chief of Police, Bryce Corner, Massachusetts sat across from Dodge Maddison, Fashion Designer slash murder suspect. "And we need to figure out *who* so we can get your ass out of here and back to your world, and my ass back to my cushy little job chasing cats out of trees and reprimanding old men for sitting on their neighbor's porch. So let's go down the list of possibilities, shall we? Let's start with Harlow."

Dodge wanted to tell Bennie how crazy that was, that Harlow couldn't have had anything to do with Dana's murder - how could he even think such a thing? But he saw the wheels turning in Bennie's head. And to be honest, he'd wondered too. Didn't believe it could be true, but had wondered about a lot of things during his long sleepless night.

"I can't believe that's a possibility and I know you can't either," Dodge said.

"Listen, as Ben Benson I know and love Harlow like a sister. As a cop, I don't know nor love anyone. Lizzie Borden's family probably loved her 'til she started wielding that axe. So, humor me. Let me do what I do best. Try to stay objective. You said she left you and Andre Chateauguy and Fletcher Ross at the restaurant just before midnight Sunday. When did you see her next?"

"Early the next morning."

"What does early mean?"

"Seven, seven-fifteen. We met in the lobby for continental breakfast."

"You didn't stay with her that night?"

"No." Dodge gave Big Ben an angry look.

"How long did you stay at breakfast?"

"We didn't. We grabbed coffees and muffins to go and went to the beach."

"Was there anyone on the beach at that time?"

"Yes. Andre was there with his crew setting up their equipment and Fletcher was already at the tent with the line."

"The line?"

"The clothing. He was organizing the clothes on the racks."

"The models?"

"They weren't there yet," anticipating Ben's next question he added, "They got there about nine."

Ben wasn't taking any notes. He was cataloguing the data in his head. "All right, let's back up a bit. What time did you return to the hotel Sunday night?"

"It must have been pretty close to two a.m."

"Alone?"

"No, Andre and Fletcher and I walked back from the Circle together."

"And you went right to your room?"

"Yes, Bennie."

"Then the last time you saw Harlow was just before midnight and then not again until seven-ish in the morning?"

"Right."

"Time of death is established at between midnight and six a.m. You were all on the same floor together, the Penthouse Suites. Harlow's room was across the hall from Dana's. Dana knew Harlow and I'm assuming she would have let her in had Harlow knocked on Dana's door, even at that late hour. Perhaps even because of the hour."

"Why do you say that?"

"Maybe she saw Harlow through the peep-hole and thought something was amiss, something important enough to bring Harlow to her door at such an early hour. Maybe she was worried about you."

Dodge didn't comment.

"At any rate, that gives her opportunity. The means is obviously the letter opener, and the motive would be ..."

"Jealousy. You think she was jealous of Dana and I?"

"Don't even try to tell me you're having a revelation. You know damn well Harlow's been in love with you for some time. Me and a lot of people. Including her. One thing we all know about women is that they're a jealous lot. Even more so if they tell you they're not."

TWENTY-FOUR

"Dodge, I'm certainly not jealous of Dana. Why would I be? What you do with your personal life is entirely up to you. Whatever makes you happy makes me happy too. I may not agree with the scenario, for obvious reasons, but you need to do what you need to do," Harlow turned from him and walked away, "You always have."

Dodge was sitting on the edge of the long, over-sized table in the Level Five Studio on the fifth floor of the Maddison Designs building in New York. Above him was his penthouse apartment with the spiral walkway to the roof where he had had an elaborate garden planted, accented with trees and shrubbery to keep him in touch with his New England heritage. Below him, on floors four and three, was where the manufacturing was done, where the pattern makers and the seamstresses fabricated his designs from sketches into reality to be shipped to boutiques and department stores worldwide, or brought downstairs to the street level boutique with the expansive staircase leading the patrons of *Lady Maddison* to the second floor mezzanine where they could dine in *Café Mad* or pamper themselves at the in-house Spa and Salon.

He stood and walked across the polished wooden floor of the old loft building over to where Harlow had gone to her desk. The open floor plan was conducive to their style of working. Her desk was on one side of the corner building overlooking the street and Dodge's was on the front side with the windows high above the main entrance to the boutique. He could stand there and watch his customers emerge from their limousines and town cars and taxicabs and enter into the building where he lived and worked and sold the fruits of his passion. He crossed the room, zigzagging between the drawing tables and design boards of his designers. They were not working on this mid-summer Sunday morning, but Dodge and Harlow were there making last minute preparations for the Paris premiere coming up this week.

Harlow had driven in from her home on Long Island enjoying the easy traffic flow of Sunday morning and the calmness of a light jazz station. She lived alone in a quaint house on the north shore within walking distance to the beach. She had tried having a pet, but her workaholic schedule with the frequent trips abroad left her cute little Bichon Frise at the neighbors home so often, that she had finally relinquished ownership to them. She visited FiFi as often as she could.

She was packed and ready to catch the Monday flight to Paris, but she had promised Dodge she'd come in Sunday to help him with a few last minute things. She hadn't anticipated helping him with his conscience. He approached her. She was seated at her desk clicking at her computer. He laid his hand onto her shoulder. She wished that her fuming anger could make the feel of his hand cold and meaningless and unwanted. But it didn't.

"What do you mean 'for obvious reasons'?"

Harlow took in a silent deep breath. She spun casually in her swivel chair, forcing his hand from her. He stood looking down at her from his lofty frame. She was wearing a flattering cotton crew-neck blouse with a silver and onyx pendant hanging from a silver chain on the outside of her top between her breasts. She was in shape and was proud of it. She was comfortable with the way her forty-year-old body wore fashion and the way men, especially Dodge Maddison, looked at her when they thought she wasn't noticing. Harlow crossed her hallmark legs in her snug fitting Italian jeans and wiggled her foot. Her sandal dangled from her toes.

"I hope you don't believe Dana's serious about you. Can't you see it's just an infatuation?"

Harlow and Dodge had each had relationships during their ten year acquaintanceship, short ones, never penetrating the armored shell of the fashion business that consumed them. They talked freely about the liaisons, compadres lending a friendly ear, coupled with an unbiased, sometimes brutal opinion. And they had successfully danced around the embers of their own smoldering relationship. It was easy when you didn't want to admit to it. Especially to yourself. And that is what they had done. Keeping a wall of professionalism erected between them. They complemented each other and worked extremely well together and were afraid to thwart a good thing with something as mundane as sexual consummation. So they pretended there was nothing there. But there was. They both knew it. But they were both stubborn. Adamantly hiding the attraction they held for each other in the folds of the fabrics they surrounded themselves with. So, they appeased their primal wants with sporadic relationships and kept at bay the building passion between them by working harder and making the business their surrogate lover.

Until now Harlow had rationalized Dodge's other 'dates', after all, she had her own from time to time. But the relationship with the super model Dana was too much. Dodge walked over to the window. The day was bright. The boutique didn't open until noon on Sunday. The building was quiet. Just the two of them there. In his heart he knew what Harlow was saying to him. But his mind held the fear of loss. One shrink had said that he'd been permanently scarred by the sudden loss of his parents when he was five. Told him time would diminish the pain, but the scar would never leave him. So he had wrapped himself in security blankets; his grandparents, best friend Bennie, his business, the fashion world, even Harlow.

His romantic relationships were short-lived and shallow, never advancing to a level that might penetrate his guarded emotions. And with Harlow, it was the fear of losing her that kept him at arms length. He believed that if they became romantically involved he would jinx the solid business relationship they shared and jeopardize Maddison Designs, the one security blanket he could control. He could control the business but could not control the whims of Fate that emotions were prone to.

At the time of this conversation with Harlow, Dodge had not lost his grandparents yet, nor had he met Annison Barrett, the one woman who would rattle his emotions sufficiently enough to allow him to drop his guard. That was all to come.

Dodge took a step away from the window. "What do you want from me?" he asked.

"Honesty," Harlow heard herself say.

"I have always been honest with you. This is why I'm telling you about Dana."

"I'm not talking about being honest with me, I'm talking about being honest with yourself. Is that what you want in your life? A young supermodel deep on looks but shallow on everything else?"

"She's not as shallow as you think. She's a very accomplished ..."

"Oh Christ Dodge! Give me a break." Harlow jabbed the 'off' button on her computer and got up from her chair. She slapped her leather briefcase onto the desktop and threw some paperwork into it. "Listen, you do what you need to do and I'll do what I need to do. Okay?" She closed her briefcase and slung the strap over her shoulder. "And right now I need to get out of here and go home to finish packing."

"Why are you angry? We've always talked about our relationships."

"No, we haven't. We mentioned them to each other but we never *talked* about them. We always danced around them, keeping them at a safe distance."

"You're surprising me. We've always been supportive of each other. What's so different this time?"

Harlow appeared to be tidying up her desk, her thin briefcase swinging from her shoulder with the abrupt movements of her arms. "Let me get this straight," she stood erect. "You're telling me you're having an affair with a twenty-year old model, a woman, a *girl* half your age, and you don't see that as different?"

"It's not an affair. I think there's really something there."

"Oh my god! Sometimes I really don't understand you, Dodge, and this is one of them."

"What do you mean?"

"Mean? What the fuck do I *mean*? I'll tell you what I mean. You've always been so level headed, so ..." She picked up her pocketbook and stood in front of him trying to breath evenly. "I can't do this right now." Harlow walked away.

"Harlow, don't do this to me. Don't walk away from me. Let's talk this out."

Why was it that she could so easily, strongly and vehemently voice her motherly opinion to him but when it came to speaking her true feelings as a woman she was so goddamn tongue-tied? Instead of standing there arguing with him, she wanted to push him down on her desk and climb on top of him. Make wild passionate love to him like no other woman ever has or ever could. Ignite him, scorch him with the raging fire inside her that burned for him. But as always, she found herself in retreat. Unable to blurt out her emotions, unable to understand this man that she felt so one-sidedly in love with. She bypassed the elevator and took the stairs to the right of it. Dodge stood at the far end of the room listening to her hard footsteps descending into the echoes of the stairwell.

TWENTY-FIVE

"You can see I'm right, can't cha?" Ben said.

"About what?"

"Jealousy. It's an age old motive."

Dodge had no response. He sat across from Big Ben at the round table in the belfry with the dominant sunshine cascading in from the southern windows.

"I know about what happened between the two of you when you were in Bryce Corner for your grandparent's funeral. And you know I know. So don't be lame with me. You and Harlow got it on. Then you immediately took up with Annison Barrett. What kind of message do you think that sent to Harlow?"

"Bennie, we have spent one night together in all this time. That's all there is between Harlow and I. She was the one who wanted to nip it in the bud, to chalk it up to unbridled lust and to move on."

"Unbridled lust? What, are you living in a soap opera? No, let me correct that, you *are* living in a soap opera. That's your problem. That's exactly why you're sitting in jail, pal." Ben leaned forward in his chair and placed his elbows on the table. He rubbed his forehead with his big hands. "Try to listen to me. I'm no shrink but it doesn't take one to realize that Harlow was hurt. She loves your ass. Maybe she got frightened, maybe she needed time to think, maybe she was testing your feelings, I don't fucking know. But what I do know is that your getting involved with another woman right away wasn't what she was thinking was going to happen."

"I didn't plan on getting involved with Annison. I didn't even know her then. That was all fate."

"Fate, bullshit. You got scared when your true emotions came out for Harlow. She probably felt that. She goes back to New York waiting on you to come to your senses and the next thing she knows, bingo, you're hooked up with another woman. You don't think jealousy comes into play here?"

"Okay. Fine. I'll give you that, but you're forgetting one thing. *If* Harlow is the perpetrator, why wouldn't she kill Annison instead of Dana?"

"Why wouldn't she if she felt Dana was still in the picture?"

"She wasn't."

"So you say. Others say different. Maybe Harlow knew you were still doing Dana, or maybe she thought you were. Maybe she transferred her jealousy for Annison over to Dana. She had an opportunity in Sarasota and she took it. One down, one to go."

"Absolutely impossible, and you know it."

"Stay objective with me. She's a suspect. She had means, motive and opportunity."

"But where's the benefit?"

"Elimination of a rival."

They were quiet. Ben sat back in the high back chair teetering on the back legs. Dodge folded his hands.

"Of course, between the two of you," Ben said, "you make the better target. You also had means and opportunity. Annnd you had five million other motives to want Dana dead. Harlow doesn't benefit from a five million dollar insurance policy and, if Dana was truly out of your life as you claim, why would Harlow need to kill her?"

Dodge looked his friend in the eye. Ben knew this look. This is how Dodge got when he was serious about something. Like the time when they were kids and he confessed to Bennie that he'd lied to him about being sick the day they were supposed to go fishing and Dodge had instead gone off with another friend to Six Flags.

"Bennie, I need to tell you something."

"I hope you do, because I need you to tell me *some*thing."

"A year ago I gave Harlow ten percent of the business."

"That's commendable, I'm sure you had your reasons. What does that add?"

"She's been an integral part of my business for a long time. It was the right thing to do. She's earned it. I wanted to show her my appreciation. And also, selfishly, I didn't want to lose her. A couple of my competitors were pursuing her at the time."

Ben stared at him. His stare said, *and...?*

"And there was a clause drawn up. If anything happens to me, she gets another forty percent."

"Fifty percent of Maddison Designs becomes hers?"

"Yup."

"Not to sound too nosey, but if you're gone, who does she share the other fifty percent with?"

"You're not going to like this."

"Try me."

"Annison Barrett."

Ben was dumbfounded.

"And I don't have to be gone. The wording was something like incapacitated, unable to perform sufficient duties relevant to the profession blah blah blah."

"Like serving a life sentence for murder? Sounds like an odd way to word a legal document."

"Not really. It was actually a standard form that my attorney filled out. I had it done last week. I had to revise a few things for the marriage and I wanted Harlow to have more than the ten percent if something ever happened to me."

"Guilt?"

"Analyzing again Dr. Benson?"

Two weeks ago Dodge had expressed his intention to marry Annison, had even asked Ben to be his best man. Ben had voiced his astonishment compiled with a lecture on sudden relationships on the heels of tragedy. He reminded him that he had only known Annison Barrett for not even two months. Added to that, Ben had pointedly asked him about his feelings for Harlow to which Dodge had responded in his classic roundabout way that avoided the issue all together. Ben thought his friend was crazy and had told him so. Nevertheless, Dodge forged on with his marital intentions. Ben's wife Carlene thought the whole thing too quick and superficial.

She believed Annison Barrett to be a nice enough person, but reserved the option of applying the label of gold-digger.

"How did you fuck up your whole life in such a short period of time?" Ben asked him.

Dodge didn't respond.

"You want my assessment?" Ben said.

"I'm going to get it anyway."

"I think you've been working so hard for so long that your brain is fried. Losing Gramma Emma and Grampa Jed pushed you over the edge. Finally expressing your emotions with Harlow scared you. Diving into a relationship with a woman you really don't even know - talking marriage for chrissake - is just some bizarre form of psychological retreat." Ben's voice was raised, "I don't believe you ended the fling with Dana. You've fucked with the minds of three women to the point where one of them is dead and the other two could own your multi-million-dollar business, and you're sitting in a dark jail cell in sunny Sarasota, just a short trial away from death row."

Dodge didn't have a reply. Ben continued, saying in a hushed tone, "You're guilty, y'know."

"What?" this got a rise out of him. "You actually think I killed Dana?"

"In a way."

"Fuck you, Bennie," Dodge angrily pushed his chair back.

"Dodge, I'm your friend, a fucking brother for chrissake, and I'll do whatever needs to be done to catch the fucker who's bringing on this collateral damage to you. But I've got to express my chagrin in you. You and I are different in our ways, and pretty much polar opposite when it comes to women. Your world is your world, its faster than mine and much more glamorous, but one thing I know for sure – women are women no matter whose world they're in. And they like to be treated right. If you're lucky enough to get a good one, you treat her right and she'll treat you right, come hell or high water. But you mix them up and all hell breaks loose. That's where I think you're at. You surrounded yourself with too much pussy and, just like those chemistry classes we had in high school, when you mix too many variables, things explode.

So, whether you want to admit it or not, your irresponsibility makes you responsible. Something you did made this happen."

The old hinges on the heavy door beneath them creaked in the narrow stairway. Footsteps scuffed on the wooden stairs. "It's Conrad Lawrence, I'm coming up."

"I think you're dead wrong, Bennie, and I don't see how whatever the fuck you're insinuating got Dana killed."

"Let me ask you a couple of quick questions. As it stands right now, you own ninety percent and Harlow owns ten percent of Maddison Designs."

"Yes."

"If something 'happens' to you, ownership goes fifty-fifty between the two women."

"Yes."

"As of right now, regardless of whether Annison Barrett is your wife or not?"

"Yes."

Conrad Lawrence's footsteps reached the landing just a few feet from them.

Bennie lowered his voice, and leaned toward Dodge, "And what happens to the vast wealth of Maddison Designs if one woman predeceases the other?"

"Whew, those stairs are steeper than I thought," Conrad Lawrence stood at the top of the stairs catching his breath. "Better get a move on. Harlow's here with clothes for you Dodge. We've got to leave for the funeral service in twenty minutes. So if you want to shower and shave, you'd better get to it." He walked over to the windows facing southwest.

Dodge didn't answer Ben. He didn't need to, the answer was obvious.

"God, it's a beautiful day," the attorney said. "Look, you can see Selby Gardens from here. Over there just beyond the giant American flag at Sarasota Ford."

Big Ben pushed his chair back. A hollow scrape filled the small room.

"You two go on ahead," the lawyer said. "I'll take a few minutes here. The guard will take you back. We'll meet at the eastside entrance of the courthouse in," Conrad Lawrence looked at his watch, "nineteen minutes. MacLaren's going to have an unmarked car waiting there. The media doesn't know what we're up to and they've all gone off to the service. We'll be arriving late to keep you in the background. This whole thing is low key, not to mention illegal. I've got my neck on the line here Mr. Maddison, so don't fuck it up."

Swearing sounded out of place for the venerable attorney, so it had an added weight of command to it.

Dodge and Ben descended the narrow stairway. Before they got to the door Ben stopped them with his hand on Dodge's shoulder. "If I miraculously get you out of this, ole buddy, I want you to make me a promise. And this will be my payment. I want you to promise me that you will seek professional help and get yourself out of this jungle you've lost yourself in."

Dodge made a move to proceed but Ben's big hand squeezed his shoulder like a vice grip.

"Okay, okay."

"I mean it, Dodge. Say it."

Dodge felt the weight of his best friend's hand lying on his shoulder. He could also feel the weight of the world beneath it. He wasn't happy in the position he was in. He'd done a lot of thinking during his sleepless night. He felt ramifications building up on him. He was, for perhaps the first time in his life, uncertain of his future. Something told him Bennie had a point.

"Alright. I'll consider it."

Ben's hand tightened.

"Okay! If it makes you happy, I'll address it after you get me out of here."

"It would make me happy."

TWENTY-SIX

Selby Botanical Gardens is a lavish tropical oasis located on the resplendent shores of Sarasota Bay. Over six thousand wild orchids intersperse their spectacular colors throughout the vast acreage of tropical plants, exotic flowers, bamboo gardens and a myriad of ponds filled with colorful species of fish. A mangrove walkway curls along the shoreline beneath grand banyan trees leading into a magnificent clearing outlined with beautiful flora. Crews had been there since early morning setting up a huge white pavilion complete with white wicker chairs, crystal chandeliers and tall ornate pedestals topped with vases of white roses.

The memorial service for the world's top fashion model was on schedule for noon. The family was seated in the front row before a long white altar covered with white silk cloth cascading in layers onto the ground. In the center stood a shiny brass urn. Large portraits of Dana were placed across the front and then randomly throughout the pavilion, representing the various stages of her short life. Thousands of rose petals were scattered about the manicured lawn. The service had been limited to two hundred guests and they had all shown up, arriving not only from her small hometown in the Midwest, but also from New York City, Los Angeles, and even the distant fashion locales of Paris, London, and Milan. Because of Dana's popularity at home and abroad, the family had allowed selected members of the media to be present, but restricted them to the outskirts of the pavilion.

The day was bright, the wind was still, the mood somber. The requiem began and those who had been standing about conversing quietly in small groups dutifully took their seats.

Unbeknownst to the mourners a car with dark tinted windows was entering discreetly through the service gates at the rear of the property.

On the ride over Lieutenant MacLaren drove with Conrad Lawrence, Esq. seated next him. Visiting Chief of Police, Ben Benson and his incarcerated best friend Dodge Maddison occupied the back seat. Lydia Lawrence had a previously scheduled court appearance and couldn't make the service. Harlow had dropped off Dodge's change of clothing and then driven the rental Jaguar over to Selby Gardens. She was seated somewhere in the pavilion between Andre Chateauguy and Fletcher Ross. The models occupied the two rows behind them.

"We're short on time," Ben said to Dodge, "so let's continue our previous conversation." The back of MacLaren's unmarked cop car was removed just enough from the dialogue going on between the front seat occupants to afford them a small frame of privacy. "Let's move away from Harlow as a suspect and onto Annison Barrett."

"Bennie, I don't see how you can even bring her into the equation. I know you're going to play the jealousy card again, but really, she had nothing to do with it. She wasn't even here, pal."

"She didn't fly home to Bryce Corner last Saturday, Dodge."

"Bennie, we drove to the Miami airport together. We dropped off the rental car at Alamo, then she took the shuttle bus to Delta and I took one to Southwest. And actually, my puddle-jumper flight was delayed over two hours, so she was probably back north by the time I got into Sarasota."

"She rented a car at Hertz."

"What?"

"At 10:45 am."

Big Ben recalled from his computer-like memory that Annison had told him she had rented a car and driven down to Key Largo to visit a friend on the day that Dodge flew into Sarasota. He told Dodge this and added, "That would have been Saturday.

Theoretically, she could have driven to Sarasota Saturday or Sunday unbeknownst to you or anyone else, gotten into the Ritz-Carlton Sunday around midnight, knocked on Dana's door, gained entry – for after all, both women knew of each other and Dana would have probably let her in – done the deed, driven back across the peninsula via Alligator Alley, and boarded a late night flight that would have gotten her to Boston in the wee hours of Monday morning. She could have then driven home to Bryce Corner and been there by the time I drove over for coffee. A stretch, but do-able."

"That's wild speculation and certainly unfounded."

"Not all of it. Delta has an Annison Barrett on their passenger list for a 5:15am flight to Logan." Ben wasn't sure if Dodge knew anything about this or not. He hoped he didn't.

Dodge got very quiet. Then he said in a very low voice, "Does MacLaren know this?"

"I don't know. If he's as good as I am he does. But if he's comfortable with you as the murderer, he may not be looking at anyone else as I am."

Dodge sat quiet: a million bewildering thoughts racing through his brain. "I'd rather he didn't know. I've got to talk to Annison first. I'm sure there's a plausible explanation."

"Like?"

"I don't know, but I'm sure she didn't sneak over to Sarasota and stab Dana, for God's sake."

Conrad Lawrence and the Lieutenant were contentedly swapping fishing stories, unconcerned with the muffled conversation going on in the back seat. Traffic on Osprey Avenue was at a dead stop due to a Florida Power and Light truck replacing a transformer box on a utility pole at Ringling Boulevard.

"What the fuck would be her motive, Bennie?"

"One of two - love or money. Love drives some people insane, y'know. It's been documented. People in love do crazy things. Remember *Fatal Attraction*? Shit like that happens."

"She's not ..."

"Wait ... hear me out. We don't know that much about her, we've only known her for two months, and you *really* don't know that much about her. She's got you so goo-goo-eyed that you're ready to change your whole life for her. First of all the love motive for Annison would be the same as Harlow's - elimination of a rival. The money motive is self-explanatory – you've written her into at least fifty percent of Maddison Designs and one hundred percent if something happens to both you and Harlow. So, actually her motive could be seen as stronger than Harlow's. There are black widows out there and some of them don't always have to kill their lovers to satisfy their needs."

"How do you sleep at night with a head full of crazy shit like that? I think you watch too many mystery movies."

"She seems like a nice enough lady, but again, what do we really know about her? She's told you she's reevaluating her life. Divorcing her husband and marrying you. She says she's financially secure, but do you know that for a fact? She may be getting cut out of whatever windfall she's expecting from the divorce. The business actually belongs to the husband's family. A smart lawyer could leave her in a cardboard box. If we dig into this and find her desperate for money, then, factoring in the quickness with which she's wrapped you around her finger, one could strongly suspect money as a motive."

"Okay, we're here," MacLaren said. Traffic had moved on and they were entering the Gardens via the back entrance at the end of Pineapple Avenue. The main entrance on Osprey was riddled with media vans and reporters crowding the main gate, cameras at the ready. The foursome had managed to slip by them, but there was the elite group of the media, the ones who'd been granted limited access to the pavilion that MacLaren and Conrad Lawrence were concerned with. They knew smuggling Dodge Maddison into the ceremony was risky, not to mention highly inappropriate.

MacLaren pulled the car between two delivery trucks at the far end of the driveway beneath a large live oak, the Spanish moss hanging down on the hood of the car. He got out and opened the rear door for Dodge Maddison. As soon as he was out of the car, MacLaren slapped the cuffs on him.

"Hey!"

"Relax, Maddison. I won't make them too tight."

Attorney Lawrence came around the front of the car. "I don't think that will be necessary."

"Hey, my ass is on the line here and I'm not taking any chances."

"It's okay, Lieutenant, I'll assume all responsibility," Connie Lawrence said. MacLaren stared at him. Lawrence was a powerful man in Sarasota with ties to many other powerful people in town and the state, including MacLaren's boss. Conrad Lawrence gave him a conciliatory look.

MacLaren took his key and placed it in the lock of the handcuff. He glared at Maddison. "I don't like this and if it wasn't for Attorney Lawrence's relationship with the police commissioner, there'd be no way in hell I'd do this. But understand clearly, Mr. Maddison, with your attorney and big brother here as witnesses, I am telling you I have a gun. And I will not hesitate to use it if you make *any* unusual moves. Do you understand?" MacLaren held the key in the lock of the handcuff and waited for a response.

"Perfectly, Lieutenant," Dodge replied.

"Mr. Lawrence, Chief Benson, are we all on the same page?"

The two of them nodded. MacLaren released the handcuffs and put them back on his belt inside his sportcoat. Dodge rubbed his wrists and walked off with Conrad Lawrence along a narrow pathway overhung with palm fronds and tropical vines. MacLaren fell in step close behind them. Big Ben came up next to him. "I think you're a little dramatic, MacLaren."

"No. Dramatic is when the EMT van comes to pick up his dead body. I'm serious about this, Benson. Keep your man in check."

The pathway narrowed and the four men walked single file, Big Ben taking up the rear, swatting away the overgrowth, with mangrove branches and pygmy palm fronds swaying in his wake. They came to the clearing and stood off to the side, fifty yards from the pavilion. Dana's sister was giving a tearful eulogy. The memorial guests were hushed and the sister's words were soft and unable to reach to where the men stood. In an attempt to conceal his identity Dodge had been outfitted with nondescript casual clothing, sunglasses and a hat. Ben and Conrad Lawrence stood on either side of him. MacLaren stood directly behind. They were silent.

Dodge looked at Dana's sister and couldn't help but think of Dana and the time they'd spent together. They'd known of each other professionally a year before they'd become romantically involved. The relationship had been spontaneous and fun, and sexually intense. In a way he was sorry that it had ended. And it wouldn't have if Annison Barrett hadn't come into his life. Annison. He hoped Bennie was wrong about her. Dodge couldn't imagine her being involved in Dana's death. Why would she? Absurd. But she had clearly stayed in Florida longer than she'd told him. They'd gone to the airport together Saturday morning. He assumed she'd flown home to Bryce Corner. She hadn't. She'd driven to Key Largo to visit a friend? What friend? She didn't get home until early Monday morning. Two days later. Over the weekend they'd texted back and forth, short messages like I Miss You, Thinking Of You, Love You, but they didn't actually speak to each other until late Monday night. Dodge had been busy with the photo shoot and then riddled with the shock of Dana's death. He'd assumed Annison had been busy with the house renovations. The conversation they did have was about Dana and the effect on Dodge's photo shoot. Annison had been mostly quiet. Maybe she was in shock too. She'd offered condolences and asked if he wanted her to come down. He'd said no, it wasn't necessary, and they'd talked awhile longer about the house and the snowstorm and other small talk. Now he wondered why she hadn't mentioned it. Maybe the news of Dana's death overrode offering whatever reason she had to stay in Florida. Maybe it had been a shopping whim, or flight problems, or some other reasonable explanation.

But he couldn't understand why she hadn't told him. He'd have to call her as soon as the service was over.

The sister concluded her eulogy and stood crying before the brass urn. It was sad. An older man rose and assisted her back to her seat; not the father, for Dodge had met him before. Perhaps an uncle. Music started playing and the mourners rose row by row and began walking past the alter, stopping to give condolences to the seated family.

The further end of the pavilion was set up with buffet tables. White uniformed chefs doled out plates of hot food to the guests to take to any of the several tables scattered across the lawn beneath the shade of the many tropical trees. Some of the guests preferred to forego the food and exit the grounds. The press approached them and some of them stood a minute talking to reporters and peering into video cameras. The questions all centered on the death of the super model and the arrest of the famous fashion designer. One of the cameramen spotted the small group of men off to the side and zoomed in on them. He didn't recognize any of them, but the guy in the middle looked familiar. He looked like Maddison incognito. He motioned to his reporter and they made as if they were closing up their equipment to leave. They walked casually away from the crowd of reporters toward the front exit of the grounds. When they were out of view they cut through the back end of the gardens and hurried unnoticed to get positioned closer to the four men.

TWENTY-SEVEN

"What are my chances of giving the family my condolences?" Dodge asked.

"None," MacLaren said. "That wasn't part of the deal. We need to get out of here as quickly and quietly as possible. If anyone finds out you were here there'll be hell to pay. The D.A. would have my ass on a platter, and yours too Mr. Lawrence. Tanya Chisholm is a real bitch and I for one don't want to mess with her. Let's go." He grabbed Dodge's elbow.

"Wait a minute," Ben said. There were two ladies coming towards them.

"Shit." MacLaren said.

Harlow was walking across the lawn with an elegant looking woman. She appeared older than Harlow. She was tall, slender, and fashionable. Her complexion smooth, polished with years of Oil of Olay. Her skin tone was a light bronze. Her long, bare legs strode assuredly from a subtle black dress, looking like they'd never had the need to wear nylons. She looked healthy with that aura of a warm sunny climate about her; like she had always lived in a place with sunshine and nearby beaches, like the L.A. she hailed from.

"I thought you were supposed to be inconspicuous," Harlow said to the men.

"We're not?" Ben asked.

The woman wore a black straw hat with a wide brim shadowing her sun-baked hair lying in soft spirals on her shoulders. She took off her sunglasses and curled her lips in a pleasant smile. "Hello, Dodge."

"Hello, Sunny."

She stepped into him and gave him a kiss on the cheek. MacLaren strengthened his grip on Dodge's elbow. The woman caught the gesture but was undaunted. She gave Dodge a motherly pat on the arm. "Good to see you again," she said. "Forgoing the circumstances of course."

"Likewise. It's been a long time."

"Yes, it has."

Dodge said, "This is Sunny Sterling, from Los Angeles."

Conrad Lawrence was the first to take her hand, "So very nice to make your acquaintance. My wife and daughter are in love with you. Their closets are full of your designs. I think my wife still has a pair of your jeans from the seventies."

"Tell her to hang onto them. They're selling on e-Bay for more than their original retail," she laughed.

Dodge introduced her to Ben and MacLaren.

"Listen," Sunny said, "I don't want to draw attention this way, so I'll be leaving. But Harlow told me you were secreted over here and I just had to come over and tell you how sorry I am about Dana. She was a lovely girl." She squeezed Dodge's arm. "And please take care of yourself, I know you'll be fine. Keep your spirits up. Good-bye everyone. It was nice meeting you all."

"Allow me to walk you out," Big Ben said.

"Did you get that?" the reporter whispered to his cameraman.

"Yeah."

"Audio too?"

"Pretty sure." They were hidden in the foliage twenty yards off to the side.

"Keep it rolling, here comes somebody else."

"Oh Christ." MacLaren said as he saw Andre Chateauguy, Fletcher Ross and another man hurriedly approaching. "We don't have time for this."

"Mi amico! Buono a vedere tu." A hearty Italian man embraced Dodge and kissed him on both cheeks.

"Good to see you too, Giovanni," Dodge replied.

Slapping the sides of his shoulders, Giovanni added, "You look thin. Are they not feeding you in this prison they have you in?" He glared at MacLaren.

"Who is this man?" MacLaren demanded.

"I am Giovanni Antonio Avenzo. The famous piece goods manufacturer from Milano, Italia. I came to be of support for my good friend, Signore Maddison. What is this travesty you accuse of him? You must let him go immediately! The American polizia are foolish in their accusations of such an honorable man."

"I assure you, Mr. Avenzo," Conrad Lawrence said, "We will have Mr. Maddison exonerated as soon as possible. I am his attorney."

"Yes, yes, I have been told of who you are, and of the other gentlemen here."

"Dodge, we have a problem," Fletcher Ross interrupted the conversation.

"More than a problem!" Andre bellowed, "A *big* problem!"

"What is it?" Dodge asked.

"The line is missing."

"What?"

"What?" MacLaren added.

"All of it. The whole fucking shebang!" Andre said. "Clothes, film, videos, your sketches, everything."

"Oh my god," Harlow said.

"Everything that we sent back to New York," Fletcher said.

"It never arrived." Andre spoke quickly, his voice agitated. "I just spoke with FedEx to run a trace and guess what?" He didn't wait for an answer. "They never picked it up."

"What?"

"They don't have any record of a pick up."

"How the fuck can that be?" Dodge was getting upset, "We sent it out overnight delivery. Guaranteed by ten a.m. Didn't we?" he glared at Fletcher Ross.

"Yes, Dodge, we did. Andre and I personally packed everything right after we finished shooting yesterday."

"And we carried it into the lobby ourselves." Andre said. "I personally filled out the paperwork. I just called the woman at the front desk and she says it wasn't the usual driver who picked it up."

"It was stolen," Giovanni said. They all looked at him. "There is no other explanation."

"He's right," MacLaren said. "If FedEx didn't pick it up then somebody else did."

"But why?" Conrad Lawrence asked.

"Espionage," Giovanni said. "An unfortunate part of the business."

MacLaren wasn't sure about that. He had a distinct feeling that it had something to do with his case. First Santiago goes missing and now the designer's line is missing? Things were adding up and he didn't like the math.

"Big Ben, huh? A fitting moniker." Sunny Sterling walked slowly next to Ben. She walked with ease, an ease he thought to be calm, even lackadaisical, as if she didn't have a care in the world.

"My football nickname," he replied.

"Dodge's best friend?"

"Yes. We grew up in the same small town."

"Mmm, small towns are nice." They walked. "The gardens are beautiful, aren't they?"

Big Ben hadn't noticed but he said yes, they were.

"Did you come down for the service?" she asked.

"No, I came to help Dodge out."

"Do you think you can?"

"If I find the killer."

"I don't envy your profession."

"May I ask you a question?"

"Surely."

"How do you know Dodge? I've never heard him mention you before."

"Professionally. One fashion designer to another. West coast, East coast, but we swim in the same small circles."

"Did you come to Sarasota for the service?"

"In a roundabout way."

Ben had to slow his usual stride to match Sunny's easy pace. She walked with a refined posture, casually breathing in the scents of the gardens. Relishing the sunshine seeping through her straw hat, and laying like a translucent shawl on her shoulders. She had an allure about her. She was a stunning woman.

"I am on a sabbatical, a pilgrimage really. This year marks my fiftieth birthday. I'm taking some time to myself, driving down to the keys, all the way to Key West."

"Looking for adventure?"

She drew in a breath of the fragrant air through her nostrils, held it for a moment and exhaled it slowly. "I've had enough adventure in my life." She smiled at him and quickened her pace ever so slightly.

He wanted to ask her more but could sense she didn't want to talk about it, so he dropped it.

"Did you know Dana?" he asked.

"Yes, she did some modeling for me. She helped launch my new jeans line a few seasons ago. She wasn't a supermodel then, but her work for me got her noticed. She became the GUESS girl and then she went exclusively to Maddison Designs. She was a smart girl. When she was with me she was always asking about designing. How I got started, what the industry was like, things like that. I think she wanted to design her own clothing line someday. It's a shame."

"Holy Shit," the cameraman said too loudly. MacLaren's head turned toward their hiding place.

"Shhh!" the reporter whispered and the two men held their breath. MacLaren turned away.

The cameraman said, "First he kills her, then has his clothing line stolen? This is mega big time shit. We gotta get over there."

"No. Let's wait. If we go over there now they'll all clam up. Just keep rolling."

Andre and Fletcher and Giovanni rambled on, trying to figure out who had stolen the line and why, and the ramifications of it all. Harlow was stunned. Dodge was silent, his business mind already far ahead of them.

"What's the status of the piece goods?" he asked Giovanni.

"I've got most of the fabric in, at least fifty percent anyway. The gray goods are in the process of being dyed. I'm on schedule, but I will need the patterns of course."

"Fletch, is there anything at the studio? Story boards, hand sketches, anything?"

"I don't think so. We had everything on the discs that we brought down here."

"No back up?" his tone was angry.

Fletcher knew Dodge was to blame for not having back ups, of anything. He was too protective of his business. Never trusted anybody, except for Harlow and maybe him. But now he needed someone to blame. Fletcher was just as startled at the news as he was. He knew it wasn't good. He also knew Dodge was under a lot of pressure. Jailed and charged with murder, and Dana gone. It all must be having a tremendous impact on him. "No, I'm sorry," he said, "but that's the way we always work. Originals, no copies, you know that."

"Sorry Fletch, I didn't mean to pass blame. It's a chance I always took. It's my fault, no one else's."

"I'll call New York and have them search their hard drives," Harlow said. "Maybe someone had something saved." She flipped her phone and walked away.

"I'll call in and get some of my people on it," MacLaren said. "It may be readily solvable."

"Fat chance," Andre said.

"Why do you say that?" the Lieutenant asked.

"They're never found. It happens all the time. More so in Europe, but it does happen in the states too."

"He's right," Dodge said. "There's a black market out there. If an unknown designer knocked off a fresh line before an established designer got his out, then two things would happen. One, the designer is shit out of luck, and two it would catapult the unknown to instant fame."

"That's piracy."

"That's the sleazy end of the business."

"But wouldn't the designer be able to prove the line was his?"

"Not in a case like this. We are always making last minute changes as we go along, that's part of why I do the photo shoot last. I need to actually see the goods on the models to make sure I'm getting the look I want. At least that's how I do it."

"Who would know that you work that way?"

"It's hard to keep secrets in the fashion business and I've been around a long time. Any number of people could know. Especially if they were dishonest. Spies operate on greed. A fresh line would bring good money."

"Why steal all the clothes, why not just take the computer discs and the film? Seems to me that'd be easier."

"Working with the actual goods would be easiest," Giovanni explained. "For example, you would disassemble the dress, lay it out piece by piece on a pattern table and make minor adjustments – thus making it a new design in its own right, different than the original. The new goods would then be sewn together and the old would be destroyed. The original designer, even if he had kept a form of proof, would now be unable to prove his design had been replicated. In regards to the other procured items, I don't believe they knew the discs and the film were in the bounty. That was a bonus."

Big Ben escorted Sunny Sterling through the visitor's center and out the side door leading to a courtyard abutting Osprey Avenue. "This way we avoid the piranhas lying in wait at the front entrance."

"Is there anything else you'd like to ask me, Chief Benson?" she smiled at him. "I knew you had a reason for offering to walk me out."

"Yes, do you know of anyone who would want to kill Dana?"

"No, I can't think of a soul."

"Any thoughts or leads that may help me?"

"I really don't have much to offer you, I'm afraid. Dodge Maddison and I are friends, but not close. I haven't spoken to him in quite a long time. It was mere happenstance that I was down here at this time. Of course, I would have flown in for the service. I liked Dana. Her zest for life reminded me of myself at that age. A tragedy. I hope you're successful in remedying this awful situation. He's a wonderful man. I'm sure he wasn't involved in her misfortune in any way."

Big Ben handed her a business card. "If anything comes to mind, please let me know." They squeezed through an opening in the shrubbery outlining the courtyard and moved onto the sidewalk.

"Where are you parked?"

"Right over there." A line of cars sat on the short block: a black Mercedes, a red Corvette, a silver Escalade and a navy blue, two-seater Lexus. She clicked a remote control and the lights on the Corvette blinked.

"Very nice," Ben said.

Another click initiated the hydraulics that raised the top and tucked it, with a light whirring sound, neatly into the trunk.

Big Ben held the door open for her. "It smells new."

"Brand new. I've only put on, oh, I don't know, as many miles as it is from Boston to here." She placed her handbag onto the passenger seat.

"Boston? Really? But I thought you came from L.A.?"

"Another story for another time," she extended her hand to him. "It was a pleasure meeting you."

"The pleasure was all mine," he shook her hand and gently closed the door when she was seated.

Sunny Sterling gave him a warm smile and started the car. She pulled out onto the street and drove away, waving her fingers into the rear view mirror. Ben watched the Corvette shrink into the illusive roadway of southern Florida. He wondered about the sense of mystery he had gotten from her. Good luck on your pilgrimage, he said.

He walked to the corner and peered at the reporters cramming the front entrance. Their numbers were growing. They'd have to get Dodge out of here now. He walked back along the sidewalk looking for the break in the bushes. A taxicab rounded the corner and came to a stop just behind him. The back door opened and a woman jumped out.

"Ben!" she hollered.

TWENTY-EIGHT

"Okay, here's what we need to do," Dodge said. "I'm not sure how much I can do from a jail cell and I don't know how much longer I'll be stuck there," he glared at MacLaren. "So, Fletcher, you need to get back to the City and start redesigning the line. You helped me do most of it, so I know the design ideas are fresh in your mind. Talk with the seamstresses and the fabricators, they'll remember the patterns they sewed and they can help you reconstruct the work. You've got to put a whole line together as quickly as possible and get it to Giovanni immediately," He turned to the Italian soft goods manufacturer. "How soon will you be back in Milan?"

"I am planning to be in New York for three days, then flying home Monday night."

"Good. Can you stop by my offices Monday before you leave and check on the progress?"

"Of course my friend."

"Fletcher, call the staff and let them know it's going to be a long weekend. By Monday we need to have some things that Giovanni can carry back with him, if not all of it, at least enough that he can get started on. That will keep us pretty much on schedule." Dodge Maddison was clearly upset. He was clenching his fists, squeezing an imaginary rubber ball. "I'll be damned if I'm going to lose this line because of some spineless bastard stealing my work!"

Andre said, "What about the catalogue?"

Dodge already knew the answer to that. "We'll have to reschedule." Andre for once was quiet. He looked forlornly at Dodge. Another shoot would be impossible. The holiday season was almost upon them. The models all had flights dispersing them to other jobs around the world, or to their homes for holiday reunions with their families. The next four weeks were down time in this industry. Andre himself had ticketed a two-week vacation. His wife wouldn't tolerate any revision of plans. They could reschedule for January or February, if the modeling agency could perform magic and get all the girls together, but by then the beach resorts of the world would be crowded with winter tourists. Shooting a summer catalogue in those months was impossible. Unless they did it inside on a set, but he knew Dodge would never go for that.

Dodge was reading Andre's mind. "I'll have to go without," he said. "I've done it before, in the beginning."

"Putting the line out without the catalogue would have a serious negative impact on sales." Harlow had rejoined them. "The catalogue represents thirty to forty percent of gross revenue." She said this as a businesswoman, yet she too knew the shoot was a lost cause. "It would be a huge loss."

"Not as much as having no line at all," the designer said. "And if we don't get it together right away, that's what we'll be looking at."

Harlow, Andre and Fletcher Ross slowly nodded their heads. They knew he was right. "So," Dodge said, "we've lost the catalogue but we're not going to lose this season. Let's move on. And move on quickly."

Big Ben came up the trail behind them. The woman with him strode light-footedly up to Dodge and embraced him. "Oh my Darling!" she said.

"Oh Christ." MacLaren said. He looked at Conrad Lawrence, "Time's up." The attorney nodded yes, it was time to go.

"Who the hell is that?" the cameraman said.

"No idea, but I can't wait to get this back to the newsroom." The reporter looked at his watch. "I can get this written and edited in time for the five o'clock lead in. Barry's going to love me!"

"Sweetheart, what are you doing here? I didn't want you to get involved with all this."

170

"I *am* involved. I'm involved with you, Darling, and everything about you," Annison hugged him harder. "I couldn't let you go through this on your own. I couldn't stand being away from you. Aren't you glad to see me?"

"Yes, of course I am," he kissed her on the lips.

"Okay, okay, it's time to wrap up old home week," MacLaren said. "This little excursion has gotten out of control. Let's move out."

Dodge Maddison did a quick round of introductions for Conrad Lawrence, Andre, and MacLaren. Fletcher had met Annison before at Maddison Designs in New York. That was also where Harlow had first met her. They said cordial hellos to each other.

As the group was turning to exit the grounds, a man dressed in a black suit, white shirt and dark tie said, "Maddison!" He walked up to him. A woman in black who wore a black hat with a sheer black veil accompanied him. Dodge recognized them as Dana's parents.

The man was holding the woman's hand. He let go of it. He looked Dodge in the eye and said, "I hope you get yours."

Dodge choked up. For a moment the two men just looked at each other. Finally Dodge said, "I ... I want to express my sincere condolences to both you and Mrs ..."

Dana's father slapped his open palm into the left side of Dodge's face. The blow made him stagger backward. MacLaren caught him and held him. There was no resistance. No one moved. No one spoke. Big Ben was ready to subdue the gentleman but could tell it wouldn't be necessary. The man took hold of his wife's hand again. "Like I said Maddison, I hope you get yours." The parents turned and walked away.

"Did you get that? Did you get all that? The reporter asked his cameraman.

"Bet your ass I did."

"Beautiful. That's a fucking exclusive. Let's go."

TWENTY-NINE

Isabella was pissed. "What do you mean it's gone?! How the fuck can it be gone?!"

"It's gone. Stolen. Caput. Eighty-sixed. Bye-bye." Andre was packing. Isabella was in his suite, upset, furiously upset, walking in circles. "So we'll take some more pictures. We'll go down to the beach and shoot it now."

"We don't have the clothing."

"I don't care, I've got clothes, and I've got a bathing suit. Come on, get your camera and let's go."

"I don't have my camera, Isabella. It was stolen! Can't you get that through your dumb-ass little head?"

"So get one! Go buy a fucking camera! Buy a throwaway in the gift shop, I don't care. Just get one and take some pictures!"

Andre was over her. He never liked her anyway. The sex had been good but he thought she was a dingbat. An arrogant little bitchy dingbat. She'd come onto him because she thought by fucking him she'd get the cover. He didn't even have to try to con her. She was easy. She'd fuck anyone and anything to get what she wanted. She thought she could instantly replace Dana. Actually, Andre thought, her looks were right up there, and her body, oh her body, Andre had tasted of that and wouldn't mind doing it again, but there were other less arrogant fish in the sea. Her body could certainly grace the cover of any magazine. It was her attitude that would always prevent her from getting to that goal. Beautiful wasn't enough anymore. You had to have a personality. Designers like Dodge Maddison wouldn't tolerate her attitude. They wanted someone who could represent their clothing line in a sophisticated way. Someone who could speak well; politely, charismatically. A supermodel was a supermodel because they went beyond looks. Dana had poise and intelligence, presentation with believability. She was likeable. Women who bought *Lady Maddison* were refined and they wanted one of their own to portray that extension of themselves. Isabella was a wild card with a choppy edge to her. Andre thought she'd do better in porn.

"It's over Isabella. The photo shoot is over. There isn't going to be any catalogue, so don't worry about a cover."

"You promised me the cover Andre!" she yanked forcibly on his elbow. "I *want* to be on the cover." Isabella dug her fingernails into his skin like an angry little girl throwing a fit. Andre pulled his arm away; the nails gouged a red trail onto his forearm.

"Listen you little bitch," Andre ignored the scratches as if they affected him no more than a feather brushing against his arm, "It's been fun but the ride is over. Now get the fuck out of my room." He snapped his suitcase shut and set it on the floor.

"You fat fuck!" Isabella raised her hand. Andre grabbed it and pushed her hard onto the bed and stood over her daring her to get up.

Her eyes were on fire. She glared at him with two hot piercing arrows. "I sucked your pathetic little cock, Andre, and let you *fuck me,* you fat skuzzy bastard!"

"Yeah, and you loved every second of it."

Isabella was leaning back on the bed, her arms spread behind her, her breasts pushed upward, rising and lowering with the quick breathing of her tempered anger. She wore a white silk blouse that highlighted her cappuccino-toned skin. No bra; nipples hard and round poking at him through the shiny material. She crossed one hand over her chest and slowly undid the three buttons on the front of her blouse, letting the silk slide open, freeing her breasts, allowing him to view her dark nipples with the brown areolas. She replaced her arm behind her, pushing her breasts towards him and shook her head, seductively tossing her long dark mane. She waited. Not long. Andre took the bait. She spread her legs and he came to her and stood at the edge of the bed.

She sat up and ran her hands over the bulge in the front of his pants. "Come on Andre," she said with a new sweetness in her voice, "let's talk about this." She began unbuckling his pants. "There's always another catalogue somewhere, right?" She pulled his penis out and began stroking the sensitive underside. His legs got weak and his knees leaned heavy into the edge of the mattress. Isabella looked up at him. Andre's eyes were half closed, his breathing heavier. "When is your next gig? Where's the location? Hmmm?" She squeezed, wanting an answer.

"In a few weeks," he lied. He'd tell her anything at this point. Anything that would get his dick into her mouth.

"Where?" she rubbed the tip of his penis between her thumb and index finger.

"Cancun," he moaned.

She gave it a flick with her tongue; Andre felt a hot shiver run through his loins. "And who's going to be on the cover, baby?" She ran her tongue around the head.

"You are, baby ... you are." His eyes were closed now and his mouth hung open.

"Hmmm, that's my boy." She took him fully into her mouth and Andre moaned loudly, swaying unsteadily on his feet. She sucked on him until she knew she had him totally in her power, and then she stopped.

"Don't stop, don't stop."

"Are you lying to me, Andre?"

"No, baby, no."

"You promise?"

"Yes, yes, I promise."

She resumed her fellatio. She knew he was lying. He was just as wicked as she was. Either of them would do whatever necessary to get to an end they desired. But he had underestimated her. Isabella didn't like to be double-crossed. She bit down hard on his penis. Andre screamed and pulled away from her, falling backwards onto the floor, grabbing his crotch. Isabella stood and kicked him between his legs.

"You fucking liar! You fucking cock-sucking liar!" she shrieked. "Fuck you Andre!" She walked off. "I'm sure your wife will be thrilled to hear what I've got to tell her."

Andre was up and after her. He caught her in the foyer and spun her around and backhanded her across the face. She slammed against the wall and he grabbed her by the throat. "You'll do nothing of the kind, you little whore."

She kneed him in the groin and pushed against his shoulders and got away, but he grabbed her by the hair and yanked her back. He went to lock his forearm around her neck but she swung her body around and slammed her elbow ferociously into his face. Quickly she went over to the writing desk and grabbed the letter opener.

"Get away from me you bastard!" She waved the sharp instrument at his face. "And don't you *ever* come near me again. Or so help me, I'll call your fucking wife *and* the fucking newspapers and cry rape."

Andre stood stock-still. He was afraid of her. He believed she was wild enough to use the knife. He let her move cautiously around him and get to the door. Still facing him she reached behind her and opened the door. She spit at him and slammed the door shut. Andre leaned his back against the wall. His face hurt, but not as much as his penis. He looked down at it. It was badly bruised. There were teeth marks on it and it was swelling up, but not in a good way.

THIRTY

Annison rode back to the police department complex in the back seat squeezed between Dodge and Big Ben, with Conrad Lawrence and Lieutenant MacLaren in front. She held Dodge's hand. "Oh God, what are we going to do?"

"We're going to be alright," Dodge said. "Mr. Lawrence and his daughter Lydia are working hard on getting me released and Bennie is going to figure out who killed Dana and then there'll be an end to this."

Ben thought, easier said than done my friend.

The ride over from Selby Gardens was short. MacLaren maneuvered down Ringling Boulevard, took a sharp left onto Washington and then a right two blocks later onto Main Street. He pulled into the rear parking lot and took the space labeled "Detectives". Attorney Lawrence looked at his watch. One p.m.

"Good," he said, "the judge should just be finishing his lunch. I'm going to go knock on his chamber door."

"Conrad," Dodge said, "do you think you could sneak Annison and I into the tower room for a few minutes?"

"Oh no," MacLaren said. "Enough is enough." He got out of the car and opened the back door. Conrad Lawrence motioned him to the front of the car. The two of them stood in an animated conversation. MacLaren threw his hands up in surrender. Conrad placed his arm around MacLaren's shoulder and the two men laughed. The lieutenant came over to the open back door and said, "Okay Maddison, you've got ten minutes." He led the designer and his fiancée into the building.

"How did you swing that?" Ben asked the attorney.

"I promised him an extra Mulligan next time on the golf course. MacLaren bargained for five, we settled at three."

When he got to his office, MacLaren jumped on his computer. He had a few things he wanted to check out, he needed to start putting the pieces of the puzzle together. He yearned for a quick conviction, but this Big Ben guy was presenting some good questions. He'd still go for Maddison, but if it wasn't Maddison, he didn't want some country cop one-upping him and getting all the credit. Wouldn't look good and certainly wouldn't help his career. He'd keep feeding Tanya Chisholm, the D.A. all that she needed to hang the designer, but he would put a contingency plan into effect just in case someone else had done the deed. As long as he got credit for the conviction, MacLaren didn't give a damn who had done it.

"Lieutenant?"

"Yeah."

"There's something on e-Bay I think you should see."

"What the fuck are you doing on e-Bay?"

"I've got it up on my screen, sir. Take a look."

MacLaren went around his desk and followed the female detective out of his office and over to her desk in the middle of the room. Several detectives were gathered around her computer. On the screen, MacLaren read, "*Dana's Death Dress.* Supermodel wearing a *Maddison Design* when she was murdered." Below the text was a picture from the neck down of someone wearing a bright red dress, complete with torn front and dangling shoulder straps. Bidding was in progress.

"What the fuck? Where is this coming from?" MacLaren asked.

"I'm working on that right now, sir," the detective at the next desk answered.

"What's it up to?"

"Just went over two thousand."

"What a scam. Someone went to Wal-Mart, bought a dress, tore it up, took a picture and put it on e-Bay."

"People will buy anything."

"Shit, I wish I had thought of that."

"Lieutenant, it's coming from Longboat Key."

Everyone got quiet. They all looked at MacLaren.

"Longboat?"

"The Vizcaya to be exact."

That didn't make sense. Scamming wasn't necessary on Longboat Key. The Vizcaya was an exclusive high-rise condominium on the Gulf side that started at three million. Started. Ground floor. Who knew what the top floors were worth? Residents of Vizcaya on Longboat wouldn't blink an eye spending two grand for toilet paper.

"What should we do Lieutenant?"

"Nothing. Let it run. Get me a name and the unit number. I'll handle it."

In the tower, with the sunny panorama of Sarasota surrounding them, Annison and Dodge stood in an embrace. Her head was nuzzled into his shoulder. He was stroking her hair.

"Ben told me something about you that I would have appreciated hearing from you first," he said.

She looked up at him. "What do you mean?"

"I thought you went home to Bryce Corner Saturday morning."

Annison sat down in one of the high-back chairs. "I meant to tell you, but with everything going on, the timing didn't seem right."

"What does that mean?"

"It was nothing, Dodge. A spur of the moment thing, that's all. You do trust me don't you?"

"Yes, I trust you, but it's easier to trust someone when they don't hide things."

"I wasn't hiding anything. I'm not. I don't ever intend to."

He wanted to believe her but he couldn't help but wonder. He waited.

"I'm sorry. I should have told you right away, but I knew you were flying to Sarasota and would be busy with the photo shoot and then I got down there and got caught up in everything and then the flight out was so early Monday morning and then I got home just in time to let the contractors in and then Ben came over for coffee and ..."

"Got down where?"

"To Key Largo."

Dodge sat down and spread his arms out, palms up.

"When I got to the terminal Saturday, the flight was delayed three hours - something about the connecting flight in Atlanta, I don't know - so I thought rather than sit at the airport all afternoon, I'd rent a car and drive down to see my friend Nina in Key Largo, spend a day with her and then fly back Sunday night or Monday morning."

"Nina was in Key Largo?" Dodge had met Annison's friend in New York before. Nina Sanderson was a successful Real Estate Broker in the City. The three of them had gone out to dinner one night not long ago.

"Yes, she has a condo there and I remembered she'd mentioned going down to the Keys the weekend we were going to be in Miami. So, when the flight got delayed, I called her and made plans to drive down for a visit. That's all it was Dodge, a spur of the moment decision that I didn't think I had to run by you. I was going to tell you about it later, next time we talked. But that was when you told me about Dana and it just slipped my mind. It didn't seem important at the time."

"Nina was there? She can vouch for you?"

"Vouch for me? You mean you don't believe me?" There was a hint of anger in her voice.

"Yes, of course I believe you. I only mean, can she verify your whereabouts?"

"Verify my whereabouts?"

"Would she be able to be your alibi?"

"My alibi?" Annison didn't know where he was going. Then it dawned on her. "Why would I need an alibi, Dodge?"

"Annison, it's just that ..."

"You think ... what? What do you think?"

"I don't think anything, but we're in a murder investigation and Ben and the attorneys need to tie up all the loose ends. It's procedure. Eliminating suspects gets us closer to focusing on the real killer." Dodge rubbed his temples. Annison could sense the emotional state he was in and she felt for him, but she didn't coddle well to being labeled a suspect.

"Do they think I am involved with Dana's death?"

"No, of course not. And once we get a statement from Nina verifying you being with her at the time, then they'll be able to move on."

"What's the time frame?"

"Sunday night between midnight and six am Monday morning."

Annison fell quiet.

"What?" Dodge asked.

"Nina left Sunday night on an eight pm flight."

An uncomfortable silence settled between them. "And no," she said "in answer to your next question, there is no one else to be my alibi. I stayed in her condo and went to bed. I got a few hours sleep before I had to drive back to Miami for a five am flight. I had no contact with anyone during that time frame."

Annison got out of her chair and went to the window. Moored in the waters of the bay front, an array of sailing boats swayed gently in the rhythmic swells of the sea, their thin reedy masts like white candlesticks reaching into the pale blue sky.

"I'm curious," she said, "how did you know about my flight change? The only person I told was Nina."

"Ben found out."

"I thought he was your friend."

"He *is* my friend, that's why he's being so thorough. MacLaren wants to fry me and Bennie's got to dissuade him, but he can only do that in a cop way. You've got to admit, your actions were suspicious."

"And now? What do you think now?"

Dodge went to her and took her in his arms. "And now I think I need to remind you that I love you." They held each other tight. "It's going to be alright. I'll tell them what you did and they'll believe it and the investigation will move on."

"Oh Dodge, I hope so. I can't bear to have you in here. What can I do?"

"You can try to relax. Go to the Ritz-Carlton, check into my room and wait for me. They're going to get me out soon. Go to the beach, the salon, shopping, anything but sitting around worrying."

"You know I'm going to worry until this is cleared up and we're back home in our new Bed & Breakfast."

They talked about that; the renovations, the weather in New England, their plans for the future, and the conversation lightened. They sat awhile, holding hands, filling the time with idle conversation, anything to take their minds off the current predicament.

THIRTY-ONE

Big Ben shuffled from one foot to the other. He didn't like standing in one spot for any length of time. He wondered how those British guards did it. The ones in the red uniforms with the fuzzy black beehive hats that stood perfectly still outside Buckingham Palace. You could taunt them and they wouldn't move. Not even crack a smile. His cell phone rang. He saw that it was Carlene and flipped it open. "Hello Sugarplum."

"Hi." Her voice was soft and pleasant. Just the way she said that one word made him smile. "How are you?"

"Fine. Bored. I'm playing palace guard. I'm not sure I can talk on a phone."

"What?"

"Just kidding," he began walking in small circles in the narrow corridor. "I'm playing sentinel at the police station. Dodge and Annison are visiting upstairs." He told her of the private room in the belfry.

"Like a castle? Wow. A bit different than Bryce Corner's P.D. huh?"

"Yeah, I'm kinda diggin' it. Sunshine, blue skies, green water, cool buildings, maybe we should transfer down here."

"Are you saying you miss this cold weather, snow, ice, black skies?"

"I'm not missing that, but I am missing you."

"Aww, that's nice, 'cuz I miss you too. How's the investigating going?"

Ben brought Carlene up to speed on things, culminating with the sucker punch at the memorial service.

"There must be some basis for an action like that. Do you think Dana's father knows something?"

Ben hadn't thought of it that way. He figured the man was distraught and angry at losing his daughter. That he needed someone to lash out at and it had been Dodge.

"Y'know, I hadn't thought of it that way. That's a good point." Ben wondered if he could talk to the family before they left.

"So, Annison is there now too? What does she have to say about her lost weekend?"

"I'm sure that's what they're talking about. I hope she's got a solid alibi. If not …?"

Footsteps were clicking around the corner on the tiled hallway. Lydia Lawrence approached Ben. She saw him on his phone and stopped a few feet away to give him privacy. She waited for him.

"Darlin', I gotta go, but can you do me a favor? Google Annison Barrett and see what you come up with."

"Good idea."

"Background, family history, credit check, everything. I'm particularly interested in her finances. I'd like to know what ground she's really standing on."

"Okay. I'll text you later. Be careful."

Ben closed his phone and waved to Lydia.

"You look like a high school hall monitor," she said.

"I feel just as stupid. How's your day going?"

"Good actually. I had a decent morning in court, won another case, minor, but any win is a good one, especially when your client has been wronged."

"Congratulations."

"Thanks. Oh, and Dad's pulling strings in the judge's chambers as we speak. Don't quote me, but we may be able to get Dodge released on bail."

"Seems like your father is a very important man around here."

"There's talk of Governor. People are cozying up to him. He's got a lot of support."

"Will he run?"

"I'm not sure. He's thinking about it. I hope he does. I think he'd be a good Governor, an honest one. He's always worked hard. He believes in people, likes helping them, and he's very smart. Doesn't take any money or any shit from the power mongers. He has an enviable record and a clean reputation."

"What does your mother think about it?"

"Mom's gone. Ten years ago. Cancer. But I know she'd encourage him."

"Be good for you too. Governor's daughter, law partner."

"I'd miss him though. He'd be in Tallahassee a lot."

MacLaren barged through the double doors at the end of the hallway. There was a uniform with him.

"Keep the bail thing on the QT," Lydia said. "The lieutenant doesn't have any idea yet and it would be better to keep him away from the D.A. until Dad can wrap it up. Tanya Chisholm's not going to like being over-ridden."

"Okay."

"Well, time's up," MacLaren said. He motioned to the officer who opened the large door with the wrought iron hinges and climbed the stairs. "I'm glad you're both here. I've got an idea."

"This should be good," Lydia said.

"Let's go fishing."

Lydia and Ben stared at him.

"The patrol boat's at the 10th Street pier gassed up and ready to go. How about you meet me there in a half hour. Are you hungry? We can get sandwiches and beer dockside, and some ice for the cooler." He was grinning. "I'm serious. Fishing helps me think. Besides, there's someone I need to talk to up on the Manatee River and there's good fishin' up there."

They still didn't respond to him.

"You do fish don't you?" This he addressed to Big Ben.

"No, actually, I don't. And I don't have time to go on a picnic, MacLaren, I've got a killer to find."

"Oh you'll want to come along on this picnic, big guy. I've got a lead on the stolen merchandise. Besides," he slapped Ben on the shoulder, "everybody in Florida fishes. You'll love it! Very soothing, kinda meditational." MacLaren disappeared through the double doors.

"You don't fish?" Lydia asked Ben.

"Never got into it."

"I'll give you a quick lesson."

"You fish?" Ben asked her.

"You betcha, Bubba. Come on, it'll be fun. My afternoon's free and you could use the break. Be good for you to get out on the water."

THIRTY-TWO

At Myakka State Park there's an observation tower you can climb that gets you high above the tree canopy. There's a grand, open-air platform with a roof over it providing protection from the sun. From here you can view the entire preserve and if you drop some coins into the pay binoculars, you feel like you're right out there in the saw grass with the gators, deer, bobcats, gopher tortoises and the other Florida wildlife.

Jeremy Nolen was out of school and on vacation with his mom and dad and little sister. Mom and sis were down at the gift shop. He and dad had climbed the tower together. Next to them a group of tourists were gathered around a park ranger who was giving a guided tour. Jeremy was standing on a pedestal box looking through the binoculars. Dad was beside him. Jeremy said, "Hey Dad, look at all those birds." Mr. Nolen looked off at the horizon and saw some birds flying in circles.

"What kind of birds are they, Dad?"

"Well, they could be eagles or osprey or even vultures, son."

"Wow. Vultures? Really? There's vultures here?"

"Sure. This is a wildlife preserve so any creature can live freely here, just like the brochure said, remember?"

"Yeah, but why would vultures want to live here?"

"Well, because it's a beautiful, safe place and there's a good food supply."

"What do they eat?"

"Mostly small animals; mice, lizards, things like that."

"Do they eat people?"

"No, people are too big."

"They don't eat big stuff?"

"Not usually. Sometimes, I guess, if a larger animal was lying dead they'd swoop down for lunch."

"Like if Boomerang was dead they'd eat her?"

"Well ..." Boomerang was their Golden Retriever back home in Ohio with the neighbors. Mr. Nolen didn't know how to answer that one.

"How come they fly in circles?"

"They do that when they've found something to eat."

"Why are there so many of them?"

Mr. Nolen was curious. "Let me see, son." He stooped down and looked through the big binoculars. The vultures became bigger in the lens, large black shapes soaring in an aerial ballet above the distant treetops, their wings spread taught. They looked like jet liners locked in a circling pattern over an airfield. "Boy, there sure are a lot of them," Jeremy's dad said.

The park ranger overheard his comment. The ranger excused himself from his tour group, took a pair of binoculars from a case on his belt and peered into the skyline.

THIRTY-THREE

The afternoon sun was high and hot. It dove into the blueways of Sarasota Bay, illuminating the sandy shallows, floating like white ribbons on the sides of the deep blue waters of the channel. MacLaren maneuvered the forty-foot DONZI Z-Tech calmly through the No Wake Zone past Mote Marine, The Old Salty Dog, into New Pass, under the drawbridge and out into the emerald green Gulf of Mexico. Big Ben was standing next to him at the center console holding onto his cap, squinting through his sunglasses past the glare on the water checking out the spots on the shoreline that MacLaren was pointing to. Lydia Lawrence was in the stern applying sunscreen to her long legs. She'd changed into a pair of white shorts and a bikini top, underneath a white cotton blouse, worn open and blowing in the wind. Ben wondered if the bikini bottom was hiding beneath the white shorts.

MacLaren pushed the throttle full forward, lurching the DONZI onto an even plane. He turned his cap around and leaned an elbow on the windshield, poking his nose into the northwest along the powdery coastline of Longboat Key, his right hand holding steadily onto the wheel. "Flat out this baby will break seventy-five miles per hour. Nine hundred horsepower coming from those triple Merc's back there. Fastest thing on the water. Except of course for the drug boats. They've got a bigger budget," MacLaren laughed. "They usually run the 450 HSV, twenty-five hundred fucking horsepower. Can you believe that? But if we get close enough, these babies slow 'em down," he pointed to the weapon mounts on either side of the hand built Government Series boat. "When there's something in them of course," the lieutenant grinned. "These DONZI hulls are fantastic, smooth riding even at top speed. Run strong and fast in big water or shallow." MacLaren was obviously proud of the police boat, but Big Ben felt a little queasy. He didn't go out on a boat much. He took a seat next to Lydia in the stern and let the refreshing salty wind stream across his face.

"Feels nice," he shouted.

"What?" she leaned into him, smoothing sunscreen over her shoulders. The cotton top had been removed.

"Feels nice," he said.

"Nicer than Boston?"

"Absolutely."

Lydia handed him the lotion and turned her back to him. Ben guessed he was supposed to apply some to her back, so he did.

"That's Beer Can Island over there," she pointed over starboard, "and Longboat Pass, and then Coquina Beach where those Australian pines are."

Ben could feel the muscles of her back relaxing, loose beneath the palms of his strong hands. She let out a sigh. Since getting on the boat she seemed like a different lady. Happier, less businesslike, less stressed. Maybe being out on the water in the sunshine was refreshing. He felt more at ease too, finally letting himself enjoy Florida. What a different world this is, he thought.

"Thank you," she said, turning to face him. Ben held out the sunscreen. She waved it off, "You should put some on."

"No, I'm fine."

"Really, put some on. Your face at least."

Ben had the parrot shirt on above his cargo shorts, and of course his yellow 'Relax' cap. He'd changed when he'd gone back to the Ritz to drop off Annison. Then he had picked Lydia up at her downtown condo and driven the mile north on Tamiami Trail in the Hummer to meet MacLaren at the boat ramp.

Lydia got up and went and stood next to MacLaren at the helm. They spoke back and forth but Ben couldn't hear them above the wind. He applied lotion to his face as instructed, and the front of his thick neck and some along his arms too. He didn't want to return home looking like a lobster. He snapped the sunscreen bottle shut, put his sunglasses back on and leaned back into the bench seat, his arms spread across the entire back. Ahh, he said, this is the life.

He looked at Lydia from behind and wondered why such an attractive, successful woman wasn't attached. She'd told him that her career took up too much of her time. She dated, but liked living alone. And now with her father entertaining a run for Governor, the burden of the law practice could eventually fall more heavily upon her shoulders. But Ben wondered. And he wondered what might transpire if he wasn't married to Carlene. He thought of his wife and he smiled. He had never been unfaithful to her. He was happy in his marriage. He wished she were here with him now, going for a boat ride in the Florida sunshine. She and Lydia would probably hit it off. Maybe Dodge should get involved with someone like Lydia. Professional, down to earth, grounded. Why couldn't he find someone solid? Why did he always have to have more than one woman in his life? He thought of Harlow, wiling away her life waiting for Dodge, waiting for something that would never happen. And Dana, poor Dana. An innocent life lost so early. And then there was Annison. Yup, ole Buddie, Ben thought, you've got it all, but you ain't got nothin' if you ain't got love. Maybe Lydia was too good for Dodge, he'd probably screw her up too, Ben decided. Or kill her.

Where did that thought come from? Naw, that wasn't in his blood. But get her killed? That was another thing. Which brought Ben back to Dana. *What* is to *whose* benefit to have Dana dead? Did it have anything at all to do with the stolen clothing line? And where the fuck was Santiago? Was he behind it all? What would be his gain? MacLaren had an APB out on him in Florida and in New York and everywhere in between. But what if he had skipped back to his home country? Santiago knew something. He was running scared. Santiago was the key.

Lydia came back and sat down. Ben moved to make room for her. "See that white sandy point way up there? That's Anna Maria Island, at the northern tip of Longboat Key. Funky, touristy, beachy, lots of little shops and cool bars, a fun little island. There's a three-story restriction height on buildings so it'll always remain a quaint little village. We should go there to celebrate when this is all over. I'll buy you a beer," she patted his leg.

MacLaren took the boat off plane and turned eastward toward shore.

"What's he doing?"

"Says he's got something to check out at the Vizcaya. That's it right there," Lydia pointed to a grand structure planted on the shoreline. It was ten stories high: Italian Renaissance, coral-colored stucco, barrel-tile roof, elaborate balconies.

"Looks expensive."

"Very."

MacLaren cut the engine and allowed the boat to drift into one of the guest berths. The dockmaster grabbed the line and secured it to a cleat attached to the side of one of the pilings. "May I help you?" he asked. MacLaren jumped onto the dock and showed him his badge.

"I need to speak to Mrs. Rosemary King-Harper, but I don't want her to be alerted. Can you take me to her?"

"I'll call security to bring you up, Lieutenant. Follow me."

MacLaren explained the e-Bay scenario to Big Ben and Lydia on the way into the Vizcaya. "I don't expect much here, but it's curious enough to check out. Should only take a minute then we can get back on the water. Manatee Landing is only fifteen minutes from here. We'll get some bait there and something to eat to take on the boat."

They got into the elevator with the security man. The paneled wood was polished mahogany. The doors were mirrored. The floor richly carpeted. When they got to the appropriate floor, security led them across the hall and rang the doorbell. An elderly woman in a purple dress and a bright red hat opened the door.

"Oh, hello Bernard, how are you today?"

"Fine, thank you, Mrs. Harper. These folks were wondering if they could speak with you for a minute."

MacLaren had his badge out. "Mrs. Harper, I'm Lieutenant MacLaren from the Sarasota Police Department, and this is Attorney Lydia Lawrence and Chief Ben Benson, visiting us from up north. I wonder if we may come in?"

"Oh my," she said, patting her heart with her hand, "What has happened?"

"Nothing Ma'am. I just wanted to ask you a question or two, if you'd be so kind."

"Well, will it take long? I'm just leaving to meet the girls for tea."

"No Ma'am, only a minute."

"Well, come in then." She brought them into the living room. MacLaren scanned the room. Ben's cop eyes were doing the same. Twenty-foot ceiling, lots of glass, grand view of the Gulf, European furniture, tiled floor, scatter rugs, Persian. Dining room to the left, galley kitchen on the right, hallway straight ahead. Lydia was marveling at the paintings on the walls. Originals.

"Please take a seat," she extended her hand to the leather couch and matching chairs sitting on an oriental rug.

"No thank you," MacLaren said. "Mrs. Harper, do you own a computer?"

"Yes, of course I do."

"Were you on it just a little while ago?"

"Heavens no. When my granddaughters are here, I can never get near it."

The lieutenant looked at Big Ben.

"Are your granddaughters here now?"

"Why yes. Franny and Fiona are in the den."

"Do you know if they have been on the computer today?"

"Lieutenant," she laughed. "When they're here, they're either on the internet, on the beach or on their cell-phones. *I* hardly get the time of day from them."

"May I speak with them?"

"Have they done something wrong?"

"No, Ma'am," he appeased her. "It'll only take a minute."

She thought for a moment, as if weighing something in her mind and then said, "Well, they're right down there at the end of the hall. The room to the left," she picked up her purse, "I really must be going. It's our monthly Red Hat Society tea and I don't want to be late. So, if you don't need me ..."

"No, thank you Mrs. Harper. Everything will be fine."

"Well then, make yourselves at home. Very nice meeting you," she said with a big smile and shook everyone's hand and walked out to the elevator, accompanied by the security guard, singing happily to herself.

Franny and Fiona were huddled together in front of the flat screen computer, their backs to the door, oblivious to the approaching trio.

"Oh my God, Franny, go for it!"

"No, it's still going higher." The e-Bay bidding was at four thousand, five hundred dollars.

"I swear to God, Franny, if it gets to five thousand you better accept it, or I'll kill you."

The room was furnished by the hand of an interior designer who had carefully picked the fabrics of the couches and chairs and curtains to beautifully match the rich earthy colors of the walls, accented by wide dark shelves supporting knick-knacks and family pictures. She would have been horrified to see the room in its present messy condition with clothing (both clean and dirty) strewn about the room, covering almost every square inch of the couch, chairs, coffee table, and carpet. The writing desk situated between the two windows overlooking the Gulf had been transformed into a vanity, clustered with cosmetics, combs, brushes, curling irons and candy wrappers. Crinkled bags with logos representing various boutiques on the islands were scattered about like a minefield. Big Ben inadvertently stepped on one of them and the crunching sound startled the girls.

"Hi," he said, reaching down and grabbing the handle to remove the bag from beneath his big feet. He held it in his hand looking for a place to put it, but ended up putting it gingerly back onto the floor. "Didn't mean to scare you."

"You must be Franny and Fiona," MacLaren said and then showed them his badge. "I'd like to ask you what you're doing at the moment."

The sisters looked awkwardly at each other. Neither one knowing what to say or do. Franny made a move to shut down the computer but MacLaren was at her side and stopped her. He bent down to get a better look at the screen. "Playing on e-Bay are we?"

Ben moved to the side of the other sister. He and MacLaren stood like bookends next to them. Lydia Lawrence was still in the doorway. There was a silk dress on a hanger hung on the door. She felt the fabric, noticing the tears, noticed the *Lady Maddison* logo sewn onto the back of the neckline. Lydia approached the computer, standing next to Big Ben. She saw the same dress on the computer screen next to a picture of Dana. Underneath that was a box with the latest bidding numbers in it. It was up to $4750.00.

"Where did you get the picture of Dana?" MacLaren asked.

"Franny scanned it from a magazine," Fiona answered. Her eyes were watering up. "We didn't mean any harm. We were just having fun." In her mind they were going off to jail. She knew it was a stupid idea. It was Franny's idea to begin with. But she wouldn't tell them that. She'd go down with her sister. "Oh my God, we are soo busted," she said almost inaudibly.

The lieutenant pulled the coffee table closer to the girls, pushed the clutter to one side and then sat on the edge of it next to Franny. "Why don't you tell me how you got the dress ... from the beginning."

Franny spilled the beans. Quickly, as if relieved to get the whole drunken escapade off her chest, she outlined the previous afternoon and evening. Everything. The bar, Roger and Mikey, the van, the bags of clothes, the bonfire at South Lido Park, the scuffle, and their escape via a kind elderly couple who had seen them on the road and given them a ride right to their grandmother's doorstep.

Ben had remained standing. He was next to Fiona. She was crying. He could tell there was an age difference between the girls, but only a year or two. The sisters looked like twins. Franny had her hair pulled back in a ponytail. Fiona's was worn down, covering her face. When she wiped a tear away, Ben could see the bruise on her eye. Lydia saw it too. She carefully pulled Fiona's hair to the side to get a better look at the bruise.

"Where'd you get the shiner?" Ben asked Fiona. She had applied extra makeup to her swollen black eye, but the purple and yellow bruise still shone through. The sisters looked at each other but didn't say a word.

"When I find him," Ben said, "will you press charges?"

Fiona looked at the floor. "No," she said quietly. "It was my own fault for getting us into this. I'll be okay. I've already caused enough embarrassment for my grandmother. I don't want our parents to find out."

Lydia subconsciously touched the scar on her jaw line. "If someone hits you like that," Lydia said, "they should be punished."

"He got his."

"What do you mean?"

"I scratched him pretty good across his face," Fiona made a gesture with her hand, like a cat claw.

"Still," Lydia wouldn't let it go, "if he hit you, he's hit others, and will continue to do so."

Fiona nodded her head but remained quiet.

"What's going to happen to us?" Franny said.

"Not sure yet," MacLaren said. "I'm going to send a police artist over. He'll work up pictures of those two men. Be as accurate and helpful as possible." Both girls nodded meekly. "I'm going to take the dress."

"Okay," they said together. "We're really sorry."

"You gonna press charges on these ladies?" Big Ben asked the lieutenant.

"Depends." Ben held his eyes fast on the lieutenant. "Probably not."

Ben took out his cell phone and held it to take a picture of the girls. He positioned it to get a good shot of Fiona's black eye. "Smile," he said. Neither one of them did.

"Five thousand," Ben pointed to the computer screen.

"What should we do?" Franny asked.

Lydia looked at MacLaren. He looked at the monitor then looked back at her and nodded.

Lydia spoke, "Accept the bid, get the money and donate it to a worthy cause."

"Like what?"

Lydia looked directly at Fiona, "Foundation for Abused and Battered Women." Fiona started to cry again.

THIRTY-FOUR

"They're scared," Lydia said. "I hope they know how lucky they were. Those men could have really hurt them."

"Maybe they learned a lesson," Ben said. "I'm glad my kids aren't filthy rich. I think it's important to learn the value of money. Rich kids never get a sense of reality. They think life's just a game. It's good to struggle and to know the struggle of others. Builds character."

"You sound like a good father."

"I try. Not easy at times."

"Give me an example of your character building." They were walking along the dock to the boat. MacLaren was lagging behind, on his cell-phone to headquarters.

"You sound like an attorney."

"Amuse me." She tripped on a raised board and grabbed onto Ben's arm for support.

"My son, Brent, wanted to get a guitar, start a band, be a rock star. I made a deal with him. I said, you buy the guitar and I'll pay for the first ten lessons."

"What happened?" her arm was still in his.

"He mowed lawns, spread mulch, and painted the neighbor's garage, stuff like that."

"And?"

"Went out and bought himself a brand new Fender guitar."

"You must have been proud."

"Still am."

"How's he doing?"

"Took lessons for a year, made some connections, started a band and now drives me and the neighbors nuts practicing in the garage," he smiled.

"What's their name?"

"Two Buck Pickles."

"Cute," she said. "I'll watch for them on the charts." They reached the boat and Big Ben helped Lydia step in.

"Those girls made five thousand dollars off of a night of foolish, dangerous revelry," Ben said. "You'd have to mow a lot of lawns to make that kind of money."

"Maybe they'll get a taste for philanthropy out of all this and learn how to put their wealth to work for the good of others."

"Optimist."

"My dad was a good role model for me too," she smiled at him. "Taught me to care for others, to use my intelligence to help better the world, one client at a time."

Ben liked her attitude.

"Okay," MacLaren untied the bowline and threw it into the boat, "Let's get a move on." A minute later they were back on plane heading along the Sun Coast, north toward Anna Maria. When you get around the point, the waterway becomes part of Tampa Bay. There was a light chop.

The DONZI slowed and turned inland, heading due east into the mouth of the Manatee River between Palma Sola and Sneads Island. Even though the boat was built for speed, MacLaren kept the throttle back and the ride smooth as they passed beneath the Bradenton bridges and cruised calmly along the mangrove shoreline. He was getting the fishing gear out.

Lydia sat next to Big Ben on the bench seat at stern. There was room, but she was close to him, her leg touching his. He thought the closeness may be due to the slight rocking of the boat traversing the river way, but he sensed better. She had had him apply the sunscreen, had held onto his arm longer than necessary when she'd tripped on the dock, and to be honest, he had wondered if their first meeting at the café may have even been orchestrated by her. Ben was an intuitive man by nature and, as a cop by profession; he had a sixth sense for things existing on the outskirts of normal. He was also a blatantly honest man never shy of voicing his opinion.

"May I be frank with you?" he asked.

"Sure."

"I sense a degree of romanticism here."

Lydia caught her breath. She was a litigator, well skilled in the art of reading body language from her clients and those seated in a witness box. She held a subconscious attraction for this man. It had just been pushed up a notch to the conscious level. She was annoyed at herself for not being smart enough to read her own body language, and to disguise it better.

"I'm sorry," she said, adjusting her posture in the seat, "I didn't mean to crowd you."

"That's alright."

"No, no it's not. I apologize. I didn't mean to be presumptuous. I'm not like that." Lydia recognized her behavior and chastised herself for it. "I guess a little bit of the schoolgirl got a hold of me."

Ben looked at her, "You're blushing."

"I feel foolish. I hope you don't think I was intentionally coming on to you."

"I'm flattered."

"It's just ... well, it's just that you're an easy man to be around. I feel comfortable with you."

"Don't be embarrassed. I just had a feeling and I thought it best to address it."

"Thanks, I'm glad you did. I guess my emotions were acting on their own. I don't mean that as an excuse, I just didn't realize it until now."

"You're a beautiful woman, Lydia, and although I haven't seen you in the courtroom, I can tell you're a brilliant attorney. If I wasn't married ..." he hesitated, "I'd be more than tempted to get to know you better, but ... y'know?" he raised his eyebrows and gave her a quaint smile.

"You're an interesting man, Ben Benson. Your wife is very lucky."

"I think I'm the lucky one."

"Wow," Lydia laughed. "Do you have a brother?"

"Wish I did. And *if* I did I'd sure like to introduce him to you. Be nice to have a lawyer in the family."

"A cop and a lawyer, then all we'd need is a crook."

"I'm sure we could find one or two of those in there." They laughed together.

The boat moved on. They chatted leisurely. Lydia's embarrassment was waning. Ben made her feel at ease. She knew it was part of his nature, part of why she was attracted to him, but she was glad that he'd called her on the carpet. Best to chill her desires early on. She hadn't consciously wanted to start anything. Maybe it'd been too long since she'd gone out with anyone. Maybe she needed a date. But the men she worked around, or the ones that her friends tried to fix her up with, were not interesting. She found most men to be superficial and into themselves. They'd say whatever necessary to get to the bedroom. Sex was one thing, but having a brain was important too. She was intelligent and needed someone she could relate to. She needed discourse, not just intercourse. And most men knew all about intercourse, but didn't have a clue as to what discourse meant, and how important that is for a woman.

"Figures," she said out loud, "I find a guy who's interesting and he's already taken," she laughed. "Why is that? No, don't answer that."

"Not many of us out there, I guess," Ben teased her. "But don't give up, I'm sure you'll find a great guy."

"How did your wife find you?"

"She looked at me. That's all it took. I was infatuated from day one."

"Love at first sight, huh?"

"Well for me it was. Took her awhile to come around. We were in high school. Carlene had transferred from out of state. She was beautiful, still is. All the guys wanted to date her. I didn't think I had a chance. I stayed in the background fantasizing. Then one day I got brave enough to ask her out and that was it. We've been together ever since."

"I envy you."

A Great White Egret flew over the bow, the wide white wingspan soaring low over the water and back-flapping into the mangroves. Lydia saw it perch on one of the higher branches next to another Egret. "May I be frank with *you*, Chief Benson," she gave him an impish smile.

Ben laughed, "I guess that'd only be fair. Fire away."

"Have you been monogamous?"

"You are *such* a lawyer, Ms. Lawrence."

"Well?"

"Yes. I have."

"Never got the urge to wander?"

"Oh, I get the urge, but then I think about 'Lene and how lucky I am and I get over it. Don't want to blow it, y'know?"

"I think that's what every woman wants, one man, one true relationship. It's so hard to find. They say birds mate for life. I think humans want to but don't know how."

He wondered if the assault on her during her college days had permanently scared her, made her afraid to follow her feelings with men, afraid to let her heart go. "Don't give up."

"Oh, I won't. I'd still like to find the right man, settle in, and have children. My dad would make a great grandfather." She watched the birds on the shoreline. "Someday."

"Funny, Dodge and I were having a similar conversation not too long ago. We've been like brothers. I'm the steady, old-fashioned type with traditional goals and he's the lofty, creative, take-a-chance kind of guy. He's always had the wild dreamy ideas. That's how he got to where he is, I guess. And he's always had the girls, but recently said he wanted to settle down, do the Bed & Breakfast thing with Annison, even mentioned having a kid or two. Said he envied what Carlene and I have."

"Did he carry that into his relationships?"

"What?"

"The take-a-chance attitude."

"I imagine so. Can't remember him ever having a steady girlfriend."

"Has he always been involved with more than one woman at the same time?"

"You mean like with Dana and Annison?"

"Dana, Annison *and* Harlow."

Ben thought about that. Lydia continued, "So we've got this successful guy, good looking, wealthy, single, international playboy reputation, always with some attractive fashion model on his elbow, with women waiting in the wings, who, all of a sudden, gets swept off his feet by a woman that he's barely met and is going to change his whole life-style to be with - a businesswoman, mind you, who is leaving her business behind - and, although she has two grown children of her own, is ready and willing to marry him and start another family? Have I got most of that right?"

"You forgot the dead girlfriend part."

"All because, what?" she wasn't finished with her train of thought, "he's having a mid-life crisis and wakes up one morning and wants to be Ward Cleaver? You know him Ben. Is he flaky? Emotionally unstable enough to kill Dana, rid himself of an unwanted child? Orchestrate the theft of his own clothing line to get out of the fashion business altogether? Could he be that devious? That disturbed?"

"You're playing devil's advocate."

"I may be playing devil's attorney."

"Are you saying he did it?"

"I'm saying for me, I've got to believe in my client. I don't prescribe to that school of defending someone by the letter of the law, with no concern for guilt or innocence. I need to believe he is innocent or I'm off the case. Let some other less honorable attorney represent him."

"Lydia, if you're having a problem with …"

"No, it's not that. I'm running in prosecution mode. You have the luxury of looking for the killer. I don't. I've got to try this case with the information that I've got, and I don't have much going our way. I'll tell you something that is privileged - I was going to have him evaluated ..."

"What? An insanity plea?"

"No. It was only to get an edge on the prosecution, and because I wanted to know. But my dad overrode me. He doesn't think the evidence is conclusive and doesn't want to mar Dodge's reputation with a psychological profile."

"And you don't agree?"

"I'd feel better if I knew more about him."

"He didn't do it Lydia," he looked hard at her, "and I think MacLaren's having second thoughts about it or else we wouldn't be chasing these leads today."

"Don't kid yourself, MacLaren's out for himself. He's only doing his job. If it's one thing I like about him, it's that he's thorough. He'll chase every lead he gets, every gut feeling he has, right or wrong. He wants to be commissioner and he knows he won't get there by being miscalculating. He won't let anything get past him."

"I'm putting in," MacLaren yelled to them and pointed the boat portside toward the wharf at Manatee Landing. He came in parallel to the dock down near the faded sign that said, "BAIT". They jumped out, MacLaren tying off the bow while Lydia got the stern.

THIRTY-FIVE

Manatee Landing was one of the original landing sites of the Scots who came to Sarasota in the mid eighteen hundreds. It is just inland of Tampa Bay on the Upper Manatee River. With the fishing being excellent it hadn't taken long before a fish camp sprung up with a bait shack built on the shoreline that, in addition to live bait, offered hot food and cold beer to a growing number of anglers. It was dubbed Rusty's Anchor. Then, in the 1960's the campground was modernized with cottages and a one-level motel in the shade beneath the large River Oaks behind the fish shack. There was never an actual Rusty, nor was there a sign (except for the BAIT sign), but there was a huge rusty anchor leaning against the riverside of the shack, since converted into a waterfront pub. People either knew about it or they didn't. The locals knew and would rather keep it to themselves. The ambience was laid-back, the people were friendly and the food was excellent. The latest owner was a native Floridian who had fished all the fresh and salt waters in and around the peninsula. She had even logged a few years captaining a shrimp boat.

Debbie Donahue was, as she fondly described herself, a tough old broad. She smoked too much, drank too much and ate too much. She didn't care about waistlines, wrinkle lines or clothing lines. The only lines she was partial to were fishing lines. And she loved her little enterprise. She worked six straight days a week, always saving Sundays for fishing. She looked a little rough around the edges; leathered skin, calloused hands, broken fingernails, straight stringy hair always in a ponytail and never any make-up. Rusty's had a bit of a reputation and was known to get rowdy from time to time, but Debbie had never hired a bouncer. If anyone got out of line, she would personally escort them off her property, or throw them into the river to sober up, which she'd done more than once.

Not much for outward appearances, Debbie had unfortunately allowed the place to fall into disarray. The cottages were falling down and presently uninhabitable and boarded up. The grounds were unkempt and overgrown, and the motel desperately needed upgrading. The property hadn't seen new paint since before Debbie had purchased it and the whole place looked run down and seedy. Hence, the motel attracted a savory, usually short-term transient clientele. Luckily though, Debbie was a fanatic about her food preparation, so the kitchen was clean and the bar and outside table area was always tidy. People came to Rusty's Anchor for Debbie's famous fish sandwich, to listen to the bands, and to just hang out in the breeze and drink.

Today she was wearing her usual garb - tee shirt and shorts. Debbie had a vast wardrobe of tees with sayings like, "I'm Rusty – lubricate me!" or "I'd rather *you* were working and *I* was fishing," or "If you can read this – DON'T!" and MacLaren's favorite, "Don't Fuck With Me – I Own The Place!"

Debbie was at her usual spot tending bar when MacLaren went around by the server's station and hugged her from behind. "Hello Beautiful," he said.

"Hey you," she turned, holding onto two Bud Lights and giving him a kiss on the cheek. "How the hell've you been? Saw the police boat pulling in. You're gonna scare my customers away with that thing," she laughed. He introduced Lydia and Ben and then said to her, "Is he still here?"

"Yup. He was going to go on break, but when I got your call I told him to stay put. Didn't tell him you were coming, told him we were too busy for him to take a break, so, he's in the back."

"Okay Deb, thanks. I'll only need him for a few minutes." MacLaren walked around the bar and placed his hand on Big Ben's shoulder, "Here's what I need you to do ..."

"Hey," Debbie said, making the Lieutenant turn around, "he's a damn good cook and I need him here. Keep that in mind."

"Yes ma'am." Then to Ben he continued, "I need you to go out back there," he pointed to the deck wrapping around the building where there were several guests eating at tables. "You'll find the back door to the kitchen on the side of the parking lot. It's usually wide open so all you've got to do is stand in the doorway. There'll be a skinny little weasel making a break for it in about two minutes. Detain him."

Ben left on his mission. MacLaren watched his watch. Debbie said to Lydia, "Sweetie, why don't you pull up a barstool and I'll make you a drink."

Two minutes later, the lieutenant pushed through the swinging saloon type doors into the kitchen. "Hello Rick," he said.

A thin man with a dirty white apron stood at the grill. He immediately dropped the skillet he was holding and bolted for the back door. Big Ben took up the entire doorway. "Hi," he said. Rick spun around looking for an alternate escape route. There was none. MacLaren came up to him. "Good to see you again, Rick."

"I ain't done nuthin' Lieutenant." Realizing he had no means of escape, Rick nonchalantly returned to his cooking. MacLaren stood between the grill and the kitchen door. Big Ben remained in the doorframe.

"Big Ben, meet Convict Rick." MacLaren said. "One of our county's most upstanding citizens and a Google of information on all things corrupt and unlawful. Isn't that so, Rick?"

"I don't know nuthin'."

"I haven't asked you anything yet."

"Don't matter, I still don't know nuthin'."

"Aw, Rick, don't disappoint me. I'm trying to show off for the big guy in the doorway. He's a cop from up north and I'd sure like to show him how cooperative the citizens of South Florida are."

"I'm clean Lieutenant. I got six months left on my probation and I ain't blowin' it. Debbie's been good to me. You ask her about me. I like it here, so don't fuck it up for me."

"I love ya, Rick, and Deb says she loves ya too. But once a convict, always a convict. You'll end up back in again, sooner or later."

"Not this time."

"Well then, help me out a little bit and if we do cross those unfortunate paths again, I'll remember what you did for me."

Convict Rick was no outsider to the outside of the law and he and MacLaren had been acquainted for several years. It was always good to have contacts on both sides. He placed the grilled grouper onto a sesame bun, slid it onto a plate, added fries and cole slaw and moved around MacLaren to the bar window. He yelled, "Bar food," and turned back towards his grill. Suddenly he did a quick two-step towards the door and MacLaren jumped to block his way. But Rick didn't go anywhere; he just laughed and went back to the grill. "Just seeing if you're still on your toes, Lieutenant."

"Don't fuck with me."

"Alright, alright," he chuckled, "what do you wanna know about?"

"Clothes."

"Clothes? I think you need to be a bit more specific than that."

MacLaren knew he didn't have to be more specific. He knew Convict Rick would know exactly what he was talking about. He didn't know how he would know, he just knew he would. Rick was like a clairvoyant. Somehow word of anything and everything illegal that went on in both Sarasota and Manatee counties got to Rick. MacLaren wished he could put Rick on a retainer. Shit, he'd give him his own desk at headquarters, if he'd stay out of jail long enough. For some reason crooks found him and opened up to him, like a shrink. He was an easygoing guy, but he was a sap too. They'd get him to run the drugs he never did and to fence the merchandise he never stole. And he was the one that always got caught and did the time. Then he'd get out, get clean and the whole mess would start all over again. MacLaren thought Convict Rick would eventually end up dead by the hands of his crook buddies that played him like a song. Too bad 'cause MacLaren actually liked the guy. He waited.

Rick pulled off a slip from the printer sitting on top of the hot line. He went into the walk-in and came out with three fish fillets. He flopped them on the grill, threw a large handful of sautéed onions into a pan and dropped the fry basket into the oil. "You must be talking 'bout that designer dude who harpooned his girlfriend at the Ritz. Then got his clothes all burned up in a campfire, 'cept of course for the dress on e-Bay this morning."

How the fuck does he know so much already, MacLaren wondered. Big Ben was impressed. Rick smirked.

"Now you didn't hear this from me …" he said.

"I never do, Rick."

"But there's been a couple of guys throwin' money around lately, buyin' everybody drinks and shit. And I got invited to an after hours private party with them last night, if you know what I mean."

"What do they look like?"

"Like a couple a guys."

As if on cue, MacLaren's cell phone beeped. He had a new text message. It was from the police artist. Pictures of Roger and Mikey came through. He showed them to Rick.

"Might be," he said.

"Where are they staying?"

"It's your lucky day, Lieutenant. They're staying right here at the motel."

MacLaren looked at Big Ben. Ben was wearing an evil grin.

"Thanks, Rick. Keep up the good work."

"You owe me, Lieutenant, big time!"

"Put it on my tab." The Lieutenant and Big Ben went back into the bar.

THIRTY-SIX

Lydia was seated with an empty stool on either side of her. She was sipping on a glass of chardonnay, watching CNN on one of the TV screens suspended above the bar. The men sat. Debbie came over, "The usual?" she asked MacLaren.

"No, not now Deb, I've got to ..." but it was too late, she placed a pint of draft beer in front of him. "And for Paul Bunyon?"

"Sure, I'll have one of those," Ben replied. "Lieutenant, can I see those pictures?"

MacLaren flipped his cell phone open, punched a few keys and handed it to Ben. Ben looked at the pictures and committed them to memory. He handed the phone back, took a long swig of his beer and said, "I'll be right back." He walked around the bar looking at faces. He went around the deck, scouted the patio where a three-piece band was cranking out tunes from the seventies. He wandered over to a group of men standing at the end of the wharf. One of them was filleting fish on a high table built into the railing. The others were watching and drinking beer and talking. Pelicans bobbed in the water waiting for scraps. The carver looked like the one called Roger, but when Ben tapped him on the shoulder to get a better look, he realized it wasn't. He moved on.

The December afternoon was hot and Rusty's Anchor was full of locals and early tourists drinking their way towards the upcoming holiday season. But no Roger or Mikey. Ben checked the men's room. Nothing. He went back through the bar. It was full. Lydia was glued to the TV. MacLaren was on his cell with one finger stuck in his other ear. Big Ben went out to the parking lot, then around to the side where the motel was. He spotted the white van pulling up to the motel. Roger and Mikey got out. One of them had an armload of grocery bags; the other hoisted a thirty-pack of Bud Light onto his shoulder and put a key into the door with a painted 5 on it. They went inside and slammed the door. Ben went over to the van. Still muddy, still had the red duct tape doubling as a rear taillight. He let the air out of both rear tires and went back into the bar.

Lydia was halfway through a fish sandwich. MacLaren was still on the phone, munching fries. A plate next to Ben's beer was covered with a lid. As he took his seat, Debbie came over and took the lid off, "Try this out, Chief. Bet you've never tasted a better, fresher fish sandwich anywhere - and certainly not in Boston. I've seen that harbor. Disgusting." She strode past MacLaren and said, "Eat it while it's hot goddamn it."

He closed his phone, and spoke between mouthfuls. "Debbie says they've been here a couple months. Always pay on time, work at the fish house next block down, packing and shipping. Thinks one of them might drive a delivery truck. They were in here late last night until she threw them out at closing time - after two a.m. Bought drinks for everyone. Said they'd hit good on a lottery ticket. Were back this morning, shots and beers, then they left in their van. Doesn't know where they went. I've got their pictures on the wire along with a description of the van from you and Convict Rick."

"They're back," Ben said, "I just saw them pull in."

"Fuck!" Lydia said. "Fuck!" she said again, louder. She pointed to the TV. CNN was on. Dodge Maddison was getting slap-punched by Dana's father. They looped it again. The caption read, "In Sarasota, Florida today, fashion designer Dodge Maddison was accosted at the funeral service for supermodel Dana. Sources say the father of the model walked up to Mr. Maddison saying, "I hope you get yours!" and then slapped Mr. Maddison across the face." The three-second scene looped again. "At the time of the assault, the service had just been concluded. Police officers and his attorney, in what has been called an unauthorized visit, surrounded the forty-two year old fashion designer, incarcerated and charged with the murder of the twenty-one year old supermodel. Neither the Sarasota Police Department nor attorneys for Mr. Maddison could be reached for comment. No charges have been filed and the incident remains under investigation." The segment ended with a close-up of the father's angry face and faded with a back shot of the parents walking away, the mother's arm over her husband's shoulders. His fists clenched.

Lydia threw her napkin onto her plate. "Well, there you have it," she looked at Ben, "Your friend has just been convicted." Her phone rang. She looked at the screen, "It's my father." She got off her stool and walked away from the noisy bar to take the call.

Big Ben pushed his plate forward and stood up. He threw some money on the bar and walked out, MacLaren fast behind him. "Where are you going?" He didn't answer. He walked at a quick pace through the parking lot toward the motel. He felt the cargo pocket on the right side of his leg. MacLaren knew instinctively what Big Ben was going to do. "You can't just barge in there, we need to get a warrant."

"No, *you* can't barge in there, *I* can. I'm just a citizen on vacation."

"Don't fuck up my case, Benson."

Ben didn't pay him any mind. It was clear to MacLaren that the big man wasn't going to slow his pace. MacLaren pulled his police weapon from its holster at the small of his back. "Geesus Christ!"

Without stopping, Ben marched right up to motel room number 5 and kicked the door in. Roger was on the couch with a clicker in one hand and a bottle of beer in the other. He jumped up just in time for Ben to grab him and push him hard against the wall. He pushed his beefy forearm like a tree branch into Roger's throat and pressed his massive weight onto his body so Roger would have no chance to kick him in the groin. Mikey came running out of the kitchen screaming, "What da fuck?" MacLaren leveled his Glock nine at him and said, "Don't move!" Mikey complied.

Big Ben was close enough to Roger to smell his beer breath. "Who set up the clothing gig?"

"I don't know what you're … "

Ben drove his left hand into Roger's kidney. "Don't make me angry."

MacLaren, still holding the gun on Mikey, reached around Ben and patted Roger down. Then he patted Mikey down. He went over to the couch and checked the cushions and ran his hand along the insides. He pushed Mikey onto the couch. "They're clean." Ben pulled Roger over to the couch and threw him next to Mikey. He reached into his cargo pocket and took out his gun. He stood over them. MacLaren went to survey the rest of the efficiency.

"I'll give it to you as plain as I can," Ben said. "We've spoken to the girls. They told us an interesting story. It didn't have a happy ending. This is the epilogue; it goes one of two ways. You give me the information I want and I don't give a shit what happens to you. You don't, and I'll help the lieutenant load you up and take you downtown to his accommodations."

"You ain't got no proof of nuthin'," Roger said.

Ben squatted and stuck the barrel of his gun into the side of Roger's knee. "You know what a 38 can do to a kneecap?"

"Hey man! Cut that out!"

Big Ben said, in his best Clint Eastwood voice, "If you were to be resisting arrest, I'll bet I would be justified in shooting your kneecap clean off."

"Fuck you!"

MacLaren came out of the bedroom holding up a plastic bag from a national discount store. "Looky here. Look what I found under the mattress – an ingenious hiding place by the way. Wal Mart's giving big cash refunds."

Ben pulled the hammer back. Mikey squirmed over to the edge of the couch, pulling his legs up and covering his knees. "Alright, alright," Roger said. "So we hit the lottery, big fucking deal."

"Stop stallin' Roger," Mikey spilled his guts. "We didn't mean anybody any harm. We picked up the clothes and took 'em to the park and disposed of them. That's all. It was an easy deal."

"Who set it up?"

"I don't know."

Ben sat his heavy weight on Roger's legs and moved his gun to Mikey's knee.

"Really," Mikey winced. "We never saw the guy. The whole deal was handled from the phone booth."

"What phone booth?"

"The one outside at the end of the motel."

"You're still not telling me who set it up?"

"I'm telling ya I don't know who it was. Rick told us …"

"Fuckin' Mikey," Roger shook his head, "Shut up! These guys ain't got nothin' on us, they don't even have a fucking warrant. They ain't got no right to be here harassing us."

"Pheew," MacLaren whistled, "I'll bet there's almost ten grand here."

Big Ben squeezed in between Roger and Mikey on the couch and put his arms over their shoulders, his gun was in his right hand on top of Roger's shoulder. "We don't need a warrant boys, 'cuz this isn't an official house call. In fact, we aren't even here. Bottom line is, we don't give a rat's ass about you two. So, if you give us what we need, we'll be on our way and you two low-life's can go enjoy another day in paradise." He squeezed their necks tightly, choking them like a vise grip. "So, what do you say?"

"Okay, okay," Mikey coughed. Ben loosened his hold. "Some guy told us there'd be a FedEx pick-up at the Ritz. All we had to do was get it and take the stuff somewhere and burn it. He didn't want no trace of it left. So we did. End of story."

"You never met with him?"

"No. It was all handled through Rick. He does a little business on the pay phone. He got a call and he passed it on to us."

"Did Rick see him?" MacLaren asked.

"No."

"How much did you get paid?" Ben continued.

"Ten grand."

"How'd you get the money?"

"It was left in a bag in the trash can next to the phone. Five grand before and five after."

"When did you get the cash?"

"The first five a couple nights ago and the rest last night."

"How did he know you finished the job?"

"He called at midnight, we told him it was a done deal and he said look in the trash can."

"Pretty trusting fellow."

"I don't think he had much experience in this sort of thing."

"Why do you say that?"

"He sounded nervous."

"Eighty-four-hundred even," MacLaren had finished counting the money. "Where's the rest of it?"

"Rick got a ten percent cut and the rest we blew."

Ben got up, towering over them, his gun at his side. "What did he sound like?" Mikey looked at Roger. Apparently he had been the negotiator.

"Like a little kid," Roger said. Ben had a quizzical look. "Like he was talking through one of those scrambling devices or something. It sounded weird. He was hard to understand."

Ben knew about those devices. You could get them off the Internet or even at Radio Shack.

"Any accent?"

"Too hard to tell."

If Big Ben were home in Bryce Corner he'd throw the two of them in his jail for a few days and make them sweat. He didn't know what MacLaren was going to do. He stood back and said, "They're all yours, Lieutenant."

MacLaren put the money back in the plastic bag. "Here," he threw some of it on the table. "Take this and get the fuck out of my jurisdiction. Today. Don't ever let me find you in South Florida again." He headed for the door.

Roger jumped up and went for the money. He thumbed through it, "Hey, what about the rest of it?"

MacLaren laughed and exited the motel room. Ben went over to Roger and said, "One more thing. I'm curious as to how you got those nice scratches on your face?"

"I cut myself shaving," Roger replied sarcastically.

Ben opened his cell phone and went to photo album. He brought up the picture he took of Franny and Fiona. He turned his phone so Roger could see the bruises on Fiona's face. "Lucky for you they don't want to press charges ... but I do Dirt Bag!" He hit Roger as hard as he could on the side of his face near his left eye. The force of the blow catapulted Roger across the room and hard into the wall. He slid down the wall and bundled on the floor holding onto his face.

"I'll sue you for police brutality, you bastard!"

"Then I may as well make it worth it," he went at him.

Roger held his hands up, "No, no. Okay, okay."

Big Ben turned and walked away. At the door he said, "Oh, and by the way, I think you might have a flat tire ... or two."

Walking back to the bar, Ben asked, "Do you believe them?"

"Yeah."

"What are you going to do about Convict Rick?"

"Nothing," MacLaren said. "I need him as a snitch. I don't want to shut down his little phone booth operation. I'll keep it under my hat for awhile."

"What about the money? How much did you keep?"

"Five grand. I thought I'd give it to Lydia to add to the girl's charitable contribution."

Ben nodded his head.

"Who do you think it was?" MacLaren asked.

"I don't know. Same suspects I guess. Although they seemed pretty sure it was a guy."

"So it could have been Maddison."

"Or Santiago or Andre Chateauguy or some guy working for a woman," Ben said, thinking of Annison or Harlow, and wondering again what motive they would have.

"Or there's the espionage angle - someone hired by some ambitious, crooked fashion designer."

"What about the little Italian guy, Giovanni?"

"Naw, why would he bite off the hand that's feeding him?" MacLaren shook his head. "Without a description we're pretty much nowhere." They walked through the grove of trees, back across the graveled parking lot and onto the deck where Lydia had resumed her seat at the bar in the shade beneath the overhang.

"I need to fish, got to think things out." Just as MacLaren said this, his cell phone rang. He stopped at the railing to take the call. The river was flowing smooth in front of him.

Ben took the seat next to Lydia. "Where did you two run off to?"

"Oh, we went to visit the neighbors."

"Yeah, right," she said. "So, what's on the agenda now?"

"MacLaren wants to fish."

"Me too. Let's get back out on the water." They bid ado to Debbie and moved toward the deck to join MacLaren.

"What did your dad want?"

"Wanted to know if I'd seen the news yet. Says we've got to push things up a bit. Too much media coverage will badly influence any jury. He's still working on getting Dodge out, and if he does, you've got to keep him away from the press. They'll be all over him. Don't let him say a word to anyone, even his fiancée. I know that's impossible but the less he says to her the better. They'll be all over her too. I'll talk to Maddison about it, but you need to reiterate the seriousness of it all and keep him low key and out of sight."

When they got to MacLaren, he was still on his cell. He sounded alarmed. "Is he dead? ... Have you touched anything? ...Good, don't. Get the tape up. Twenty-five-foot radius. Don't let anyone near the car. Sit tight, I'll be there in fifteen minutes. Oh, and Sergeant, put a call into the M.E. as soon as you hang up."

"We gotta go!" he said to Ben and Lydia and headed for the boat. "Park Ranger over at Myakka called in an unresponsive person in a car." He went immediately for the bowline and released it from the cleat. Lydia hopped into the boat. Ben untied the stern. "Sergeant Reynolds ran the tags. Rental car, Alamo, Sarasota Airport." MacLaren fired the engines, Big Ben climbed in and stood next to the two of them at the helm. MacLaren pushed lightly on the throttle and the powerboat moved carefully away from the dock. "Rented two days ago to a Mr. Carlos Santiago." He threw the throttle full forward and the boat roared into the river way.

THIRTY-SEVEN

By the time Annison got to the Ritz Carlton, her luggage had already arrived from the airport and her clothes had been neatly closeted away in Dodge's penthouse suite. The maid had set out her toiletries in the master bath and a welcoming bottle of chardonnay sat in a silver ice bucket on the living room table. She started the shower and stripped out of her clothes and placed them in the wicker hamper. The suite was cool with the air conditioning, so she allowed the hot shower time to steam the bathroom. She donned the complimentary terry robe with the embroidered *RC* crest and went to pour herself a glass of wine.

It had been a distressing day. First Annison had traveled an hour east, on the bumper-to-bumper Mass Turnpike, to Logan International in Boston to board the morning flight to Sarasota. There'd been a stopover in Atlanta with an hour delay, and then a smoky cab ride to Selby Gardens with an arrogant driver oblivious to the No Smoking policy. Arriving at the memorial service, anxious to see Dodge and jittery due to the circumstances, her nerves were on end. Later, she was jostled by Dodge's inquisition at police headquarters. She had never thought she would be viewed as a suspect in this thing and was inanely upset by it. Thankfully, Ben had filled the drive over to the hotel with cordial small talk and hadn't pressed her on anything further. Annison wanted to be a strong, positive support for her fiancée, so outwardly she appeared upbeat and hopeful, but underneath the facade she was worried and upset.

High above the shoreline, Annison stood at the sliding glass doors sipping her wine and looking at the breathtaking view of the ocean with the white waves inaudibly rolling onto the sandy white shore. She hoped to God they'd let Dodge out soon. She wanted to hold him in her arms, to feel his embrace, to hear him tell her everything was going to be all right.

The shower was refreshing. She let the hot water cascade over her shoulders and run down her back, loosening the tension in her muscles. In the bedroom she sat on the bed deep in thought, finishing her wine. With her mind on overload and the softness of the bed beckoning, Annison succumbed to the pleasant atmosphere of the suite and fell asleep.

When she awoke an hour later, she was hungry. She dressed in shorts and a loose cotton top, twirled her hair into a bun and covered it with a floppy straw hat she had purchased in the gift shop. She left the penthouse suite in search of a chicken Caesar salad.

On the patio on the beach, guests were seated in mesh chairs beneath oversized umbrellas, enjoying the sun and salty air, nibbling hors d'oeuvres and sipping colorful cocktails. The afternoon Tiki Bar was crowded and all the tables were full. Fletcher Ross was the first to see Annison approaching. He saw her hesitate, looking for a place to sit and motioned to her from the table he was sharing with Andre and Harlow. He acquired a chair for her from the adjoining table and Annison sat down between the two men, directly opposite Harlow.

"Get settled in okay?" Fletcher asked.

"Yes, thank you. The suite is very nice."

A server arrived and asked the new guest if she'd like a drink.

"Yes, please. I'd like a glass of Kendall Jackson chardonnay."

"Would you like a menu, Ma'am?"

"Actually I'd love a chicken Caesar salad."

"Sure thing."

Annison noticed the others were not eating. "I'm sorry, did I order out of turn?"

"No, not at all," Andre said. "We've already eaten. You go right ahead, we'll keep you company with our cocktails."

The table fell quiet. Fletcher sipped his drink, Andre gazed at the beach and Harlow stared at Annison from behind her dark sunglasses. When the server placed Annison's glass of wine on the table, Andre made a swirling motion with his hand signaling another round. He was drinking a frozen Margarita, Fletcher was sipping Knob Creek on the rocks and Harlow was having seltzer water with a splash of cranberry. She had chastised herself for drinking last night and embarrassing herself in front of the attorney, Lydia Lawrence.

Not a word was spoken. The mood was awkward. All four of them were wondering who would speak first, and what they would say. The server reappeared with the fresh cocktails, took the empty glasses and disappeared. It was Annison who spoke first.

"This is difficult for me. I feel like the outsider."

"No, please," Fletcher offered, "you shouldn't feel ..."

"It's okay, Fletcher, I'm okay with it. I know all of you are part of Dodge's world and have been for quite some time. And I know I'm still new to you all and I imagine the news of our relationship has been ..." she hesitated looking for the right word. She looked directly at Harlow and said, "Startling?"

Harlow's eyebrows said, "To say the least."

"But all I want to do is to fit into his world, to make him happy. To have all of us get along, especially now that he needs us so."

That he needs *us* so, Harlow had a hard time digesting *that* word. She felt Annison wasn't part of the *us*. Had no right to be, should have no claim on the man she'd spent loving and caring for and protecting for the past ten years of her life. She wished Annison would just go away, go back to whatever hole she had crawled out of. She could do just fine without her. And so could Dodge. She'd had it with keeping her feelings at bay. It was time to air the laundry.

Boldly she said, "Would you gentlemen mind giving us a moment?"

Andre looked at her and then to Annison and then raised his eyebrows at Fletcher. Fletcher pushed his chair back and said, "By all means." The two men took their drinks and walked over to the Tiki Bar.

"I've tried to accept you and to accept the fact that Dodge wants to marry you, but I'll be blunt with you Annison, I don't like it - for a myriad of reasons, but mostly because I'm in love with him. Maybe I should have been more forthcoming with my feelings earlier, years ago, whatever. But I will express them now. To him, and to you. You say you want to fit in. Well you know what? You don't fit into his world. You never will. I don't know what type of hold you have on him but I'm sure he'll come to his senses soon enough."

"I don't have a hold on him," Annison responded. "He is who he is. I'm not stupid, I know you have feelings for him and I'm sorry if you feel slighted by his affection towards me but I really can't help that. You'll just have to learn to deal with it."

Harlow removed her sunglasses and leveled a stare across the table. "Don't patronize me."

Impossible in the tropics, but the air between them actually froze.

"I know all about you, Harlow. Dodge told me about your little *fling*."

If a stare could be lethal, Annison would be dead. "It was much more than that. Much more than you'll ever know." Harlow was more than ready to spar with this charlatan. "And you know what Annison Barrett? We don't need you here. The best thing you could do for Dodge right now is to leave him."

"You'd like that wouldn't you? But it's too late. You've had your chance." Annison raised her wine glass to her lips and took a short sip. She saw the fury in Harlow's eyes and she wasn't intimidated by it. In fact she was glad she had come to Sarasota to be with Dodge. And she wasn't afraid to stand her ground. "It's your own fault, Harlow. If you waited too long, that's *your* tough luck. Dodge is in love with me. So your feelings for him are moot. We are going to be married, we are opening the Bed & Breakfast, and we have a plan for Dodge to cut back his time spent in New York."

Harlow felt a knife twisting in her gut, and she was wishing it were twisting in her rival's gut instead.

"I feel sorry for you," Annison continued. "I really do. But I at least want you to know that I truly do love him. You can rest assured about that."

"Rest assured? Are you fucking kidding me? Who do you think you are?"

Annison glowered, "I'm his fiancée, Harlow."

THIRTY-EIGHT

MacLaren maneuvered the boat into the narrow waterway among the reeds where the Myakka River enters the remote end of the State Park. A hundred yards in, one of the park rangers stood waving on the shoreline. He helped them secure the boat to a mangrove outgrowth and lead them into the dense foliage. They came out onto a sandy, double-rutted road and followed that a ways to where the rental car sat off to the side in a small clearing surrounded by yellow crime scene tape. A flock of vultures circled ominously above. The ranger truck was there next to an ATV. Blue lights were blinking in the hot sunshine on top of a police cruiser. Behind it, a white boxy step van was rumbling towards the crime scene, its sides scraping against the foliage. The large blue lettering on the box over the cab announced the arrival of the *FORENSICS UNIT.*

Big Ben lifted the yellow tape and went toward the car.

"Hey!" an officer shouted.

"He's okay," MacLaren said, then asked the officer, "Who was first on the scene?"

"The park ranger over there sitting on the tailgate. He's kinda shook up."

Lydia Lawrence stood in the shade watching Ben survey the crime scene. He was focusing on the tire marks leading up to the car. It was a light gray Toyota Camry with tinted windows. She thought that was odd for a rental car. Black vultures were perched on the roof and hood; they were also watching the man. Lydia noted that for such a large man, Ben carried himself with a certain concentrated power of movement. She liked the way he moved. She tried not to focus on that.

"Some kid on the observation tower spotted the vultures and got the attention of one of the rangers. I got the call at the station and jumped on the ATV to come check it out. I thought it was going to be a rabbit or a baby gator or a raccoon or something. That happens a lot out here, but there were so many of the birds circling around. Huge bastards, four-foot wingspans, I figured it had to be something big." The ranger coughed into his hands. MacLaren noticed a water bottle sitting on the tailgate and handed it to him.

"Thanks," he took a sip and wiped his mouth with his bare forearm.

"When I saw the car, it was loaded with them," the ranger continued.

"Them?"

"The birds. They were all over it. Must have been fifty of 'em. Some in the trees, some in the air, some on the ground, but there was a shitload of 'em on the car. That's called a venue, when they're in a group like that. When they're circling in the air it's called a kettle, I don't know why." He was talking fast, nervous, his vocational tan looking pale in the circumstances. The ranger took a long swig of the water. "They were pecking away at the windshield and the glass, especially the back window on the far side. I could see 'em perched on the edge of the roof there, fighting for position. They were flapping their wings and shrieking like I've never heard before." He took another sip of water. "When I got to the other side of the car, that's when I saw the broken window. They had ... they had gotten into the car."

"They broke through a window?"

"Yeah. Buzzards are strong, prehistoric creatures. They're incredibly adept at scavenging. They can get at food. The smell of carrion drives 'em crazy. Their beaks are powerful ripping tools. They can rip through tough cowhide in seconds. The window was partially open, just a crack. There's a hose running in there. It goes to the tailpipe. I think the guy did himself in. Anyway, there was enough space for them to get their beaks in and rip it back. One side of it is pulled out at an angle; the rest of it is shattered. They made enough room to gain access ... and they got to him, the poor bastard."

The ranger looked over to the car. MacLaren's gaze followed his. Big Ben was approaching the vehicle. The vultures stood their ground.

The ranger continued. His voice lowered in a whispered reverence, "I got as close to the car as I could get. I couldn't shoo the birds away. They were fearless. I could see him sitting in the driver's seat; his head back against the headrest. The birds were all over the place. They had ripped off pieces of his scalp and they were ... they were fighting over the pieces ... and the eyes ... they always go for the eyes." He clutched his stomach and got off the tailgate and went around to the front of the truck.

The forensics van pulled to a stop. Two men got out. One was the Medical Examiner. "What do we have here, boys?"

MacLaren told him.

"Who's that big oaf inside the tape? He's walking all over my scene."

"He's cool, vacationing Chief of Police from a snow state. He won't disturb anything."

Just then a loud *crack!* echoed across the terrain like a bullwhip snapping. Lydia jumped.

"Geesus Christ!" the M.E. shouted.

The vultures leapt off the car and took flight, followed by their brethren in the trees.

Then came another loud shot. Big Ben was discharging his weapon. He blew out the side window of the car. The Camry's tinted windows that Lydia had noticed earlier began to evaporate as the vultures hastily exited the car, taking with them the thousands of flies that had blackened the interior. It was like a cloud of black smoke seeping into the sky.

The M.E. hurdled the yellow tape and ran toward the big man standing at the side of the car with a gun in his hand. "What the fuck are you doing?"

Ben stood with his .38 at his side letting the two-and-a-half inch barrel cool before he'd replace the gun into the cargo pocket of his shorts.

"You're disrupting my crime scene, pal."

"I'm preserving it. A few minutes more and those bastards would have ripped your vic to pieces."

The M.E. looked inside. MacLaren joined him. They saw the man, the bloodied head with the black ponytail. Big Ben said to them, "I think we've found Santiago, or what's left of him."

Even at the distance she was at, the rancidness of the scene, stirred by the wings of the retreating buzzards, overwhelmed Lydia. This wasn't her schtick. She decided to walk back to the boat.

She followed the pathway through the hammocks with the moss hanging down like long wiry ponytails, stagnant and unmoving in the dead wind. This wasn't helping her case any. She had hoped that they could find Santiago and that he'd shed some light on things. But not now. Shit. This was getting too weird. Another questionable suicide slash murder. She'd have to wait for the cops and the M.E. to figure that out. Meanwhile, she had a case to put together quick. Innocent until proven guilty, right? Bullshit. It was guilty until proven innocent, a line her father had instilled in her.

Big Ben and MacLaren moved off to the side away from the stench emanating from the blown out windows. The Medical Examiner and his assistant donned white facemasks and latex gloves and got to work.

"The ignition's in the on position," Ben said. "Fuel is gone. Battery's dead. How long ago did he rent the car?"

"Two days."

Ben looked up toward the sun, "Must have been over a hundred and twenty degrees in there."

"Yeah, he's ripe."

"Here," Ben pulled a piece of paper out of his pocket. "Found this in his lap."

MacLaren unfolded the paper and read, *Santa Maria, perdoname. Y ahora llenare mi ogligasion. Yo estare con ello. Yo los quidare a ellos.*

"What does it say?" Ben asked.

"Forgive me St. Maria. Now I will fulfill my obligation. I will be with them. I will take care of them."

"What's on the other side?"

MacLaren turned the note over. In smaller letters written almost illegibly, he read, "*Mira en de vidrio* ...Look on the glass."

"What the fuck does that mean?"

"It's a clue."

"No shit, Sherlock."

Ben took the note from the Lieutenant. "Look at the main body of the writing here," he held it open. Then he folded it and turned it to the smaller writing on the back. "And now look at this. See how different this writing is? Same hand, but looser. He'd already written the first part and folded it and was holding onto it in his lap. The carbon monoxide was getting to him, his mind was foggy, motor activity impaired with the intoxication of the fumes. He must have been having second thoughts about something and scribbled the clue as an afterthought."

"Or a final thought."

"Have them check for a glass in there," Ben nodded toward the car.

"Let's hope he didn't mean the window glass, big guy." MacLaren walked over to the car.

Ben realized he'd been holding onto his gun all this time. He put it back in his cargo pocket. The barrel had cooled.

The county sheriff's car approached. An older man with a bushy white mustache got out. He wore dark sunglasses and adjusted his hat against the sun. "Howdy, MacLaren. Heard on the radio you were having a party here. Thought I'd come by and check it out." They shook hands.

"Good to see you, Ray. I thought you'd be retired by now."

"Well, you never know," he chuckled.

"Sheriff Ray Burati, Chief Ben Benson."

The two men shook hands.

"Old Ray used to work S.P.D. until Myakka got hold of him. How long's it been now?"

"Pretty near fifteen years."

"Boy, it sure doesn't seem that long. Ray was my partner."

"Yup, when MacLaren was just a rookie. Taught him everything he knows."

MacLaren said to Ben, "I'd tell him he was full of shit except he's absolutely right," he laughed.

"So, what's going on?" Sheriff Burati asked.

MacLaren started telling him. Ben looked around for Lydia and didn't see her. "Excuse me gentlemen," he said.

"Hang on a second Ray," then MacLaren spoke to Big Ben, "You and Lydia go on back. I'll ride in with the M.E."

"Okay."

They spoke another minute then Ben said good-bye to Sheriff Burati and walked off toward the trail they'd come in on.

THIRTY-NINE

Harlow's cell phone jingled in her pocket book. She retrieved it and looked at the incoming number. Private call. "Hello," she said.

"Harlow, this is Conrad Lawrence, I've got some good news."

Annison sat across from her, eavesdropping. Harlow picked up her sunglasses and slowly slid them onto the bridge of her nose. Her eyes sending a penetrating scowl as they disappeared behind the polarized tint. The scowl said *this isn't over yet.*

"Yes, Mr. Lawrence," she said to Dodge's attorney, making sure her rival recognized the role of authority in her voice, "What is this good news you have for me?"

Annison hadn't necessarily disliked Harlow when Dodge had introduced them last month in New York City. In fact she thought her to be very pleasant. But when Harlow had declined to join their luncheon table that day, Annison had felt the chill. The way she strutted away from the table told her that the pleasantries were over.

"Dodge is going to be released. The judge set bail at one million dollars. We're in the process of transferring funds as we speak, but it will probably take another hour to wrap up the red tape."

"That's wonderful. I'll plan on picking him up in an hour then."

"Fine. I'll see you then." Conrad Lawrence disconnected.

"They're letting him go?" Annison said excitedly.

"They're arranging bail now. I'm to pick him up in an hour," Harlow slid her cell into the side pocket of her bag and pulled out her wallet. "I think I'll go freshen up."

"That won't be necessary. I'll pick up my own fiancée, thank you very much."

"Listen Annison, I'm giving you strong advice. Get out of Dodge's life and stay out. If you think …"

"I don't scare that easily, Harlow. I've waited all my life to find this man. I'm not going to let him go now. Make no mistake; your loyalty to him is during business hours only. His personal time belongs to me. And you know that to be true, whether you want to believe it or not. So stop playing the pathetic injured lover and face reality."

Harlow placed some money on the table. Her emotions were wired. She felt the jagged edge of her nerves poking through her skin. She was angrier with herself than Annison. Knowing that Dodge was planning a life without her was too much to bear. She could feel her heart tearing, the pain of it ripping across her breast and seeping into her very core. Suddenly everything crashed over her like the crescendo of the waves behind her. Harlow felt herself being tugged beneath the undertow of lost hope and dragged into an unsettled sea. Lately her emotions were like a pendulum of extreme highs and lows. She could do no more battle with this woman. Something inside her told her to retreat before she completely lost her temper.

"I can't do this right now," Harlow dug into her pocketbook and retrieved the keys to the rental car. Abruptly she stood and threw them on the table. "Top floor of the parking garage. It's the silver blue Jaguar near the penthouse entrance. Go ahead, you go get him. I'm over it."

Annison sat alone at the table. The Tiki Bar was thinning out, the patrons walking onto the beach to put their feet in the sand. Andre and Fletcher had witnessed the scene of the two women from their position at the end of the bar. They looked at each other and shrugged their shoulders.

FORTY

Big Ben stepped onto the gunwale and boarded the boat. The DONZI rocked in the shallow water of the shoreline. Lydia sat beneath the Bimini top watching the narrow river way darken in the descending sunlight.

"You okay?" Ben asked.

"That was a horrible scene. I've never been that close to death before. My job doesn't start until after the crime scene has been cleaned up. I only see the pictures. Some of them are gruesome enough but to see it first hand like that, to realize how it happened and to see those damn birds like that," her voice wavered, Ben laid a hand on her shoulder, "and to think of what they were doing … and to smell it … and all those flies …" Lydia reached a hand up and placed it over Ben's.

He put his other hand on her other shoulder and squeezed them both. "I've witnessed my share of morbid crime scenes," he said, "and you never get used to it. It's not like in the movies where the cops stand around being cool and cracking jokes. Sometimes death can be a messy business."

An alligator ventured out of the tall grasses on the shoreline and slid into the water. They watched it swim up river and disappear into the reeds on the other side, the wake from its massive reptilian tail rippling into the gentle stream.

"MacLaren's going to stay here 'til they wrap things up," Ben said. "He says we should go on back to Sarasota and berth the boat. You know the way?"

Lydia leaned her head back and looked into his eyes and smiled, "Aye, Captain."

"Good," Ben released his hands from her shoulders and stepped off portside. "I'll untie her."

Half an hour later, Lydia steered south into Anna Maria Sound leading to the Intracoastal Waterway and Sarasota Bay. The sun was setting on the other side of Longboat Key and the lights of Cortez Village were illuminating off to starboard.

Lydia's cell phone alerted her to a voicemail message. As she pressed the key to dial up, it rang. Pressing answer on the keypad, she said, "Hello, Dad."

"Did you get my voice mail?"

"No, I was just retrieving messages now."

"I've been trying to get hold of you. Where are you?"

"We're in Sarasota Bay coming back from Myakka State Park. We're in the police boat heading for Marina Jack."

"We?"

"Ben Benson and I."

"What's up in Myakka besides poor cell phone reception?"

"Carlos Santiago's dead body." Lydia brought her father up to speed on the discovery and the cryptic suicide note.

"Dammit," Conrad Lawrence said. "He was a key witness."

"I know and the contents of the note are perplexing."

"Do they believe it to be a suicide?"

"Right now, yes. They'll be more certain once the autopsy is done and the handwriting analyzed."

"What was in your voice mail message?" Lydia asked her father.

Ben had taken the wheel and stood at the helm holding the speedboat at quarter throttle. The wind was calm and the bay smooth. The lights were on under the Ringling Bridge and Sarasota loomed in the twilight. Marina Jack was up ahead. Ben brought the throttles back for the No Wake zone. Lydia was seated beside him on the phone with her dad.

I will fulfill my obligation. Ben thought, obligation to whom? *I will be with them. I will take care of them.* He needed to know more about Santiago, his background, and his family. Did he have someone he was supporting back in his home country? How would killing himself support them? Ben remembered the cut Santiago had on his face and the excuse of bumping into his equipment, substantiated by a fellow videographer. He made a mental note to check with that person. Something wasn't right. There was something going on at that fashion shoot that Santiago knew about. That Dana was privy to. But what? And if they were killed by the same person, what would that mean? And if Santiago had indeed killed himself *to be with them*, who was he with?

The other thought swirling in Ben's investigative mind was the possibility of a murder/suicide. Perhaps Santiago had killed Dana and then himself. But why two days later and what would have been the motive?

Look on the glass. MacLaren and the M.E. had searched the car and found nothing. They would dust the windows for a message of some sort, except for the two Ben had shot out. Those windows were tempered and had fragmented into thousands of tiny pieces. But Ben didn't think there was anything to be found in the car. His analytical intellect was formulating an idea.

"Okay Dad, I'll make sure he's there in the morning. See you then. Bye." Lydia closed her cell phone and stood up next to Ben. "Dodge has been released. Annison picked him up a few minutes ago. In light of the Santiago situation, Dad wants to meet with Dodge at nine o'clock tomorrow morning in our office. You too he says. He wants to plan our defense strategy."

"I hope he's got one."

"Me too."

The DONZI pulled alongside the pier and the Dock Master extended a hand to help Lydia out of the boat. He jumped in and held onto the piling while Ben disembarked. The Dock Master would berth the boat.

"What are you going to do?" Lydia asked Ben.

"I'm going to go have a long talk with my buddy Dodge Maddison. You?"

"I need to get to the office. It's going to be a long night. Could you drop me?"

"Sure thing."

They walked past the dockside restaurant entrance and saw that the tables were full. It was a beautiful evening to be dining on the bay and patrons were queued at the hostess stand. They crossed the brick roundabout where the valets were parking expensive automobiles. Ben's Hummer was parked out in the main parking lot. He held the door for Lydia, climbed in his side and started the vehicle. They never heard the explosion.

FORTY-ONE

The bomb had been set in the front wheel-well beneath the hood, a place that held the least risk for occupants.

"Whoever set it was clearly an amateur," the bomb squad guy was giving his initial assessment. "Or ..."

"Or what?"

"Or else someone very adept at explosives."

"A pro?"

"Sending a message. Didn't want to kill you, just wanted to scare you."

"Okay, he scared me," Ben said. "But now I'm pissed."

The sheer shock of the blast had instantly rendered Lydia unconscious. Ben had seen the hood coming at him in enough split second timing to raise his arms against the shattering of the windshield. It didn't shatter. It cracked from the bottom up in deep lines like a little kids drawing of a sunrise.

"Black powder residue everywhere." The bomb squad guy was short and compact, his head shaved as bald as a billiard ball. G. Gordon Liddy mustache. His name was Jack Barney; he looked to be about fifty and said he'd been on the force for twenty-five years. His black tee shirt stretched over his pecs like a body tattoo. Ben figured that when he wasn't out chasing bombs, Jack Barney was in a gym. "Looks like the container was a plastic to-go mug wired to a spark plug. You turn the key and boom, big flash, but no fire. Not much damage really, except for springing the hood and cracking the grill and the windshield. Lucky. Could have been much worse. Fatal if he'd of wanted it to be."

"Or she."

"Could be. The bomb was primitive, easy to make, simple to set up. All this arson stuff is on the Internet. Hell, there are guys on You Tube showing you how to do it. Did you know the average age of an amateur bomber is thirteen to seventeen? Scary shit."

"What's your gut say?" Ben was speaking loudly. Jack Barney knew that was because his ears were traumatized and ringing from the explosion.

Barney smoothed his trim mustache with the thumb and forefinger of his right hand. "I don't think it's a kid screwing around in a parking lot. I know what you're mixed up in Mr. Benson and I think someone just gave you a warning. They don't like you poking around in this case. Now ..." more mustache playing, "I'd say it's an amateur. A pro would be smoother, leave some telltale sign of their work. They're proud of what they do. Even if someone had contracted them to send a message, it would be hard for their ego to set off such a small charge. They would have wanted a bigger bang. Would have used a command detonation so they could set it off by their own hand, they like that kind of control. I think it's someone you know Chief."

Ben didn't even have to ponder that idea. He wasn't one to believe in coincidence. "Also," Barney added, "covering all bases, it may not have been meant for you. Could have been meant for the attorney."

Lydia Lawrence sat in the EMT van, her pallor ashen and her hands shaking. Someone had gotten her a coffee and she was holding onto that for dear life.

Ben stuck his head in the side door, "Are you okay?"

"Yes, just a little shaken up. And my ears won't stop ringing."

"That'll go away in awhile."

Lydia reached a hand toward him and Ben took it. He could feel the cool pulse of terror in her palm.

"It's going to be alright," he assured her.

She smiled. "How are you doing?"

"To be honest, a little shaky too, but I'll be fine." The reality was that his adrenaline was spiking and the minor shakes he was exhibiting were not as much a result of the incident as they were a desire to get his hands around somebody's neck and kill them.

"Dad insists I go to the hospital for a thorough check up. He's on his way there now to meet me. The consummate lawyer," Lydia managed a chuckle, "maybe he sees a law suit in here somewhere."

"I'm sure he's concerned about you. It's a good idea," Ben squeezed her hand and released it.

The EMT technician came in the back doors, closed them and took a seat next to Lydia. He grabbed a clipboard and took her free arm in his, strategically placing his fingers on her wrist to attain her heart rate.

"You should come too," Lydia said to Ben.

"No, I'm fine. You will be too. They just want to be sure. Your dad probably has a whole team of doctors waiting at the ER door right now," he smiled. "Get some rest. I'll call you in the morning."

"I just want to go home," she said, "take a shower and curl up with a good book. Nothing suspenseful, maybe a comic book." They laughed together, a sign of relief, a shared thankfulness that they were both still alive. Ben shut the side door and the van pulled away.

Big Ben was riled. He didn't like being threatened, especially by a coward with a car bomb. He thirsted for closure on this and right now he pretty much didn't care who he had to have it with. Dodge's image flashed into his mind's eye. He felt sick that he even considered his friend being involved in anything like this, but he couldn't help but sense that Dodge was connected in some way, either voluntary or involuntary. Something going on in Dodge Maddison's world had now infringed upon Ben Benson's world and he didn't like it. Ben's first thought was to confront him. He was tired of wondering if his old friend was being truthful with him or not. He wanted answers.

His second thought was wiser, crafted with less anger. If Dodge was in front of him right now, Ben was afraid he'd beat the shit out of him first and ask questions later. So he decided on plan B. He floored the Hummer and squealed out of the parking lot and cut into traffic. Big Ben set the GPS for Manatee Landing.

FORTY-TWO

The jet-black Hummer cast an ominous image racing through the streets of Sarasota. The hood was missing, the windshield was cracked and the fractured grill grinned into the night with its chipped and broken chrome teeth. Ben sped east along Fruitville Road out to I-75 north. Minutes later the big all-terrain tires squealed off the 224-exit ramp, cut through the river road and screeched to a halt in front of Rusty's Anchor. Convict Rick was still in the kitchen when Ben barged through the swinging saloon-type doors.

"What the …" was all that got out of Rick's mouth before Ben's big fist slammed into it. Convict Rick went flying against the prep island knocking over a full tray of appetizers and sending a screaming waitress out the door.

"Whoa! Whoa," Rick held his open palms up in front of Ben's assault.

Ben grabbed Rick's shirt by the neckline and lifted him onto his tiptoes. "Where are your friends?" he grumbled.

"What friends?" Rick said.

Big Ben kneed him in the groin and lifted him off his feet and held him against the wall next to the grill. A mound of onions sizzled next to a pair of hamburgers. "Don't make me ask again."

"I don't know man. They're gone. They left right after you guys did."

"Where did they go?"

"And they're not my friends, okay?"

Ben held Rick against the wall and cocked a fist.

"Wait, wait, wait …"

"You're trying my patience, Rick."

"After you left they came into the bar. They talked to Debbie for a minute and then they split. Deb said they were talking about New Orleans. Said they wouldn't need the motel room anymore. That's all I know."

"What do you know about the car bomb?"

"What car bomb?"

Ben smashed his fist into the wall next to Rick's head.

"Cut the shit man!" Rick yelled. "I don't know nothin' about no car bomb, I swear."

"Hey! What the hell's going on in here?" Debbie said.

"Just having a friendly talk with your cook," Ben answered.

"Yeah, well it don't look too friendly to me." She grabbed Ben's cocked arm and said, "I know MacLaren'll vouch for you but I don't think he'd vouch for your actions. You got a problem with my cook, you come to me first."

Big Ben relaxed his grip on the cook. Rick's feet settled to the ground. He brushed off the front of his shirt. There was a trickle of blood coming from his lip.

"You've got a temper, Chief," Debbie said. "They teach you that at the Police Academy?"

"I'm sorry, Deb."

She looked at Convict Rick. "Here," she threw him the bar rag she had tucked into her waist. "Wipe your lip. You've got burgers burning."

Debbie took Ben's arm and led him out the side door to the deck. Outside the night air held a soft breeze. They leaned their elbows on the wooden railing. Traffic streamed over the Manatee River Bridge, white lights coming at them and red dots fading into the southern distance. Water lapped against a houseboat moored fifty yards out.

"What's this I heard you say about a car bomb?"

Ben told her what had happened at Marina Jack.

"And you figured Rick had something to do with it?"

"I figured he'd know something about it. Maybe he'd even set it up."

"Listen, let me tell you about Rick. I like him. Pity him a little, maybe, but I think he's okay. He's nothing more than a sucker. Gets wound up in schemes he shouldn't, but he doesn't have the heart to hurt nobody. He wouldn't be messing with anything as violent as a bomb. I know that. He's a kid who needed a chance to straighten out his life and I'm the one who's giving it to him. I took him in and put him under my wing. He's doing all right here and he knows it. He's not going to chance losing it all and ending up back in the pen again."

"What about those other two, Roger and Mikey?"

"Well," Debbie watched the river moving along with the wind pushing intermittent waves across the surface, "I wouldn't put a lot past them, but my gut says no. I can read people. I've been in this business a long time and if it's one thing I've learned, it's how to read people, even the losers. And that's all those two are. Hell, they ain't smart enough to blow up a balloon, never mind a car. Besides, they're long gone. Probably halfway to Louisiana by now. You and MacLaren put the fear of God into them. I think you're barking up the wrong tree, Chief."

Ben had a feeling she was right.

FORTY-THREE

"Debbie just chewed me a new asshole, Asshole." MacLaren sounded angry. "What the fuck's got into you? You can't go around beating up my citizens."

"I know, and I apologize. I apologized to Deb and to Rick and now you. I was a little shook up, that's all, and I over-reacted. I'm having a tough night."

"So I heard," MacLaren said into his cell-phone. He was driving back into Sarasota with the M.E. Santiago's body was zipped up and riding in the back of the van. At Myakka, a tow truck was hoisting the rental car onto its flatbed. The park ranger was swatting at mosquitoes as he tore down the crime scene tape. In a few minutes the humans would be gone and the creatures of the wild prairies would reclaim their sovereignty. The night would go on as if nothing had happened.

"Where are you?"

"On 75 heading back to the Ritz," Ben said.

"You okay?"

"Yeah."

"I spoke with Conrad Lawrence. He's at the hospital with his daughter. She's fine. He's taking her back to his home for the evening."

Ben remained silent.

The Lieutenant continued, "I also spoke with Jack Barney. He thinks the bomb was a little love note addressed to you. Any ideas?"

"I'm thinking on it." Ben didn't offer any more than that.

"Okay, well, we've got to stop at the morgue. Then I'm going to go get my car. I'll meet you at the Tiki Bar. I think I need to buy you a drink."

"I'll be there."

A tall thin figure of a man stood outside the main lobby of the Ritz-Carlton as Ben pulled up and got out of the Hummer.

"What happened to your car?" Fletcher asked.

"Minor modification. I thought you were Dodge for a minute. Is he here?"

"No, but they should be any minute."

"You waiting for him?"

"Yeah, I need to talk with him about what he wants me to do. I'm leaving for New York in the morning."

"Everybody else gone?"

"Except for Andre and Isabella."

"Isabella? I thought she left with the other models."

"Apparently not."

"Andre at the bar? I'd like to talk with him."

"I saw them getting into the elevator when I came down a few minutes ago."

"Andre and Isabella?"

"Yeah."

"What's up with that?"

"I don't know. I think there may be something going on between them."

Ben thought that was an interesting twist.

Fletcher said, "There's smoke coming out of your grill."

"Yeah, small hole in the radiator."

A white limo pulled up and the driver got out to open the back door. An elegantly dressed woman exited and walked past them as if they were invisible and went through the automatic revolving door. She carried a miniature dog in the crook of her arm. It wore a diamond-studded collar. Probably real, Ben thought. The uniformed driver followed behind her with an armload of luggage. There was more luggage in the trunk.

243

"Fletcher, you've worked for Dodge awhile, right?"

"Five years."

"Fashion consultant."

"Head designer, actually."

"And there's a bunch of other designers?"

"Mostly interns and sketch artists."

"Are you in charge of them all?"

"Yes."

"So who actually designs the line?"

"Dodge and I work together."

"And Harlow? Where does she fit in?"

"She runs the day to day operations; the boutique, shipping and receiving, bookings for fashion shows, travel arrangements."

"Does she get involved with the designing?"

"Only peripherally. She's not a designer, but we like to get her opinion on things from time to time."

"Who stole the line?"

"I have no idea."

The limo driver returned to retrieve the balance of the bags from the trunk. As he walked away the lid closed automatically.

"How about Andre? How long has he been involved with Maddison Designs?"

"He did the Fall catalogue for us …" Fletcher thought for a moment, "two seasons ago."

"And since then?"

"He's done them all. He also works our fashion shows and premieres. Dodge likes his work."

"Can you think of any reason why anyone would want to kill Dana?"

"No I can't."

"How do you feel about it?"

"I think it's bizarre. This whole thing is crazy."

"Any idea why Santiago would want to kill himself?"

"What?" There was a snap of concern on Fletcher's face. "Santiago's dead?"

"Yes. We found him this afternoon. Looks like suicide."

The limo driver walked past them and got into the car and drove away. A light blue Jaguar convertible pulled up and took its spot. Dodge Maddison got out of the passenger's side. "Bennie! God it's good to see you," Dodge embraced his friend and then extended his hand to Fletcher, "Hey Fletch, how are you?"

"Okay."

"Man, it feels good to be out of there." Dodge took in a deep breath of the sea air. "Did you guys eat yet? I'm starved. The county accommodations don't have much to offer on their menu."

Apparently Dodge didn't know about the car bomb. Ben figured he'd fill him in at dinner, but first he needed to get him alone to ask him a few questions.

"Dodge," Annison was seated behind the wheel of the Jaguar. The convertible top was down. She wanted his attention. He held up his index finger, "One minute, Baby."

"We need to talk, Dodge," Ben said.

"Yeah, I know, they've found Santiago's body. What the hell is going on, Bennie?"

"There's more. Let's get a table."

"Dodge ..." Annison was impatient. He turned to her and said, "Are you hungry? Let's get a bite with Bennie and Fletcher."

Annison hesitated. She wanted to be alone with him. They hadn't been together since last weekend and she longed for him. She had wanted to go right to the suite and jump into bed with him. She was hungry, but not for food. She wished that Ben and Fletcher hadn't been standing there when she drove up. Making love to her fiancée would have to wait until later. "I want to freshen up first," she said. "I'll go park and then go to the room."

"Park it inside the garage on the penthouse level. I'll be right up, I want to change my clothes."

Dodge turned to his companions, "Do you think someone murdered Santiago?" Dodge asked his companions. "Fletch, you knew him, would he kill himself? What possible reason would he have?" He looked at Big Ben. "I don't like it. First Dana and now Santiago? Nothing's making any sense."

Annison started the Jaguar. The three men stood in silence and watched her drive to the end of the building and enter the parking garage. The night was warm. Temperatures were in the seventies. Clear sky, lots of stars, a perfect night to dine outside on a beach in southern Florida. Ben missed his wife. He wished Carlene was with him now, getting a table with him, holding his hand and listening to the soft roll of the ocean. "Come on," he said. "Let's get a table."

"I'm really not hungry," Fletcher said. "I think I'll call it an early night."

"Come on, Fletch. You don't have to eat, come and have a drink with us."

"No, that's okay. I'll talk to you in the morning. Good night." He turned away from them and walked into the hotel.

"Well, I'd certainly like a drink. Go grab us a table Bennie and I'll be right down."

"Look, I know you must feel liberated and would like a drink to celebrate, and you've got Annison here and I'm sure you want to spend some time with her, but you and I need to talk about a few things, alone."

"Like what?"

Ben looked his friend straight in the eye and said in a stern voice, "Conrad Lawrence wants to meet with us at nine a.m. tomorrow morning and I need to get some things straight. So, go change and get your ass back down here. We'll have dinner and keep it pleasant, but afterwards you need to get rid of Annison so you and I can have a heart to heart. I'll reserve a table and be waiting at the bar." Ben walked away without giving Dodge a chance to respond.

FORTY-FOUR

The bartender at the Tiki bar recognized the big man standing at the end of the bar. "Scottish Pale Ale?"

"You bet."

A front was stirring in the Gulf of Mexico and the landward edge of it was bringing a slight breeze to the shore. The horizon was still visible in the clear night sky, but faint wisps of clouds were starting to put their mark on it.

"Gonna be a windy night," the bartender said, placing Ben's beer atop a bar coaster.

"Storm coming?"

"Nothing serious, little wind, little rain maybe, but it'll pass over quickly. It's Florida in December. Be another beautiful day tomorrow."

Ben was finding Florida an interesting state. The weather was pleasant and warm and predictable, and even with the diversification of the big cities and the little towns, the high rises, sprawling enclaves and the wide-open plains of the cattle lands and citrus groves, there was an openness, a bare honesty to the country. Here I am, what you see is what you get. Yet, he was also getting a sense that Florida held her own secrets, ones that no one could predict. From her sandy beaches to her reedy prairies she was teasing him, keeping her secrets close while dangling just enough suspicion to keep him intrigued. Florida was seducing him.

Maybe it was the sea breeze or the sultriness of the salt air or the mystique surrounding this case, but he felt invigorated. Even the car bombing had excited him, had charged him up. He felt alive again; away from his ho-hum desk and the monotony of Mayberry

RFD. Ben was doing the thing he liked best, using his analytical brain. Chasing an unknown, being in the hunt, playing hide and seek with a killer. He was picking up pieces of a puzzle and snapping them into place until a clear picture formed and his mind became satisfied that he had solved the illusion, had tricked the trickster.

Tonight he felt closer to an answer. There was resolution coming in on the sea wind. Ben held up his beer glass and toasted the shoreline. "To Florida," he said and took a healthy taste of his beer.

"Talking to yourself now?" MacLaren said breaking into Ben's reverie. He motioned to the bartender, pointed at Ben's beer and held up two fingers.

"Y'know, Lieutenant," Ben leaned his back against the bar, his elbows on either side of him on the bar rail, his gaze out to sea, "a guy could get used to this life down here."

"Yeah, well I've been here forty-four years and I haven't got used to it yet."

The Tiki Bar was full. A three-piece band was playing island music behind the easy banter of the bar patrons. The smells of the fresh cooked cuisine scattered on the beachfront tables wafted pleasantly through the air.

"Think I'm starting to like it here."

"You're going to like it even better when you hear what I've got to tell you."

The beers came, MacLaren said, "Salut-," and downed half his beer. "Ahh, I needed that. Thank God for making hops."

"So?" Ben asked.

"So, I ..."

A blood-curdling scream pierced the air. It was unmistakably human but it was so shrilling and high pitched that it could have only come from an animal whose leg had just been cut off by a bear trap. It came again, impossibly louder, horrifying. Everyone heard it. Conversations stopped, the band hushed and the shrieking amplified in the new silence.

Big Ben was first on the run, MacLaren a step behind. They raced through the crowded dinner tables and hit the beach at a full run. Sand spewed behind them like a rooster tail from a high speed racing boat. The screaming wasn't stopping. They ran toward it, cutting through the tall sea grass at the edge of the parking lot and rounding the corner of the hotel, past the entranceway and following the eerie sound echoing from the concrete and steel of the parking garage.

FORTY-FIVE

Annison wove the Jaguar from one end of the parking garage to the other, climbing level to level until she reached the penthouse parking area on the top floor. Her thoughts were on Dodge, on the two of them being together. Getting beyond the madness of Dana's murder and the effects that was having on their relationship. She could sense Dodge's trepidation and knew he was worried about the future of Maddison Designs. But she had plans for them. Plans that would take him away from that world and bring him comfort in a new world that they could build together. She'd love it if he sold out and got away from the rat race of the fashion world and New York City. They could make a living with the Bed & Breakfast. She was sure of it. And they'd have his lake house to retreat to for relaxation and romance. And what a great set up - the B&B, the lake house, quaint Bryce Corner, Massachusetts – for raising their child.

Annison pulled into the reserved spot marked Penthouse 1. The front of the car nudged the concrete half-wall on the outside perimeter of the parking garage. She put it in reverse and backed up, hoping she hadn't done any damage to the rental car. Annison put the gearshift in park and turned the key off. Impulsively she checked her image in the mirror. She looked good, her skin tight and youthful despite her advancing biological age. Forty-two was still childbearing age. And to be honest, she missed her children. They were grown now. No longer needing mom to coddle them and teach them about the world. Her son and daughter were out of the nest with their own lives to live; J.J. traveling the world with his Air Force career and Sarah in D.C. in her new marriage. She'd be having a baby soon, but a grandchild wasn't the same. Annison wanted a baby. She couldn't wait to marry Dodge and begin their new life together. She mused at what their baby would look like. They were both good looking. They'd have the cutest baby. The mirror told her she needed to reapply her lipstick and brush out her hair. She'd do that in the suite. Maybe Dodge was there already.

Annison grabbed her pocketbook and reached for the door handle. The top was down. There must be a button here somewhere. Yes, on the dashboard below the radio. She pushed it and waited for the retractable top to rise and lock into place. She wasn't too keen on having dinner with anymore of Dodge's entourage, but she would go through the motions and after dinner she would have him all to herself, finally. She closed the windows and got out of the car, pushing the remote lock. The Jaguar chirped. Annison set her pocket book on the hood and bent over the front of the car to inspect for damage. Luckily there wasn't any. Thank God.

The force came from behind and hit her hard as she was straightening up. The wind was knocked out of her as her stomach was driven into the barrier wall. A rib cracked. She tried to scream but nothing came out. Hands clasped her ankles and her body was hoisted up and over the short wall. Her legs came over her head like she was doing a cartwheel in the school playground. Her hands grabbed frantically at something to hold onto, digging into the gray porous concrete. The momentum of her flailing body was too strong to maintain a grasp. Her fingernails broke and the flesh was ripped off her fingertips, leaving bloody red lines etched across the top of the wall and disappearing into the night. She was flying like in one of those dreams where you feel like you can and you want to soar in the air, holding your arms wide and flapping to keep aloft. But you feel the pull of gravity and you know you're going to fall, but you pump harder and harder to stay in the air, knowing all along you'll be okay, that you'll wake up any minute in the safety of your own bed.

The woman was hysterical. Her screams were deafening. Ben recognized her as the society dowager who had been chauffeured to the hotel earlier. Her lap dog was standing next to the body, sniffing at the wide crack in Annison's skull. Its leash, dropped from the hands of its mistress, was trailing through an expanding pool of blood on the sidewalk. The woman was shaking and jumping up and down like in some crazy dance, her hi-brow façade abandoned as she clutched her face with her hands. There were red spatters on her hands and her clothes and her bare legs.

FORTY-SIX

Midnight. It had been a long day. But it wasn't over yet. MacLaren was driving home. The Medical Examiner was carting another body back to his laboratory. Harlow, exhausted from the questioning all of them had gone through, had taken a sedative and gone to bed. Andre was in his room packing for New York. Isabella was in hers - speed-dialing the latest macabre development to her model friends back in the City. Fletcher paced his suite, scotch-on-the-rocks in hand, contemplating his future. Dodge was a mess. Deep in shock. Annison had come so quickly into his life and had now so quickly left it. Where would he go from here? What road was he upon? Still accused of Dana's murder. Facing an uncertain trial, and now this.

Big Ben walked along the sandy path that led to the deserted Tiki Bar. Patio lighting stuck in the sand guided his footsteps. The beachfront patio was deserted. The all weather chairs had been propped against the sides of the all weather tables, the umbrellas down for the night. The storm, which hadn't been much of a storm, had blown over. The sea was calm and the wind was traveling toward the central part of the state, perhaps swaying the reedy grasses of Myakka.

"Hey."

"Hey," Ben responded. He hadn't noticed the bartender in the darkness, lowering the shutters on the Tiki Bar and locking them for the night. "How are you doing?"

"Okay. I've never been interviewed by a detective before. Never been this close to a tragedy like that. Thank God I wasn't any closer than I was. I pity that poor woman who was walking her dog. What an awful nightmare."

"Yeah."

The bartender said, "You want a night cap?"

"No, close up, go home."

"You knew her, right?"

"Yeah."

"That fashion designer, Maddison, you think he really did in the model chick?"

Good question, Ben thought. All of a sudden the nightcap sounded like a good idea. "You got any bourbon back there?"

The bartender smiled, "I thought you'd never ask." He lifted the wooden gate and reached onto the top shelf of the bar. He fumbled for glasses and grabbed a bottle of Knob Creek. "Don't have any ice, neat okay?" Without waiting for an answer he poured generously into the glasses. "No one's here. I'm the last guy out at night," he took a healthy swig and shook his head with the sting of the bourbon. "Whew, I think I needed that."

Ben pulled out a twenty from his wallet.

"No, man. Don't worry about it. This is just between you and I."

"Keep it. I'm sure you lost some tips by all the commotion."

"Actually, I did okay tonight. Once the cops shut everything down and made everyone wait to be interviewed, the bar filled up. People were nervous. A few of them had even gone over to look at the ..." He took another drink. "I was one of them." The bartender poured another finger of bourbon into each of their drinks. He replaced the bottle, locked up the bar, and downed his drink in one last gulp. "I'm going to go home and hug my wife." He left his glass on the bar top and walked away, leaving Ben alone in the night with the stars above him and the muffled sound of the waves rolling onto the midnight shoreline.

His cell phone chimed. A new text message saying, "I can't sleep. I miss my big teddy bear."

Ben smiled and speed-dialed his wife. "I miss you too, Sugarplum."

"Mmm, that's nice."

"Can't sleep Babe?"

"Can't stop thinking about my favorite crime-stopper. I hadn't heard from you and I was wondering how things were going."

Ben thought about being next to Carlene, snuggling with her and talking about their day like they usually did. He was glad he had her in his life. "It's been a busy day," he said. He told her about Annison.

"Oh my God, I don't believe it."

He told her all of it and the way he felt about it, his despair augmented by the quietude of the night and the fresh void left by the cleansing storm.

She let him get it all out, sensing his concern, knowing he was taking it personally. "There was nothing you could have done. Don't beat yourself up over it."

"I've allowed my better judgment to be clouded by my friendship with Dodge. I don't think he's telling me everything. For the first time in my life I'm questioning his veracity. I keep running off on other tangents, yet my cop brain always circles back to him, and I don't like it."

"Stay focused. Treat it like any other case."

"I know."

"I'm really sorry to hear about Annison. We didn't get a chance to know her did we?"

"Not enough."

"Dodge seemed so happy with her and their plans to move into town. I feel guilty, like I should have given her more of a chance. I would have liked more time to get to know her."

"There's more." Ben told her about the car bomb. Carlene didn't speak as he related the story. She knew he had a dangerous job. There had been other harrowing instances and there would be more. She knew that acting the part of the horrified wife would only make him worry; dull the edge that he needed to do his job right and to stay alive. They were each other's support. Sometimes support came in the form of prudent silence. She only said, "How's Lydia Lawrence doing?"

"She'll be fine."

And then, "I'm glad you're both okay."

Another breeze picked up and Ben wondered if something else was stirring in the Gulf, the bartender had said something about passing bands. Or maybe Sarasota was just breezy at night.

"Are you outside?" Carlene could hear the wind in Ben's cell phone.

"Yeah."

"On your balcony?"

"No, on the beach."

"What's it like?"

"Still warm. Small breeze coming in off the water. Waves are small too. Quiet. Everyone's back in their rooms. I'm the only one out here. Actually, foregoing all that's been happening, it's kind of romantic here."

"Looking for romance?"

"You are my romance."

"Aww, you say the sweetest things when you're two thousand miles away."

"I miss you, darlin'."

"Miss you too. Like to be there with you."

"Someday."

"Let's make it soon, Bennie."

Ben walked over to the lee side of the Tiki Bar and paced behind the shuttered bar away from the approaching winds. "What I can't figure out is why Annison? Why Dana for that matter? These relationships are all intertwined and Dodge is smack dab in the middle. There has to be a connection. Jealousy, retribution, bare bones anger? I don't get it."

"I think you're too close, Bennie. Remember that saying? You can't see the forest for the trees? You need to stand back and look at it from the distance."

"You're at a distance, what do you think?"

"First of all, I think you're right about being too emotionally involved. I know you; you're better than what you sound like now. Walk out of the woods and tell me what you see."

"I see a guy who's involved with three women and now two of them are dead."

"You're stuck on the relationship thing again."

"What do you mean?"

"I don't think it's about the relationships. There's something else at work there, some other evil."

FORTY-SEVEN

Carlene's comment hit him. Ben had been thinking that, but wasn't allowing himself to see it. The relationships were the common denominator pointing to Dodge Maddison's guilt. But sometimes the obvious is too obvious. Dana's death, the theft of the clothing line, the Santiago suicide, the car bombing and now Annison's murder didn't feel right to him. Didn't seem to be components of the same puzzle. But he knew they were.

"What other motive usually surfaces?" Carlene asked.

"The biggest one is money."

That's what MacLaren had said. They were watching the Medical Examiner going about his business for the second time that day, his ominous black valise sitting on the pavement next to Annison's lifeless body.

"I'm back to your buddy," MacLaren said. "It's making more sense to me now." Big Ben didn't have a reply.

He had consoled Dodge when he'd come on the scene and saw his fiancée on the ground. Dodge stood like a statue, stiffened by the reality of what he was seeing, Ben's hands on his shoulders holding him away from her. Ben didn't want him to go to her, to touch her, to contaminate the scene. Didn't want any more incriminating evidence stacking up against his friend. Ben and MacLaren had been the first to get to the body (save for the hysterical society woman and her dog) and they didn't want anything disturbed.

Fletcher was standing in the crowd of spectators. Ben motioned to him. He came, put an arm on Dodge's shoulder and walked him away. Andre joined them and took the other shoulder. Harlow followed behind as they made their way through the parting crowd. Isabella was next to her, her head turned back at Big Ben, something in her eyes. A deputy, taking orders from Lieutenant MacLaren, began assembling the bystanders for statements. They moved en masse toward the hotel lobby.

After the pictures were taken, the CSI team spread out another body bag. MacLaren rubbed his forehead, "I've got a headache."

The M.E. joined them. "I'm done here. You want to ride back with me on this one?"

"No," the lieutenant said. "You going to work on her tonight?"

"No, I'm beat. I'll do it in the morning."

"Well, let me know when you get a final. I'm sure the cause of death will be a push." MacLaren shook his head, "Two murders at the Ritz-Carlton in the same week."

"She could have jumped," the M.E. said.

"Yeah, or she could have stubbed her toe and fallen over the barrier by accident. Get the fuck out of here."

"Good night, Lieutenant." He picked up his valise and walked away. "Oh Lieutenant," he turned, "the Santiago case, preliminary findings - carbon monoxide poisoning. No sign of foul play."

"Thanks."

The two cops stood together watching the CSI techs zip Annison Barrett into the black body bag. Ben thought of her kids. He had never met them but he knew they'd take it hard. He had two kids of his own and wondered why he chanced putting a big hole in their lives on a daily basis. That car bomb could have ended it for him tonight. His inspiration had been his uncle, a generation ahead of him, who had been a cop in Bryce Corner and had attained the chief's position that Ben now held. Ben had asked him once why he'd become a cop and he'd said being a cop wasn't a career that you chose; it was a destiny that chose you. Ben hoped that if anything happened to him his kids would understand that, but he doubted it.

MacLaren said, "I've got to get statements from all those people."

"You want some help?"

"Sure."

They walked along the sidewalk with the light scent of the sea wafting over them. MacLaren said, "It's the money. He gets five mill off the model." He was back to railroading Dodge.

"And what does he get by killing Annison?"

"He doesn't have to share the five mill."

Ben looked warily at MacLaren who continued, "Maybe she knew something. Maybe she found out he killed Dana for the money. Maybe his business isn't as lucrative as it appears to be - I'm going to dig into that. Maybe he told her, talked in his sleep, or maybe they plotted it together. Five million dollars would set up one hell of a Bed and Breakfast. Or maybe he's just paring down his stable, who knows? But all of a sudden, for one reason or another, the fiancée became a liability and he had to get rid of her."

Ben frowned. "That's a lot of maybes."

"Yeah, well if those maybes were arrows, he'd have a back full of them. Hey, come on big guy, you were the one who implied he hasn't been in his right mind lately. What did you say? Too caught up in the pressures of the fashion world, family crisis, blah blah blah. *And,* any guy who's fucking around with three women at the same time is *definitely* fucked up. If you ask me, I think he's lost his marbles."

"What about Santiago's suicide? How does that fit in?"

"I don't know yet, but I'll figure it out."

"So the Lieutenant thinks it Dodge again?"

"Yeah."

"Do you?"

Ben couldn't even bring himself to give his wife an answer.

Carlene continued, "You're too distraught. Get some sleep. Tackle it in the morning. You'll have a clearer head."

Ben was turning his snifter of bourbon around in a circle on the wooden railing. "Maybe you're right."

"You've had a lot happen to you in the short time you've been in Sarasota. Your mind is on overload, Big Bear. Give it a break."

"Probably a good idea." Ben had hardly sipped the bourbon. He tossed the amber liquid into the white sand that looked gray in the night. "I just wish I had a fucking clue."

"You do. What about the glass?"

FORTY-EIGHT

Ben slid the magnetic card into the slot, pushed on the door and ducked beneath the crime scene tape. It had been easy getting the key card from the front desk. After midnight only the night auditor is on duty, straining his eyes through thick lenses, tallying the daily receipts. He'd hardly looked up when Ben flashed his badge and said he needed to get into the cordoned penthouse suite.

The room was dark. He decided to leave it that way. There was enough light coming into the suite from the outside lighting to get his bearings. He didn't know what he was looking for, but he knew he was looking for something. Ben perused the suite. There were glass sliding doors, a glass tabletop, and several mirrors adorning the walls. A glass vase, a glass Dolphin on a glass pedestal on a glass end table. There was even a fucking glass chandelier. *Look on the glass.* What glass? He decided to go for the obvious.

Ben entered the kitchen. It was darker here; the light from the balcony doors didn't penetrate this far. He opened the refrigerator, empty, but the light carried well and he left the door ajar as he opened the cabinets. Empty, not a glass to be found. The investigation team had bagged everything and taken it downtown. Thorough down here in Sarasota, he thought.

He shut the fridge door and walked through the darkened suite. It was cool with the air conditioning and he could feel the lingering coolness of death surrounding him - the after presence, the veiled telltale mark of the satisfied Grim Reaper. It was outside on the sidewalk too and had been in the black heat of Myakka. He had felt it, crawling on his skin and raising the primal hairs on the back of his neck. Ben never felt comfortable around death. How could you? An unpleasant, chilling reminder that you could be next. Sometime, anytime, unexpectedly next.

He went into the bedroom where the light smell of Dana's perfume still hung in the air. What thoughts did she have on her last evening of life? Was she happy? Content in her innocence, unaware that her soul was about to take a predestined journey? The door to the master bath was open; Ben crossed to it, reached for the switch and illuminated the white tiles and the granite vanity. Fine traces of fingerprinting powder reflected on the mirror, lay on the vanity top, and spotted the handle of the shower door.

Ben followed the ray of light to the unmade bed with the dark stain of Dana's blood in the hollow of the ruffled sheets. He stood there in the cold silence trying to sense what had happened. There was a presence here, a story yearning to be told, a discovery wanting to be found. The lighting crept across the plush carpet and curled beneath the bed. Ben squatted on his good knee, forever favoring the old football injury. His right leg stretched behind him as he lifted the bed skirt and peered underneath, almost expecting the killer to be hidden there with a psychotic grin on his face and a pointed gun barrel about to explode.

As he pressed on the mattress, bench-pressing his body off the floor, his leg swung into the edge of the bed and he heard a clink. A single solitary sound, one tinny musical note disrupting the hidden silence. Ben looked under the bed again and ran his hand along the carpet into the corner beneath the headboard. His fingers touched something and the clinking sound resounded again. Carefully he felt for the object. A glass with a stem. Ben pulled it out by the bottom edge of the stem, careful to not place his fingerprints anywhere on the glass. He stood and turned the champagne flute into the light from the master bath. Even in this dim light he could make out several distinctive fingerprints.

The blackness came hard to him and he fell to the ground with the heavy weight of the pile upon him. The tackle had slammed into the back of his head. His brain ignited with a thousand flashing lights, sparkling like a grand finale of fireworks behind his clenched eyelids. As he slipped into the chasm of unconsciousness he wondered why he didn't have his helmet on. Stubbornly he grasped the pain. Feel the pain, his coach had said, feel the pain and get up. He rose off the floor and steadied himself against the bed. The champagne flute was gone from his hand. Someone was running fast across the marble tiles in the foyer. A door swung open and crashed loudly against a wall. Ben scrambled to his feet and took off after his assailant. By the time he reached the hallway it was empty. The door at the far end was gliding shut and Ben ran to it. The parking garage was brightly lit. A slate blue Jaguar convertible screeched out of a distant parking spot, burning rubber in reverse and then peeling out toward the exit ramp as the transmission snapped into drive.

The Hummer was eleven flights down parked in the roundabout outside the entrance. Big Ben yanked open the exit door and took the stairs two, then three at a time, cringing each time his bad knee impacted the concrete staircase. He could hear the squealing of the Jag's tires as it spiraled down the exit ramps, two, then three, then four flights ahead of him. By the time he exited, out of breath and his knee throbbing, the Jag was spinning sideways out of the Ritz driveway onto Ben Franklin Drive. He fired up the Hummer and roared after the Jag.

Like the chase scene from Bullitt, the two vehicles raced at full throttle through the streets. Except this wasn't hilly San Francisco, this was flat land Sarasota with lengthy straight-aways for gaining speed. And Ben was gaining on the Jag along the beachfront road. The Jag ignored the stop sign and flew on two wheels around St. Armands Circle and powered down Ringling Boulevard reaching a speed over one hundred miles per hour going over the Causeway bridge. The black, angry looking Hummer was close behind.

Post midnight, the streets were luckily barren of the obligatory senior citizens crawling in their expensive, shiny, over-sized cars. They were safely tucked away in their condos and million-dollar downtown residences, oblivious to the speeding currents cutting through the salty air. Two lone denizens of the night heading for an unknown, yet inevitable climax.

Onward they sped into the city, to the tee intersection of route 41 North, taking the ninety-degree turn far too fast and nearly careening into the monolith structure of blue glass known as One Sarasota Tower. Tamiami Trail stretched ahead of them with classy high rises on the right and the Van Wezel Performing Arts Center to the left. "Where do you think you can go?" Ben said to the red taillights looming in front of him. "You're dead meat." He had the accelerator glued to the floor. He was staying right with the Jag, but unable to gain on it. Smoke was coming out of the hood and Ben swore. "Shit!" the temperature gauge was in the red. Ben had intended to put water into the radiator when he'd gotten back to the hotel, but had forgotten with all the commotion of Annison's death. Now, as they passed by the old single-story Florida motels, he could feel the Hummer struggling to stay alive, bogging down, starving for power. The Jag was inching ahead, increasing its lead.

Someone ahead of them had their blinker on, crossing lanes to the entrance of the Palm Tree Motel. The Jag clipped them in the rear quarter panel and the car spun like a top in the middle of the road. Ben had to swerve to the right and climb the curb to avoid hitting it. He could see the terrified faces of the tourist family screaming through the windows. The Sea Breeze Inn, Sun Dial Motor Lodge, Cadillac Motel and the Flamingo Inn lined both sides of the roadway in their lost glory from the fifties. Once the cute art-deco Mom and Pop lodging places for weary vacationers, these now seedy and dilapidating relics of the past stood away from the glorious architecture of the new Sarasota, preying on unsuspecting snow-bird families with their low rates and false accommodations - like the Bates Motel from Psycho. Would you like a room?

They were running all the red lights. Two miles north, the Trail metamorphosized back into a cultural landscape with the John and Mable Ringling Museum of Art, the Ca' d'Zan and the University of South Florida campus. Then at University Parkway a County Transit bus pulled into the intersection. The Jag's brake lights lit up and it went sideways, smashing into the rear of the bus and spinning around directly into the path of the Hummer. Ben was going to ram it. He kept his foot on the gas pedal and braced himself for the crash. But at the last second, the Jag came to life and squealed off across the sidewalk and entered the access road to the Sarasota/Bradenton Airport.

They were at the far end of the airport, away from the SRQ terminal, racing in the grass skirting along the rusted fencing. A cloud of dead grass and dust spewed behind the cars. Faded red "Restricted Area" signs were wired onto the fence at fifty-foot intervals, some of them had lost their anchoring and lay askew, flapping in the tail wind as the cars breezed by. Ben's Hummer was struggling, the engine gasping for water, the scorched pistons melting into the heat of the engine block. He knew the engine would soon seize, or blow, but he was so close, only feet from the Jaguar. Ahead of them appeared the old entrance gates to the airport storage area, chained together and blocked in front by two yellow poles. One was listing at a forty-five degree angle. Ben figured that was due to age and loose soil. Still, he thought, the Jag'll never get through, crazy to even try. But the car wasn't stopping, or deviating from course. Dead set on the center of those gates. "Crazy bastard," he said.

It was like a game of chicken, who would give up first? "You'll never make it," Ben said as he took his foot off the accelerator pedal and started tapping the brakes. Desperation breeds desperate acts and the aerodynamic Jaguar, with nowhere else to go, plunged forward like a guided missile striking the metal posts and slicing through the rusted gates like a hot knife through butter. The convertible top sheared off as the gates sprung off their hinges, slid over the roof of the Jaguar and bounced to either side of the tarmac. "I don't fucking believe it." Ben said. He pushed on the gas pedal, begging the Hummer to respond.

The Jag was listing to one side, the right front tire blown out by the impact. Good, Ben thought, that'll slow you down. The chase went on with both adversaries injured, the Jaguar limping and the Hummer wheezing and out of breath. Beside them, in compact rows to either side, sat ancient Quonset hangers, now used for storage and airplane repairs by Dolphin Aviation. Tonight they were closed and dark. The only lights at the airport came from the terminal across the runway and the lights from the Boeing 747 on its landing approach.

"What the fuck?" the pilot yelled to his co-pilot. They hadn't seen the headlights scanning across the runway like a weakened flashlight until it was too late. They held their breath in unison as the Jaguar cleared the forward wheel by inches. "Geesus Christ!" the co-pilot said. Ben had hung back, almost hoping the plane would hit the Jaguar, but nevertheless holding his breath too as the maniac in front of him surged on in a dead run to the terminal.

Ben couldn't let that happen. He didn't know who was in that car, but whoever it was, was a desperate and dangerous person who had to be stopped at any cost. "This is it, baby. Give me all you've got," he pleaded to the Hummer. "You're supposed to be indestructible, right?"

The baggage cart came out of nowhere from behind the passenger plane at the gate, a long chain of carts linked together like a herd of elephants tail to trunk, trunk to tail. The Jag saw it and made to cut to the left, but the blown tire made its turn unmanageable. A collision was inevitable. Big Ben saw his chance. He maneuvered to the left and swung the Hummer in a wide arc toward the Jag. The baggage cart operator jumped from his lead car and rolled onto the tarmac. Ben came around like a left-handed hook and slammed the Hummer full speed into the side of the Jaguar. They hit the caravan in the center and the baggage carts curled around the mangled cars like an angry snake.

The impact of the crash jammed Ben's knee into the dashboard. His bad knee. He winced with the sharp pain but the adrenaline kicked in and he pushed the door open and exited the Hummer drawing his gun. As soon as his feet touched the ground his knee gave out and he fell to the concrete. The Jag driver leapt out of the convertible, clambered over the baggage carts and ran full speed toward the airport entrance not fifty yards away. Big

Ben got up and shouted, "Halt! Police. I will shoot. Stop now!" But the man kept running. Ben's gun was in his hand. He didn't know if the running man had a weapon or not, but he had to make a decision quickly. In a few more seconds he'd be in the terminal and endangering innocent people. Ben's cop brain juggled the pros and cons of shooting this person and despaired over the endless questioning that would result. He needed to be stopped. Lines from his instructors at the Police Academy echoed in his head, "Shoot to stop. Terminate the crime."

Ben fired a round into the side of the Jaguar. The sound of the Smith and Wesson .38 was loud. It was a noisy gun. It was also a close-range weapon, and every running step the perpetrator took diminished the accuracy of it. He didn't stop. Ben couldn't let him reach the airport doors. "Middle mass. Shoot at the center of the mass," his instructors shouted. "A clear and eminent danger. Shoot to stop." Ben limped to the overturned carts and leaned down on his good knee, steadying his two-handed aim on the frame rail and sighting on the center of the runner's back. "Halt! I will shoot. Halt!" Ben squeezed the trigger, dropping his wrist a fraction of a second before the gun fired. He couldn't shoot him in the back; he wanted to take him alive. The bullet stung into the fleshy thigh of the runner and hammered against the femur bone, instantly producing a web of hairline fractures. Ben had stopped him.

But only temporarily. Big Ben, holding his gun with both hands stretched out before him, approached the man. Ben's knee was throbbing and he was limping badly. "Stay down!" he yelled. "Place your hands behind your back."

A family of four exited the airport into the windy night air. The two small children ran along the sidewalk waving to their grandparents sitting in a car at the curb. Mom and Dad were holding hands. With her free hand Mom curled her long hair behind her right ear against the effects of the wind. Dad heard a moaning and saw a man lying on the ground. He left his wife to go lend a hand. He reached down to help the man get up.

"No! Don't."

Dad hadn't seen the big man with the gun and was immediately taken aback by it. Fear overtook him and he froze. The running man was on his feet. He pushed Dad into the path of the big man and ran like a wounded deer directly to the woman. Mom screamed as he grabbed onto her. Her husband swore, "Get your hands off her!" and made to go after him. Big Ben held onto him with one arm, still aiming the snub-nose at his target. More people came through the airport doors, at first oblivious to the scene, and then becoming aware of the man pointing a gun. In an instant, chaos broke loose. Happy travelers were emerging, and scared people were pushing back against them trying frantically to re-enter the safety of the airport. Ben saw people scrambling in every direction. The man held the screaming woman in front of him like a shield, his arm squeezed around her neck and his face hidden by her hair blowing in the wind. Ben still didn't know if the man had a weapon or not and at this point he didn't care. There were already three people dead in this fiasco and he couldn't allow this man to claim any more. Big Ben was done fucking around with this guy. All he wanted was one clear shot. And if he got it, this time he would shoot to kill. He hoped to God it wasn't Dodge.

But he couldn't get a clear shot. He knew it and so did the man. Slowly, almost casually, the man backed through the doorway with his human shield. Inside, out of the wind, the woman's hair fell and Ben got his first glimpse of who he was chasing.

"You son of a bitch," he said as Fletcher withdrew into the airport.

FORTY-NINE

Dana couldn't believe he went to the door. She had waited all evening for the two of them to be alone and had set the mood with candlelight and champagne. She had wanted it to be a romantic moment when she told him she was pregnant with his baby. Something they could remember together and someday tell to their kids and grandchildren. She was so happy. So focused now on her life and her future. She was happy, but at the same time perturbed. Upset that he had jumped up and gone to the door. How could that possibly be more important that what she had just told him? Christ! She couldn't believe him sometimes.

Santiago looked through the peephole and saw who it was. He stood back staring at the door. The knock came again. He looked back to the bedroom; saw Dana crossing the room, her delicate form in the candlelight. Heard the door to the master bath close. He looked into the peephole again. He was still there. Santiago buttoned his shirt, flipped the light switch illuminating the foyer and opened the door.

Fletcher barged in. "I knew you were here!" He stormed into the suite.

"Why are you here? You'll wake everyone up with your knocking. What is it you want?"

"What do I want? What do I want? What the fuck do you think I want, Santiago darling?"

"Fletcher, we've been over this. Why are you still pursuing this? It's been a long time now. We parted amicably. We said we could work together again without any problems, remember? That we could go on with our separate lives and still be friends."

"I know, but I can't. I can't bear to think of you with her, can't bear seeing the two of you playing your silly little game, being so fucking secretive and childish. It's sickening. You don't know what you've done to me."

They stood in the hallway, Fletcher leaning against the wall with his arms crossed in front of him and Santiago beside him with his arms at his sides.

"I'm sorry, Fletcher. What happened between us shouldn't have happened. I made a mistake and I'm sorry. I never meant to hurt you."

"A mistake? You call six months of fucking a mistake?" His voice was raised.

"Please be quieter. You're going to wake up the others."

"Fuck them!" Fletcher sprang off the wall and strode into the living room.

"Listen," Santiago said to him "you've got to go." He placed a hand on his elbow. "We'll talk about it tomorrow."

"No. We'll talk about it now. You need to come back to my suite with me. You owe me that much." There was a longing in his eyes.

Santiago didn't feel that way. What he had shared with Fletcher had started innocently as a friendship that had grown into something else, something that he was ashamed of and trying to get beyond. "I was at a difficult time in my life. You gave me friendship and understanding. You helped me pull myself up from my depression. For that I will always be grateful. Please, can we not be friends again, as we started?"

"You shared my bed with me, now you share hers," Fletcher lifted his chin at the bedroom. "How do you think that makes me feel?" He had been drinking and the intoxication was fueling his anger. "I need a fucking drink."

There was no stopping him when he got like this. Santiago was sorry he'd opened the door. He would placate him, give him a drink and get him to leave. "Here," he said going to the kitchen, "let me make you a drink to take back to your room." But Fletcher had gone into the bedroom.

271

"Well," he said, "isn't *this* cozy? Candlelight, champagne, silk sheets, all any slut could want." Fletcher reached for the champagne flute standing on the nightstand. He downed the liquid in one gulp and went to pick up the champagne bottle. Santiago intercepted him.

"Enough." He took the glass from him and put it back on the table. "You must go. You're drunk. I'll speak with you tomorrow." He pushed him back through the bedroom doorway into the great room.

Dana came out of the bathroom with a white terry robe wrapped around her. She knew about Santiago and Fletcher, he had told her early on when their relationship started getting serious. Santiago wanted to be up front with her about his past. And he had gotten himself tested before they started having sex.

Dana and Santiago had worked together for nearly two years on photo shoots all over the world. Glamorous in the public eye, but grueling, tiresome and lonely in the real world of fashion modeling. They had become friends in an easy and comfortable way, like a brother and sister, keeping each other company and making each other laugh when they were over-tired from the long hours of work. In order to not jeopardize their professions with tabloid gossip - the super model and the videographer - they kept a low profile, and when Dodge and Fletcher were present on the shoots, they hardly saw each other. But since their subsequent break-ups, Dana and Santiago had come together naturally. Now they were more than friends, more than lovers, they were to be true partners, beginning a family together. But first they had to get Fletcher beyond his insane affliction.

Dana was leaning against the door jam. She could see that Fletcher was drunk. She wanted him out of there. "Fletcher, this isn't the time or place."

"Well, if it isn't the queen slut herself."

"There is no need for that talk," Santiago warned.

He paid no attention and moved to Dana, placing his face an inch in front of hers. "I'm going to take your little boy-toy back over to my side for awhile."

"Eww! Your breath stinks," she pushed him away.

"Don't push me you little cunt." He put his palms on her breasts and pushed her hard. Dana lost her balance and slid along the wall and fell to the floor.

Santiago was enraged. He yanked Fletcher by the arm and pushed him forcefully into the hallway. "Get the fuck out of here," he said sternly. He went to Dana and helped her up. "Are you okay, baby?"

"Yes, I'm fine." He escorted her to the couch. "Sit for a minute. I will take care of him."

"Watch out!" she yelled.

Santiago turned just in time to catch the lamp that Fletcher had thrown at him.

"Don't touch her!" Fletcher was saying through clenched teeth. "Don't put your hands on that cheap filthy little whore. Can't you see she's no good for you? She's playing you for a chump."

"What is the *matter* with you?" Santiago went up to him. "Have you lost your mind?"

"She's nothing but a low class, fag-sucking whore. She only wants ..."

Santiago's fist smashed into the side of Fletcher's face. He staggered and then caught his balance. "Oh, you want to fight with me you little bitch?" He backhanded Santiago across the cheek, cutting the flesh with his ring.

They went at it, punching and kicking their way to the floor and rolling on the carpet, viciously entwined and frantically trying to overpower one another. Fletcher got the upper hand and put a chokehold on Santiago, squeezing his forearm into his windpipe and making him gasp for air. Santiago hammered his elbows into Fletcher's sides, to no avail. Dana picked up the table lamp and pounded it into Fletcher's back. "Stop it! Stop it!" She was holding it by its base, swinging from the side like she was backhanding a tennis racket. The cinch tie on her robe had come undone and now the long length of the robe was getting caught in her swings, making them ineffective. She should have held the lamp by the top and slammed the base of it into his head, but she didn't think of that. In the moment she was scared and unable to think, reacting by primal impulse. She'd never been in a fight before and was ill prepared for logistics.

Santiago was turning blue. The lamp kept getting caught in her robe. She put it down and jumped on Fletcher's back, beating him with her fists. She grabbed his hair and pulled savagely, sinking her nails into his scalp. Finally he let go of Santiago and reached for Dana. Santiago, nearly unconscious, rolled onto his side coughing and massaging his neck, begging his tortured windpipe to open the flow of air to his starving lungs.

Fletcher threw Dana off him and dragged her to her feet. He went to backhand her but she ducked and he swung around losing his hold on her. Dana saw the fury in his eyes; he came at her like a mad dog. She backed into the desk in the corner of the room. There was a letter opener sitting atop it next to a pen set with hotel stationary. She clutched it. "Get back you bastard. Stay away from me."

He laughed, "What are you going to do with that, princess?" His hideous laughter made her skin crawl.

She stood erect pointing the letter opener at him. "Get out of here," she snarled. "Get out of here right now."

He turned away from her and saw Santiago still on the floor gasping for air. Abruptly he spun around and grabbed for the letter opener. They scuffled. He tried to wrestle it from her hands and she tried desperately to stop him, to stab him, to end it. He was a deranged maniac. Dana lifted her leg to kick him in the groin but again the robe got in the way and her foot deflected off his leg. He twisted her wrists and reversed the point on the blade. She tried to push him away. Her arms went higher and higher as she pushed against his strength, grappling to keep control. But he was stronger and he encircled his hands around the handle and with a powerful thrust, Fletcher plunged the long, thin blade deep into Dana's chest.

FIFTY

Chaos broke out inside the terminal. Everyone was aware of the big man with the gun limping after the guy with the woman hostage and they scrambled to get out of the way, running to the sides, barricading themselves in the rest rooms and jumping over the counters, peering over the top with frightened eyes. This left the walkway clear of travelers, with only Fletcher, the woman and Big Ben occupying the center. The woman was terrified, tears streaming from her wide eyes, locked on her husband, walking cautiously behind Ben's outstretched arm. "Stay back," he said to him, then resumed his two-handed grip on his gun.

"Give it up Fletcher!"

He had a choke hold on the woman. His other arm was behind her back. Ben wasn't sure if he had a gun in her ribs. If he had a knife, he'd be holding it at her throat, and usually with a gun, the perpetrator would nuzzle it into the temple. Ben wasn't sure, and he didn't care. If he got the shot, he'd take him out. The woman was panicked. Her eyes beseeched him to save her, to shoot the man dragging her, threatening to leave her children motherless. Oh my God, she thought, I hope the kids aren't watching this. She scanned the terminal; saw the crowd standing in the entranceway. They weren't there. She remembered they had run down to her parent's car before the man had grabbed her. Please let them be safely inside the car, away from this.

Her motherly instinct was taking precedence over her panic. She began to feel anger. Who is this bastard disrupting my family? What is he pressing into my back? It doesn't feel hard like a gun or sharp like a knife. The red trail of his blood meant that he was bleeding badly. By his limping she knew his right leg was the injured one. She lifted her leg and kicked back as hard as she could. Fletcher screamed with the pain and stumbled, losing his grip on her. The woman pushed herself free and ran into the arms of her husband.

Ben took aim at Fletcher's chest. He wanted to shoot him. It could have been his wife Carlene that he was terrorizing, or even his daughter. He was a murderer and guys like this needed to be put down. Ben's trigger finger was itching. "Put your hands up!" he said angrily. Fletcher obliged and Ben saw that he was unarmed. There was only twenty feet between them and Ben was closing in. Fletcher smirked at him like a wild man, then turned to flee, hopping like a three-legged dog down the terminal. Ben really wanted to shoot him. He's an unarmed man, he thought, and then said, "Goddamn it!" He tucked his weapon into his cargo pocket and hobbled after him, his knee throbbing with each step. He could hear his coach saying, Run through it! Run through the pain, make the tackle! And he did. Ten yards later he dove into Fletcher's back and took him down.

"A guy can't get any decent sleep with you around," MacLaren said. "Can't you solve crimes in the daylight?"

He was at the airport. Fletcher had been arrested and was on his way to Sarasota Memorial Hospital. Ben was sitting on a bench outside the entrance taking the pressure off his knee.

MacLaren sat down next to him. "I was in the middle of a dream. I was fishing. Did you hear me Benson? You made me lose a twenty pound grouper."

Ben laughed. "Sorry Lieutenant, but somebody's gotta do your job."

"Yeah, well ..."

The husband came over to them. He shook Big Ben's hand. "Thank you."

"Thank your wife. She was the brave one." His wife was standing at the back door of the grandparent's car holding both her children in her arms. She smiled at Ben. The husband nodded and went to his family.

"Well, now what?" Ben rubbed his knee.

"Now we head down to the hospital. I want to interrogate that prick while he's still in pain. I told them to hold off on painkillers and not to dig out that bullet until I got there. Plus, you should get that knee checked out."

"Probably, but I already know what they're going to say. 'Stay off it and go to physical therapy.'" He stood and carefully put pressure on it. He'd be limping for awhile. "His lawyer going to be present?"

"Didn't ask for one."

"You read him Miranda?"

"Yup."

"He waved his right to an attorney?"

"Yup."

"You're shittin' me?"

"Nope."

"Then let's get our asses down there before he changes his mind. I got a few questions I want to ask him too."

Fletcher was a beaten man, riddled with guilt and reeling with the psychotic crash from the insanity that had captured and controlled him for the past few days. He was in tears when Big Ben and MacLaren got to the E.R. He had a tourniquet on his leg and an I.V. in his arm. When they approached, he turned his head in shame and bit his lower lip. They didn't have to coax anything out of him - he spilled it all. Starting from that fateful Sunday night in Dana's suite he told a story of jealousy that spawned the anger that went to rage, then so quickly and uncontrollably to murder. "I didn't mean to do it," he said, "I didn't mean to hurt her ... and Dodge," he broke down again, "he is my mentor. And my poor Santiago, what did I do to you?"

The DNA results would later prove the tiny fetus in Dana's womb to be Santiago's, releasing that suspicion from Dodge Maddison. But the sorrow that Santiago felt, feeling responsible for losing his own baby and his cherished Dana, had broken him. He could not live with that pang of guilt. He would honor his obligation and join them and take care of them in heaven.

In the hotel suite that night, only he, Santiago, knew that Dana was pregnant. He was deeply in shock. On his knees he prayed over her at her bedside, holding her hand and begging for forgiveness. Fletcher was busy eliminating all signs of a scuffle. He was in a state of panic. The whole ordeal had happened so quickly, lasting only a minute or two. No one seemed to be aroused by the commotion, but he was afraid someone would be pounding on the door any second. He needed to get them out of there. The idea of staging a suicide was the first thing that came to him. He carried Dana to her bed and positioned her. Santiago was no help, bewildered and unable to comprehend what was transpiring around him. Fletcher spoke harshly to him to help him, but he knelt there, immobile and weak, feeling a painful hollowness.

Fletcher shook him, "Help me," he pleaded. "We must get out of here quickly. What did you touch in here?" He squeezed his shoulders and raised him to his feet then handed him a hand towel and told him to wipe every surface that he had touched. Like a limp marionette, Santiago walked aimlessly around the room carrying out his orders. He picked up his champagne flute and wouldn't remember slipping it into his pocket until much later. Fletcher found Dana's cell phone, wiped it clean, then pressed her fingertip on the keyboard, entering the text message to Dodge. He thought that would clearly make it look like a suicide and remove any suspicion of foul play.

Santiago moved listlessly about the suite, swiping surfaces. When he got to the foyer he saw two room cards on the little table. He put one in his pocket, a loose train of thought suggesting he could sneak back in later and hold Dana's hand. But that would not happen. He would slip further into shock and despair and then unconsciousness as the night went on.

Fletcher gave the suite one last look-over then joined him at the door. "Come on, let's get out of here." He grabbed the towel from Santiago, opened the door slowly and looked into the empty hallway. He wiped the door handles and even the front of the door where he had been knocking. They rushed away.

MacLaren was getting all this on a hand held tape recorder. "What about the stolen merchandise?" he asked.

"Gentlemen," the E.R. doctor interrupted, "we need to cut this short."

MacLaren waved him off, "Just two more minutes, Doc."

As events escalated the next day, Fletcher told them he tried to erase the prior evening from his mind. He took advantage of Santiago's lingering shock and disorientation by threatening him. "If I go down, so do you. You were an accomplice." Thus he believed he had him under control and instructed him to go about business as usual.

Initially Fletcher just wanted to eliminate himself and Santiago from any suspicion. But when the staging of the suicide was found to be a ruse and Dodge was implicated, he saw an opportunity to come out from Dodge's shadow and become the designer he'd always wanted to be. With Dodge incarcerated for the murder of Dana, and Maddison Designs a tarnished name in the fashion industry, the new and untainted name of Fletcher Ross Designs could emerge and stand on its own.

As Fletcher spoke unabated to the lieutenant, Big Ben could see the story unfolding. Having broken the seal by committing murder, all the other evils lurking beneath the surface in Fletcher's psyche could gush forth, like still waters surging in a wild rage from a broken dam, a flow of evil aspirations that would lead to more deviousness and death.

"Lieutenant, I've really got to get this man on a table," the doctor threw a set of x-rays on the bed and motioned to an orderly to help him with the gurney. "He's lucky. An inch more to the left and that bullet would have missed the femur bone and severed the femoral artery. He'd have bled to death before the EMT's got to him." Ben and MacLaren stood to the side as they wheeled Fletcher out.

Ben moaned, "I knew I should have aimed an inch more to the left."

"Come on, sharpshooter, I'll buy you a coffee."

FIFTY-ONE

They sat at a table in the hospital cafeteria. MacLaren was stirring in lots of sugar and cream. Big Ben took his black. "Do you believe him?" MacLaren said.

"I don't know. People snap all the time. Maybe once he got started he couldn't stop, just a guy that got caught up in a bad thing that went worse. Then he got a taste for glory." He blew across the top of his coffee cup and took a sip. "Having the line stolen was kind of clever though," he put the cup down on the Formica table top, leaned back in his chair and folded his arms. "That not only threw us off, maybe even put more suspicion on Dodge, but it certainly worked in his favor, set him up to re-design the line. That's what he really wanted all along and that greed became his driving force. "

"Crime of passion gets mixed into lust for power and glory and he spins out of control."

"They all do. That's what makes them fuck up. He should have left it alone. Flipping Annison over the railing was what did him in."

"I can't believe he thought that was a good idea."

"He wasn't thinking straight. Psychopaths are diabolical and clever. Fletcher was just warped, demented maybe. It came on him fast, he wasn't a seasoned killer. Dana was a mistake, not premeditated, but Annison was premeditated. He became focused on destroying Maddison Designs in order to do his own thing. That was all he could see ahead of him. All he wanted was a name for himself. He had probably resented Dodge all along."

"Illusions of fame and fortune – getcha all the time."

"One way or the other."

MacLaren was flipping through his notes. He had tape recorded and taken notes at the same time. Not a bad idea, Ben thought, he'd try that next time. First shift nurses were straggling in, getting their morning cup of joe before starting their seven a.m. rounds. Ben had gotten an ice pack earlier and that sat on his knee numbing the pain. He was hungry; he couldn't remember the last time he ate. He wanted a doughnut.

"So he thought that getting Annison out of the way would what?" MacLaren was flipping through his notepad.

"Two for one deal. He figured Harlow would take the rap for that. She'd be the prime suspect after the overt jealousy and anger she had displayed during her argument with Annison on the restaurant patio. Fletcher and Andre and any number of nearby guests would substantiate that."

"Then, with Dodge and Harlow both out of the picture, and Annison unable to lay any claim to the Maddison empire, it'd be clear sailing for Fletcher Ross, super designer."

"Exactly."

"But how did he get into the room? I forgot to ask him that. You said you got a key from the front desk. Did you leave the door open?"

"No, I definitely shut it."

"So he was either already in there or snuck in afterwards."

"That's easy," Ben said.

"Enlighten me."

"Did you find the master key that Dodge got from the desk clerk the morning he and Fletcher discovered Dana?"

"Good point. You figure he lifted it then?"

"Sure. Dodge was distraught. Probably threw the key on the hall table or kitchen counter. He didn't know what he was going to find, but Fletcher did. He would have been looking for any telltale signs they hadn't gotten rid of before. Grabbing the key would have been a smart move. That'd give him access later if he needed it."

"Like to clobber you over the head when you found the champagne glass?"

Ben just grunted at that remark.

"That was an interesting thing," MacLaren said. "Why do you think Santiago went through the trouble of hiding the glass and then leaving such a cryptic message on his suicide note? He could have just said 'Fletcher did it'."

"That'll remain a mystery, I guess."

Ben's coffee cup was empty. He wanted another one, but his knee was comfortable and he didn't feel like getting up. Besides, he needed some sleep. Another cup would wire him for hours and all he wanted to do was get to a bed, call his wife and then get some sleep. MacLaren closed his notebook and downed the rest of his coffee.

"Let's blow this popcorn stand," he said.

"Good idea."

On the way outside, Ben asked, "Whatever happened to that anyway?"

"What?"

"The champagne glass."

"I don't know. It wasn't in the Jag at the airport, so he must have tossed it when you two were joy riding along the Trail. Probably in a million pieces. At any rate, as it turns out, we didn't need it anyway."

"Well, it was still the straw that broke the camel's back."

Outside, in the fresh sea air of dawn, the two men walked side by side in the parking lot. MacLaren was walking; Big Ben was more like ambling.

"What's next for you?" MacLaren asked.

"Back to the snow, I guess."

"And Mayberry R.F.D.?"

"It's not as dull as that."

MacLaren raised an eyebrow.

"Well, not all the time. We do have a murder or two," he paused, "every century or two."

"You know what I was going to tell you earlier at the Tiki Bar, before all hell broke loose, was that Ray Burati told me he was putting in for retirement next year. Myakka City will be looking for a new police chief."

"Throw your name in the hat." Ben said to MacLaren.

"Oh no. I'm perfectly happy right where I am."

They walked along in silence. Big Ben took in a deep lungful of fresh salty air. Wheels started to turn.

"What about your buddy Dodge?" MacLaren asked. "He's a free man now, but not unscarred by all this."

"I'm not sure what he'll do. I'll talk to him and give him my support, but he's had a lot of tragedy the past few months. I don't know how he'll come off of that. Probably delve back into his business, I'd expect."

"If he's got any left."

"Time will tell."

They reached the side of the parking lot where the car sat beneath a stand of coconut palms with their fronds gently rising in the morning air, like they were yawning in the new day.

A few feet from the car, MacLaren pressed the remote and released the door locks. When he got to the door, he turned and looked at the sky. The sun was just clearing the skyline and starting to stretch across Sarasota Bay, chasing the faint western stars over the horizon of the Gulf of Mexico.

"Another beautiful Sarasota sunrise," he said.

Ben had to agree with him, "Sure is."

"Y'know," MacLaren said, resting his forearms on the roof, "you might want to think about that Myakka gig. Chief Burati says he's only going to give it one more year. You could be a real asset down here. I'll bet you'd like it. Hell, I could even teach you how to fish."

Ben smiled and looked at the sky.

"Or at least come back for a visit, see how your wife feels about Florida life. Love to get the wives together. My Lorraine's a helluva cook. You should taste her blackened grouper. Phenomenal. Think about it, we've got plenty of room."

"You're not coming onto me are you Lieutenant?" Big Ben laughed.

"Not a chance," MacLaren returned the laugh, "Besides, you're not as cute as you think you are."

They got in the car and left the hospital. Traffic was light at that hour and the ride up 41 along Gulf Stream Avenue was smooth. They were quiet, tired and exhausted, but satisfied that they had solved the case. Sometimes that doesn't happen, but when it does it's a rewarding thing.

MacLaren took a left and headed over the Ringling Causeway with palm trees and pelicans rising into the sky. At the arch of the bridge you get a breathtaking view of the emerald waters of the bay spreading into the gulf, and in the near distance, the white sandy beaches of the coastal islands.

"Y'know, Lieutenant," Ben said, "I just might take you up on that offer."

EPILOGUE

ONE YEAR LATER

If Harlow was perfectly honest with herself, it was that morning, that very morning when she had mustered the courage to take the EPT test, that she had decided to keep the baby and to keep the knowledge of it from Dodge. After all, he was engaged to Annison and would soon be moving out of his apartment atop the Maddison Designs building in New York City and living with her back in Bryce Corner, Massachusetts. Their life, Harlow and Dodge's, was about to change. No longer would their coveted working relationship be the same. Nor would her heart. She had lost him. Yet even with that foreboding awareness, Harlow could have never foreseen the unimaginable events that were forthcoming.

No one had come away unscathed. Although, with all things considered, perhaps she was the lucky one. Harlow had lost the man she was in love with, but had gained a part of him to keep for the rest of her life. Now, a year later, she had a new life in California with her son. They were decorating their condo in San Diego for baby's first Christmas. Mom was hanging ornaments on the tree as baby slept peacefully swaying back and forth in his swing in front of the picture window. He had just received his early morning feeding and had returned contentedly to his dreams.

"Here comes Daddy. Want to say good morning to Daddy?" The sun was rising over the distant mountain range and Harlow liked to pretend that it was Dodge coming to say good morning. Foolish, she knew, but she was up each sunrise with the feeding and thought of him, wondering how he was doing and imagining that he had sent the sun to say good morning to them. The ritual wouldn't last forever. The baby was six months old and hopefully wouldn't need mommy so early in the morning much longer. But it had become a quiet and intimate ceremony for her and she wanted to hold onto it a little while longer.

"Good morning," whispered Harlow.

Dodge was far away in Italy. Living with Giovanni and his family outside Milan. He was a man with a broken spirit. Dana's death had injured him, but losing Annison and the dreams they had, had all but destroyed him. And then the most fatal of all happened and sealed his demise. *Maddison Designs* crumbled. Even though Dodge was acquitted of all wrongdoing, his reputation had been forever stained and his customers fled him, taking their fickle loyalty and their pocketbooks to some other designer.

Dodge now occupied the guest cottage at the rear of Giovanni's estate nestled in the open fields and colorful countryside of northern Italy. He found a subtle peace in the rejuvenation of his artwork and was slowly exorcising his demons through the bristles of his paintbrush. Occasionally he would venture into the city with Giovanni and help out in the factory – no designing, just menial labor on the manufacturing floor. Maybe someday he'd get back into the fashion world, but for now he was content in his self-imposed exile.

Harlow had left the business shortly after Sarasota to have her baby in secret. Someday she would tell him of his son, but now his father needed time to heal. If he did come to them one sunrise, she wanted it to be true, not because of a false sense of responsibility, but because he wanted to.

Fletcher had pleaded guilty and was in jail serving out two life sentences. His dream of being a famous fashion designer had come true, but not in the way he had hoped.

Andre Chateauguy was still in New York shooting photography, but no longer uptown on the plush runways of the fashion world. He was in a tiny studio down in Greenwich Village. His focus had turned to pornography. He started his own magazine called *The Naked Lens*. Isabella was on the first cover.

MacLaren was still chasing crime in his paradise city and dreaming of spending more time fishing.

Lydia Lawrence had put her legal career on hold to become campaign manager for her father's bid for governor.

Ben and Carlene Benson were on a plane heading for Sarasota. Ben had kept in touch with MacLaren and was taking him up on his fishing offer. Carlene had developed a cyber friendship with Lorraine MacLaren and was looking forward to meeting her and savoring her famous blackened grouper. She was excited to be on vacation with her husband, just the two of them without the kids, and was resting her head on his shoulder, thinking how wonderful this second honeymoon in sunny Florida was going to be.

The plane was on its descent and Ben was in the window seat gazing at the emerald waters with the fishing boats etching bright white lines across the surface. He was quiet. Big Ben had something up his sleeve. He was considering the job of Chief of Police of Myakka City and was flying down for an initial interview. One morning while the girls were on a shopping spree, the boys would be on a "fishing excursion" to Myakka. Ben wasn't exactly keeping anything from his wife; he just wanted to check it out first - to see how he felt about it. Then, if he were interested, he'd broach the topic with Carlene. Anyhow, that was the plan.

She snuggled into his chest and looked out the window. "It's beautiful." He put his arm around her. "I'm so happy we're doing this," she said and kissed him on the cheek. "I love you, Big Bear."

Ben squeezed her shoulder and smiled. *I hope so.*

ACKNOWLEDGMENTS

When writing a story you go on an adventure in your own mind and it's easy to get lost in a fictional world. Thankfully there are times when you have to step back into reality and ask for help – even if it's just to remind you that there's still a real world out there. Thanks to all those who keep me on the planet:

My family and friends, who have always wondered where I was - even when I was with them; the Kindiegarten Club for comic relief, Trud, Dave, Jimmer, Bobbo, Billy, Bobby C, Cowmup, J.T., and Whit; Toucann for his unbirdlike patience; BettyAnn for just being there, and with gratitude EBF,

Fellow writers for their words of encouragement; Michael Connelly, Robert B. Parker, Stuart Woods, Randy Wayne White, H. Terrell Griffin, Don Bruns, Ray Ryder, Wayne Barcomb, David Hagberg, Tom Corcoran, the Sarasota Fiction Writers Group, and Deb Stowell and Eric Lamboley, booksellers extraordinaire, Circle Books,

The professionals; Chief Tom O'Donnell W.B.P.D., Brian Strout S.P.D. Arson Squad, Coach Moe, Chris and Earl at DONZI Marine, Graham Kendall of Dolphin Aviation, and Kevin McG for the harrowing ride in the Hummer,

Nothing is possible without the glue that holds me together – for my daughters Jennifer and Jillene,

And especially … to my "pusher" Paula Marie, for minding the momentum and keeping me steady on all the turns - the even keel to my divergent bow.

To the moon, Nila!